Praise fo

Nominated for *Romantic*
Awards for Career Achievement in Urban Fantasy

Winner of the *Romantic Times* 2008 Reviewers' Choice Awards for Career Achievement in Urban Fantasy

"Keri Arthur's imagination and energy infuse everything she writes with zest."

—Charlaine Harris

Praise for *Full Moon Rising*

"Keri Arthur skillfully mixes her suspenseful plot with heady romance in her thoroughly enjoyable alternate reality Melbourne. Sexy vampires, randy werewolves, and unabashed, unapologetic, joyful sex—you've gotta love it. Smart, sexy, and well-conceived."

—Kim Harrison

"*Full Moon Rising* is unabashedly and joyfully sexual in its portrayal of werewolves in heat . . . Arthur never fails to deliver, keeping the fires stoked, the cliffs high, and the emotions dancing on a razor's edge in this edgy, hormone-filled mystery . . . A shocking and sensual read, so keep the ice handy."

—*TheCelebrityCafe.com*

"Keri Arthur is one of the best supernatural romance writers in the world."

—Harriet Klausner

"Strong, smart and capable, Riley will remind many of Anita Blake, Laurell K. Hamilton's kick-ass vampire hunter . . . Fans of Anita Blake and Charlaine Harris' Sookie Stackhouse vampire series will be rewarded."

—*Publishers Weekly*

"Unbridled lust and kick-ass action are the hallmarks of this first novel in a brand-new paranormal series . . . 'Sizzling' is the only word to describe this heated, action-filled, suspenseful romantic drama."

—*Curled Up with a Good Book*

"Desert island keeper . . . Grade: A . . . I wanted to read this book in one sitting, and was terribly offended that the real world intruded on my reading time! . . . Inevitable comparisons can be made to Anita Blake, Kim Harrison, and Kelley Armstrong's books, but I think Ms. Arthur has a clear voice of her own and her characters speak for themselves. . . . I am hooked!"

—*All About Romance*

Praise for *Kissing Sin*

"The second book in this paranormal guardian series is just as phenomenal as the first . . . I am addicted!!"

—*Fresh Fiction*

"Arthur's world building skills are absolutely superb and I recommend this story to any reader who enjoys tales of the paranormal."

—*Coffee Time Romance and More*

"Fast paced and filled with deliciously sexy characters, readers will find *Kissing Sin* a fantastic urban fantasy with a hot serving of romance that continues to sizzle long after the last page is read."

—*Darque Reviews*

"Keri Arthur's unique characters and the imaginative world she's created will make this series one that readers won't want to miss."

—*A Romance Review*

Praise for *Tempting Evil*

"Riley Jenson is kick-ass . . . genuinely tough and strong, but still vulnerable enough to make her interesting. . . . Arthur is not derivative of early [Laurell K.] Hamilton—far from it—but the intensity of her writing and the complexity of her heroine and her stories is reminiscent."

—*All About Romance*

"This paranormal romance series gets better and better with each new book. . . . An exciting adventure that delivers all you need for a fabulous read—sexy shapeshifters, hot vampires, wild uncontrollable sex and the slightest hint of a love that's meant to be forever."

—*Fresh Fiction*

"Pure sexy action adventure . . . I found the world vividly realized and fascinating. . . . So, if you like your erotic scenes hot, fast, and frequent, your heroine sassy, sexy, and tough, and your stories packed with hard-hitting action in a vividly realized fantasy world, then *Tempting Evil* and its companion novels could be just what you're looking for."

—*SFRevu*

"Keri Arthur's Riley Jenson series just keeps getting better and better and is sure to call to fans of other authors with kick-ass heroines such as Christine Feehan and Laurell K. Hamilton. I have become a steadfast fan of this marvelous series and I am greatly looking forward to finding out what is next in store for this fascinating and strong character."

—*A Romance Review*

Praise for *Dangerous Games*

"One of the best books I have ever read. . . . The storyline is so exciting I did not realize I was literally sitting on the edge of my chair. . . . Arthur has a real winner on her hands. Five cups."

—*Coffee Time Romance and More*

"The depths of emotion, the tense plot, and the conflict of powerful driving forces inside the heroine made for [an] absorbing read."

—*SFRevu*

"This series is phenomenal! *Dangerous Games* is an incredibly original and devastatingly sexy story. It keeps you spellbound and mesmerized on every page. Absolutely perfect!!"

—*Fresh Fiction*

Praise for *Embraced by Darkness*

"Arthur is positively one of the best urban fantasy authors in print today. The characters have been well-drawn from the start and the mysteries just keep getting better. A creative, sexy and adventure filled world that readers will just love escaping to."

—*Darque Reviews*

"Arthur's storytelling is getting better and better with each book. *Embraced by Darkness* has suspense, interesting concepts, terrific main and secondary characters, well-developed story arcs, and the world-building is highly entertaining. . . . I think this series is worth the time and emotional investment to read."

—*Reuters.com*

"Once again, Keri Arthur has created a perfect, exciting and thrilling read with intensity that kept me vigilantly turning each page, hoping it would never end."

—*Fresh Fiction*

"Reminiscent of Laurell K. Hamilton back when her books had mysteries to solve, Arthur's characters inhabit a dark sexy world of the paranormal."

—*The Parkersburg News and Sentinel*

"I love this series."

—*All About Romance*

Praise for *The Darkest Kiss*

"The paranormal Australia that Arthur concocts works perfectly, and the plot speeds along at a breakneck pace. Riley fans won't be disappointed."

—*Publishers Weekly*

Praise for *Bound to Shadows*

"The Riley Jenson Guardian series ROCKS! Riley is one bad-ass heroine with a heart of gold. Keri Arthur never disappoints and always leaves me eagerly anticipating the next book. A classic, fabulous read!"

—*Fresh Fiction*

Praise for *Moon Sworn*

"Huge kudos to Arthur for giving readers an impressive series they won't soon forget! 4½ stars, Top pick!"

—*RT Book Reviews*

"The superb final Guardian urban fantasy saga ends with quite a bang that will please the fans of the series. Riley is terrific as she goes through a myriad of emotions with no time to mourn her losses. . . . Readers will enjoy Riley's rousing last stand."

—*Midwest Book Review*

Praise for *Darkness Unbound*

"A thrilling ride."

—*Publishers Weekly*

Praise for *Darkness Rising*

"Arthur ratchets up the intrigue . . . in this powerful sequel."

—*Publishers Weekly*

By Keri Arthur

THE DAMASK CIRCLE SERIES

Circle of Fire

Circle of Death

Circle of Desire

THE NIKKI AND MICHAEL SERIES

Dancing with the Devil

Hearts in Darkness

Chasing the Shadows

THE RIPPLE CREEK WEREWOLF SERIES

Beneath a Rising Moon

Beneath a Darkening Moon

THE DARK ANGELS SERIES

Darkness Unbound

Darkness Rising

Darkness Devours

Darkness Hunts

Darkness Unmasked

Darkness Splintered

THE MYTH AND MAGIC SERIES

Destiny Kills

Mercy Burns

THE RILEY JENSON GUARDIAN SERIES

Full Moon Rising

Kissing Sin

Tempting Evil

Dangerous Games

Embraced by Darkness

The Darkest Kiss

Deadly Desire

Bound to Shadows

Moon Sworn

Circle of Desire

KERI ARTHUR

DELL
NEW YORK

Circle of Desire is a work of fiction. Names, characters, places, and incidents either are the product of the author's imagination or are used fictitiously. Any resemblance to actual persons, living or dead, events, or locales is entirely coincidental.

2014 Dell Mass Market Edition

Published in the United States by Dell, an imprint of Random House, a division of Random House LLC, a Penguin Random House Company, New York.

DELL and the HOUSE colophon are registered trademarks of Random House LLC.

Originally published in trade paperback in the United States by ImaJinn Books, Hickory Corners, MI, in 2003.

This book contains an excerpt from the forthcoming book *Memory Zero* by Keri Arthur. This excerpt has been set for this edition only and may not reflect the final content of the forthcoming edition.

ISBN 978-0-440-24657-2
eBook ISBN 978-0-345-53908-3

Cover design: Lynn Andreozzi
Cover illustration: Juliana Kolesova

Printed in the United States of America

www.bantamdell.com

9 8 7 6 5 4 3 2 1

Dell mass market edition: April 2014

ONE

AIR HISSED THROUGH THE SILENCE. TENDRILS OF SMOKE began to curl past the window frames, its color luminous yet sickly. Katherine Tanner tugged one of the two white ash stakes strapped to her jeans free and clenched it tightly. On the opposite side of the room, a little girl slept on, oblivious to the smoky slivers of evil beginning to slip past the window. Kat hoped she remained unaware, but how likely was that, given her kidnapper seemed to be targeting children born into shifter families? While not all shifters were sensitive to magic, many were. It was a part of their soul, after all, even if a child this young would not be able to shift form. Not until puberty, anyway.

Kat was keeping her fingers crossed that this kid *did* get the chance to hit puberty.

Because if Gwen's premonition was right—and her grandmother's premonitions usually were—this child would be the next to go missing. They'd done everything they could to prevent that. They'd nailed the windows shut, they had cops patrolling close by, and warding stones had been placed around the child's bed to prevent any magic from coming close.

But these wards weren't designed to stop evil itself—

and that's what was seeping into this room tonight. Kat's stomach began to churn. Though she'd spent the last ten years hunting the rogue elements of the supernatural community that preyed on humans, she'd never come across anything that went after kids the way this thing did. She had never met anything that did to them what this thing did.

She closed her eyes, fighting tears, trying not to relive the moment two nights before when they'd stepped into that old factory and found the body of the second missing four-year-old. Daniel had been unmarked except for two small puncture wounds on his neck. Though he'd been drained of blood, this was not what had caused his death. Only those gifted with psychic sight would ever see *that*.

Something had stolen his soul—had ripped it from his body between the beats of his heart. He'd died quickly, but in pain. Terrible, terrible pain.

She didn't want to face the thing that could do something like that. No one in their right mind would. But she had no choice, simply because the Damask Circle's resources were stretched to the limits right now, and there was no one else free to make the trip to Oregon.

She gripped the stake tighter and watched the smoke draw together and find shape, becoming a scantily clad, extremely beautiful woman.

Evil came in all shapes and sizes, but for some reason Kat hadn't expected it to take the form of such Oriental perfection. And maybe it was just her own maternal instincts coming to the fore, but she just couldn't understand how *any* woman could harm a child—particularly one so young.

But this *was* the thing snatching the kids. It had the same sense of deeply entrenched corruption that she'd felt in the other bedrooms.

The woman stepped toward the child. Kat tensed but fought the urge to move, sensing the show wasn't over yet. Her fingers ached with the force of her grip on the stake. She had no idea whether it would actually kill the soul-sucker or not, but at the very least it would do some serious damage and give her time to yell for reinforcements.

A cold smile touched the woman's bloodless lips, then she turned and tried to open the window. It didn't budge, held steady by the nails placed there earlier. The woman stepped back and energy surged, crawling like fire across Kat's skin. The nails slithered from the wood and dropped softly to the floor. The woman lifted the window and leaned out.

A gaunt, dark-haired figure appeared, and the sensation of evil increased tenfold. The vampire's dead gaze scanned the room, stopping when it reached the shadows in which Kat stood. Though she was certain he couldn't see past her grandmother's wards, he really didn't need to. Not with the frantic beat of her heart.

He snarled softly, revealing stained canines. The soul-sucker spun, the malevolence in her dark eyes overwhelming any lingering impression of beauty. With an inhuman growl, she leaped for the sleeping child. Kat raised her hand, thrusting a lance of kinetic energy at the soul-sucker, flinging her away from the bed. The woman hit the wall with enough force to dent the plaster and shatter the nearby window. As glass fell to the floor, the child woke, her shriek almost ear-piercing. Hurried footsteps began to echo down the hallway, but it was doubtful the cops would get here fast enough to even see this thing, let alone catch it.

As the child's screams continued, the woman's gaze met Kat's. In the dark depths of the creature's eyes, she saw the promise of retribution. A chill chased through her soul and she shivered.

Then the woman's form disintegrated, becoming little more than mist that eddied out the open window. Kat cursed and ran across the room. The woman had regained shape near the back fence, and though the vampire was nowhere in sight, the scent of his evil stung the night.

The bedroom door burst open and police poured in. They called to her to stop, but their voices were almost lost beneath the child's continuing screams. So Kat ignored them and climbed out the window, simply because she had no other choice. By the time she stopped to explain what had happened, the soul-sucker and the vamp would have disappeared. Besides, she doubted the cops would believe her anyway. The only person who *would* understand would probably be scrying right now, staring into her crystal ball in an effort to track the creatures and perhaps discover their daytime hideaway.

Smoke swirled up the wooden fence and disappeared over the top. Kat scrambled after it and sprinted down the alley, her footsteps a lone echo in the night. Ahead, streetlights shimmered and traffic rolled, but it all felt a world away. The creature she chased wanted seclusion and darkness—at least for the moment.

It turned left into another small alley. She followed,

leaping over the rubbish and battered trash cans strewn across her path. She was tempted to shift shape and hit the night sky in her raven form, but she didn't dare risk it with the stakes she carried. And she wasn't about to leave them behind—not when the vampire still lurked. Her quarry ran past one of the gates leading into an old factory. Metal creaked, as if stirred by a wind that didn't exist, and another chill ran down her spine. The vampire was out there, pacing her. Watching her.

If he was the soul-sucker's partner, why didn't he attack?

The smudge of vapor continued on, moving toward a squat-looking building at the end of the alley. Kat slowed and half wished she'd brought a flashlight. The moon above was almost full, yet its light struggled to touch the shadows lining the small alley. Though her night sight was generally better than a human's, even she would struggle to see through the pitch blackness inside that warehouse.

The soul-sucker wrapped itself around a window and disappeared. Kat stopped and scanned the outside of the building. It was a two-story brick structure, though the color of the bricks had long since been lost to thick layers of dirt and graffiti. Most of the windows on the lower floor had been boarded up, and the upper ones were all smashed. There was a small door to her right. The thick chains that had locked it were shattered.

An invitation, if ever she saw one. But an invitation to what? Was she walking into a trap, or had she merely found the most recent hiding place of these creatures?

The pounding of boots against concrete echoed against the night—probably the cops coming after her. She couldn't let them find her. The vampire could take out a dozen men in the blink of an eye. Even her powers gave her no certainty against him, despite her experience and psychic senses. Especially with that other thing wandering around.

She flipped the stake in her hand, then walked across to the entrance. Raising her fingers, she sent a sliver of kinetic energy at the door and pushed it open. It didn't creak. It didn't make any sound at all, not even from the chains that swung gently back and forth.

Her unease stirred anew. She stepped to one side and studied the darkness. Though the moon caressed the outer wall with light, no brightness shone through the doorway. It was as if a blanket of night hung over the entrance, sucking in all light.

She stepped inside. Nothing stirred the blackness except the wild beat of her heart. Yet she wasn't alone. The vampire and the soul-sucker were both here—along with someone new. Another shapeshifter.

Taking on two was tempting fate; three was inviting a trip to the nearest morgue. But she couldn't retreat. Not when the image of little Daniel Baker rose in her mind.

She edged forward. The farther she moved into the warehouse, the heavier the air became. The scents of age and rotting rubbish mingled with the ripe aroma of evil, turning her stomach and making it difficult to breathe. Breathing through her mouth didn't help, either. The air tasted as bad as it smelled.

Her foot hit something solid, and metal rattled

across the concrete floor, the noise deafening in the silence. She cursed under her breath, but the night seemed to amplify her words and echo them across emptiness. Laughter answered, deep but feminine.

She hesitated, her gaze sweeping the night. The soul-sucker wasn't running anymore. It was out there, watching Kat struggle through the dark. Waiting for her slightest mistake . . .

Despite the chill in the air, sweat trickled down her back. A white ash stake suddenly seemed woefully inadequate against the creatures that waited ahead.

Her fingertips touched a wall. It was wet and slimy, even though there didn't appear to be any water running down its surface. She skated her hand across it, using it as a guide as she moved deeper into the darkness. Concrete eventually gave way to metal—a staircase, leading down into a deeper gloom.

Down to where they waited.

God, she *so* didn't want to go down there. She didn't want to confront these things. In ten years of fighting evil, she'd never been this scared, and she'd faced some pretty foul beings during that time. But none of them had the power to suck the essence from her body and destroy all that she was, all that she could be—both now and in future reincarnations.

Once again the image of Daniel rose, and she took a shuddering breath. He would have been just as scared. And he'd certainly deserved more than four years of life. While she and Gran had been placed on the trail too late to save him and the other two kids, they were here in Springfield, Oregon, now. They had a chance stop this.

All she had to do was go down into that darkness.

She took another deep breath, then felt for the edge of the step with her toes. She kept hold of the banister for guidance and repeated the process, moving slowly down.

The chill in the air grew until it felt like she was breathing ice. Her fingers were so cold they ached, and despite the fact that she'd put on extra-thick socks, her toes felt numb.

Or maybe it was just fear, paralyzing her from the extremities up.

She reached the bottom and stopped. Nothing moved. Her breathing rattled across the silence, and the wild beat of her heart echoed in time with it. The vampire and the soul-sucker stood to her left. The shapeshifter was more distant and to her right. There was no sense of evil coming from his direction, just wave after wave of anger and hostility. It didn't seem to be aimed at her, or even at the duo she chased. It seemed to be aimed at the world in general.

And it was odd that she was getting such a strong impression of a man she hadn't even met.

Evil stirred, splitting up as it moved forward. She backed away until she hit a wall, her grip on the stake so fierce her knuckles ached.

Air rushed at her from the left. She slashed the stake across the night and felt the slight resistance as the sharp point tore into flesh. The vampire howled but didn't stop. She dove out of his way, hit the concrete with a grunt, and rolled back to her feet. Tendrils of softly glowing smoke reached for her. She hit it with kinetic energy, momentarily fragmenting it.

The darkness stirred, then lashed out, connecting hard with her chin. The force of the blow sent her sprawling backward. Her back hit the floor, and her breath left in a whoosh of air. For a moment, stars danced in her vision.

Then, the weight of another hit her, pinning her in place. Though gasping for breath and fighting the blackness invading her mind, she still heard the vampire's snarl. She looked up in time to see the shadows unravel around him. His dead brown eyes were inches from hers and his teeth were extending, dripping blood in expectation of a feed. Tendrils of smoke gathered above him, pulsing red. *Excitement,* she thought. *Need.*

With as much force as she could muster, she smacked the heel of her palm into the vamp's nose. At the same time, she sent a surge of kinetic energy at the vapor, again tearing it apart.

"Bitch!" The vampire's voice was hoarse, his breath full of dead things.

"Bite me," she said—and yelped when the bastard did. She stabbed the stake into his side, using kinetic energy to force it deep.

Blue fire flickered, and the smell of burning flesh rent the night. The vampire howled and slashed at her, not with his teeth but with fingernails as sharp as claws. They tore across her face, and she cursed him fluently. Kinetic energy surged, but before she could release her weapon, the vampire was torn from her.

"You all right?"

The voice was rich, husky, and called forth fantasies of long nights and silk sheets. She blinked, wondering where the hell her mind was. "Yeah."

A hand appeared in front of her eyes. "Then get the hell up, because that thing is coming back."

The shifter's fingers were a furnace compared to hers, and he pulled her up with an ease that spoke of strength. He was a warm, solid presence she could feel but not see. A man whose emotions she could taste as easily as she tasted the evil of the other two.

And she had no idea why. Empathy with the living was not one of her talents.

"Thanks." She pulled her hand from his, and the emotive swirl died a little. But his hostility lingered, mixed with some deeper emotion she couldn't quite define. Yet it stirred her senses. Made her pulse race.

"Get out of here," he said. "This place is too dangerous for a woman. I'll keep the creature occupied."

"It's not alone," she retorted. "And this place is just as dangerous for a man who has no idea he has two opponents rather than one."

"Listen, lady—"

"No."

Tendrils of smoke formed behind the shifter's solid presence, ready to caress and kill. Kat hit the soulsucker kinetically, dissipating it yet again, then was flung sideways by the shifter.

She flailed her arms, battling to keep her balance, then heard a grunt as the shifter was hit by the vampire. Blue fire flickered across the darkness—evidence that the stake was still buried deep in the vampire's flesh. So why didn't he damn well die, like all bad little vampires should?

She dragged the second stake free and clenched it tightly. The two men were slugging it out, the shifter apparently giving as good as he got. But he obviously knew he was up against a vampire, so why didn't he just grab the stake and thrust it into the bastard's heart?

Surely he *had* to know it was the best way to stop a bloodsucker? Going toe-to-toe with one generally never ended well—for the attacker, not the vampire. Hell, the only reason he could even *hit* the vampire was the stake holding it in human form.

She shifted her weight from one foot to the other and fought the need to move. She didn't dare attack until the shifter was clear. The stake she held was just as deadly to him as the vampire, and the slightest mistake could prove costly.

The mist began forming again. She swore and slashed it with the stake. The air howled—an inhuman sound that sent a chill down her spine. The vapor disappeared, and the sense of old evil retreated, flowing up the stairs and out the door.

If she didn't follow it, she'd lose it. But she couldn't leave the shifter here alone, either. Not when instinct suggested he would not come out of this warehouse alive if she did.

"Back off, shifter, and let me at it," she said.

"Like . . . hell." His words were punctured with the smack of flesh against flesh.

"Hitting it is not going to damage it." Exasperation edged her voice. If she lost the soul-sucker's trail because of this man's stubbornness . . .

"He's injured. Bleeding."

"And already dead," the vampire snarled. "As you and the bitch will be by the time I'm finished with you both."

"As I said to the lady, like hell."

His words were emphasized by a grunt of effort and another smack of flesh. The vampire made an odd sound deep in his throat and staggered backward. It was the break she'd been waiting for. She reached deep, drawing on all her remaining kinetic strength, and flung the shapeshifter back—far back, across the warehouse. Surprise whisked around her a moment before he smacked against the wall, then all emotion died. *He hit his head.* At least she didn't have to worry about him getting in the way.

She raised the stake and ran at the vampire. He snarled and tried to dodge, but his movements were slowing, and he was nowhere near fast enough. She drove the stake through his chest into his black heart, then leaped sideways as he lashed at her with clawed hands. His fingers slithered down her leg, tearing through her jeans and into flesh. She cursed and kicked him, shoving him backward.

He hit the ground with a splat and didn't do anything more than writhe. Blue fire encased his torso, and the smell of burning meat churned her stomach. She climbed to her feet, brushed the dirt from her hands, and watched the vampire incinerate. She felt no elation at her victory. She couldn't. Not when there was one more horror still running free.

When there was nothing left but ash, she turned and ran for the stairs. The shifter was safe enough now that the vampire was dead, and with any luck, Gran and she would be well gone by the time he awoke. Because if the hostility he'd projected was anything to go by, it wouldn't be pleasant to be within a ten-mile radius of the man when he eventually stirred. Especially after she'd knocked him cold.

The moonlight seemed abnormally bright after the shuttered darkness within the warehouse. She blinked and hesitated, searching for some sign of the soul-sucker. Evil was a distant echo, moving away fast.

She shifted shape and flew down the alley, skimming past the cops who raced toward the warehouse. This time, the creature headed for the main street. Perhaps it hoped the noise and motion might loosen any psychic hold she had on it—which was a definite possibility after all she'd been through tonight.

The soul-sucker hit the street, its ethereal form getting lost in the warm glow of lights. It whisked away to the right, and the psychic leash she had on it snapped with a suddenness that had her plummeting to the ground.

She hit with a grunt, then shifted shape and rolled onto her back, staring up at the moon.

She'd lost it.

ETHAN IMPATIENTLY THRUST THE PARAMEDIC'S HAND AWAY. "Enough, already. The cut is not that bad."

"Sir, the wound needs stitches—"

"It's stopped bleeding, hasn't it?"

"Yes, but there's still the possibility of concussion—"

If the ache in his head was anything to go by, it was more than a possibility. But right now, he had no intention of going anywhere—as much as the paramedics and the captain might wish it. "I haven't got a concussion, and I have no desire to go to the hospital."

"Sir—"

"Goddamn it, Morgan." The second voice rose out of the night, cutting through the paramedic's words like a foghorn. "I thought I told you to keep away from this investigation."

The captain huffed to a stop three feet away, nose and cheeks beacon-bright in the stark light coming from the ambulance's interior. Ethan knew the cause was not so much the cold as blood pressure. This case would kill Benton if they didn't solve it soon.

"You didn't tell me to keep away from the warehouse," he said with a calm he certainly didn't feel. "It's not my fault one of the suspects decided to head my way."

"I told you to stay *completely* away. That means out of the whole damn area."

Benton dragged a stick of gum from his pocket and undid the silvery wrapper. He offered it to Ethan, who shook his head. The captain had given up smoking two months earlier—in an effort to save some money more than save his health—but he now appeared to be spending more on gum than he ever had on cigarettes. And his health hadn't improved either—although this case certainly wasn't helping anyone's physical or mental well-being.

"Just what the hell happened in that warehouse?"

Ethan shrugged. "As I told Mark, I heard the man and woman enter the building. I wasn't sure who they were or what they were doing, so I waited. When the man attacked the woman, I intervened, but the woman somehow managed to knock me unconscious. You know the rest."

Benton grunted. "Was there anyone else in the warehouse other than those two?"

"No." Though he'd certainly had a sense of something else, something he couldn't exactly define. "Why?"

"Because the woman claims there was."

"From what I saw, that woman isn't exactly sane." Refusing to run after he'd pulled that man off her, *then* knocking him unconscious? What sort of stupidity was that?

Benton snorted. "Ain't that the truth. She and her grandmother are the oddest pair you're ever likely to meet."

And meeting them was next on his priority list—as much as the captain was likely to disapprove. He crossed his arms. "They're certainly not cops, so why the hell are they on this investigation?"

"Pressure from higher up." Benton shrugged. "I'm not happy about it, but I've got no choice. And they did save the kid tonight. You have to give them that."

Yeah, but there was no guarantee tonight was connected to the other kidnappings . . . murders. The word sat like a dead weight in his gut. He rubbed a hand across his jaw and caught a scent that reminded him of summer rain. The woman. Even though he'd barely touched her, her fragrance branded his skin. His pulse quickened and lust rose, as hot as anger.

He took a deep breath, battling for control. *Damn the moon's rising!* It couldn't have come at a worse time.

"Are they FBI?" He wouldn't have thought so—not with the way the woman had acted in the warehouse.

"No, they're psychics. Working for an organization known as the Damask Circle."

"*Psychics?*" Scorn edged his words. Such mumbo jumbo was *not* what this case needed right now. "The press are having a field day already. What are they going to do if they discover we've resorted to psychics?"

The captain sighed. "I know. But as I said, I don't have a choice on this one. Besides, I'll use whatever—and whomever—I can to stop the bastard doing this."

Amen to that. Ethan grabbed his jacket and stood up. "You mind if I go talk with Mark for a few minutes?"

"Like it's going to make any difference if I say no." Benton unwrapped another stick of gum and shoved it in his mouth. "But a few minutes is all you're getting, then I want your ass out of here. As of tonight, you're on leave."

This time it was anger that rose in a red tide. He struggled to keep his voice calm as he said, "Captain, you know I can't—"

"You're too involved, Morgan."

Of course he was too involved—three days ago his goddamn *niece* had become one of the missing kids. And he'd promised Luke—his brother, and the only family member he acknowledged these days—that he'd find her, and bring her back safely. Which was a stupid thing to do, but he just couldn't help it. Luke and his family were the one truly good thing remaining in his life.

He flexed his fingers and took a deep breath. Anger wouldn't help his cause. It would only confirm the captain's opinion that he couldn't keep a clear mind. "I know this case better than anyone. And I've got a better nose for hunting down killers than anyone else in the squad." Which was certainly more accurate than the captain would ever know.

"I'm not denying either of those facts." Benton paused, beady eyes narrowing. "But when was the last time you slept properly?"

Ethan didn't answer. He didn't need to.

"And when was the last time you ate a decent meal?"

"Cap, that has nothing to do with my ability—"

"That has *everything* to do with it! You're running

on anger, Morgan, and nothing else. God, man, you look like *shit*."

Wasn't *that* the truth! But the cause wasn't just lack of sleep or food or his missing niece. It was the heat of the moon pounding through his blood.

"Your few minutes are ticking by, Morgan. Move it."

Ethan put on his jacket and pushed past the paramedic and captain.

"Morgan?"

He hesitated and looked over his shoulder.

"Leave. If I catch your ass in the area again, and I'll lock you up until this thing is over."

Ethan's smile was grim. With the full moon rising, there wasn't a prison cell in the country that could hold him. "Sure, Cap."

The moon caressed his shoulders as he walked away—a touch that burned clear through to his soul. The darkness stirred deep within, and hunger boiled through his veins. He thrust clenched hands into his jacket pockets and tried to ignore the moon-spun fever. He didn't have time to quench his physical needs right now. Not when every minute that passed brought the reality of Janie's death one step closer.

Not when the fiends behind these kidnappings were so close he could almost smell them.

He walked into the warehouse and made his way down the stairs. Floodlights had been brought in an hour ago, and the shadows had long since fled. Oddly enough, the room looked smaller than it had when encased in darkness. Forensics methodically searched for the smallest of clues, but he doubted they'd find anything beyond the oddly human-shaped smudge of ash.

Mark Fairfield, his friend and partner of the last three years, squatted near the dark stain on the concrete floor. Ethan stopped next to him.

"They figured out what that is yet?"

"Human, if the small bits of bone they've found are anything to go by." Mark's voice was grim.

"A fire hot enough to do this to a human would have killed me, too."

"Yeah. And made a mess of the warehouse, too." Mark looked up. "By your reckoning, you were only unconscious for three to four minutes. Not enough time for this to happen."

"No." But the fact was, it had. "You questioned the woman?"

"Katherine Tanner? Yeah. She's not saying much, but I have a feeling she knows exactly what transpired."

Her name was Katherine? Odd. He'd expected something more . . . feisty. "Is Benton taking her downtown for questioning?"

"Nah. Apparently the pair of them have friends in high places, and he's walking on eggshells around them. Besides, until we know for sure what this is and how long it's been here, what the hell are we going to question them about?"

They could try asking just what this thing had been before it burned. He'd hit the creature with every ounce of strength he had. No human could have stood up to those blows, because *he* wasn't human.

No, he thought bitterly, he was something a whole lot *less* savory.

"Nothing else in the warehouse?"

His effort to keep his voice carefully neutral failed, and Mark's expression became sympathetic.

"No," he said softly. "Nothing at all."

Ethan nodded. At least he could hold on to hope just that little bit longer—however false he knew it to be.

"Are the two women still here?"

"Benton let them go about half an hour ago."

"Do we know where they're staying?"

Mark considered him. "Benton told you to keep away from this case."

"Would you?"

"I guess not." Mark rose. "They're at the Motel Six down on Beach Road."

"Thanks."

Mark nodded. "I'm guessing you want me to keep you updated on anything that happens?"

"You said it." Ethan hesitated. "As of tonight, I'm on leave. Don't call me from the office."

"I'm not stupid." His partner looked past him. "Benton's headed this way."

"Which means my time is up. Keep in touch, partner."

"I will if you do."

Ethan swung around and raised his hands. "I'm outta here, Captain."

"Good. Go home and rest, Morgan. Let us catch this bastard."

He nodded and looked at Mark. "I'll see you Saturday."

"Morgan, I'm warning you—"

"It's my wife's birthday," Mark cut in. "No business allowed."

"Leave," Benton said, stabbing a finger in Ethan's direction. "Now."

Ethan went.

KAT FLOPPED ONTO THE SOFA AND PLACED THE AROMATIC herbal pack on her forehead. Though the trembling had eased, every muscle still felt weak, and her head boomed. Right now, she needed sleep, she needed coffee, and she needed chocolate—and she was likely to get only one of those in the near future.

A soft sigh filled the silence. She cranked open an eye and looked across the room. Her grandmother sat at the laminate table, chin resting on palms, as she stared at the small crystal ball in front of her.

"No luck?"

"Not a damn thing." Gwen leaned back and rubbed her forehead. Moonlight danced across the multi-colored stones decorating her gnarled fingers.

"It's been a long night. Maybe you'll get something once you take a break."

"Maybe." She met Kat's gaze and smiled. "I did see one thing, though."

Kat had seen that smile before, and it usually meant trouble headed her way. Wariness edged her voice as she said, "What?"

"Your werewolf is on the way here."

Kat frowned at her word choice. "Werewolf?"

"The man you met in the warehouse."

"He's a werewolf?" It would certainly explain the anger she'd sensed in him. And her own, somewhat surprising, attraction to a man she couldn't even see. Werewolves were sexually alluring when the full moon was rising. "So why didn't I sense that? I thought he was a shifter."

"No, he's definitely something more than a shifter. But the question is, what type of werewolf is he?"

Kat raised an eyebrow. "There is more than one type?"

Gwen laughed softly. "Of course. There are those who are born and those who are bitten."

"Really? I didn't know." Mainly because they'd never actually come across any werewolves in their travels for the Circle. A couple of wolf shifters was as close as they'd ever gotten.

"Those who are bitten are the ones responsible for all the bad press werewolves get." Gwen rose, her movements stiff as she hobbled over to the kettle. "They're usually bitten well after puberty and don't have the experience or knowledge to control the sexual and emotional turmoil the rising moon causes. And of course, the physical change makes most quite mad."

"And those that are born?"

Gwen filled the kettle and plugged it in, then grabbed three cups and spooned instant coffee into them. "The werewolf born can generally control the worst of his urges. And they can generally shift shape anytime they want."

"Does the moon still force the change?"

"Always. That's part of the legacy that can never be escaped."

Like the weakness and headaches she got after using her abilities to the fullest. Like the arthritis ravaging her grandmother's body. "So why is he coming here?"

"He's one of the cops on the special task force. And his niece is one of the missing kids."

"Oh, great." A werewolf seeking vengeance was not what they needed right now. The kettle's shrill whistle sounded. She put the herbal pack on the coffee table and swung off the sofa. "And you didn't answer my original question."

"No." Gwen hesitated. "He seeks us out because he thinks we know more than we are saying."

"Which we do." Kat grabbed the kettle and poured the water into the three cups. "Does he take milk?"

Her grandmother shook her head. "Three sugars."

"Black syrup. Yuck."

Gwen smiled and continued. "And because he's desperate for a miracle and willing to chase even the craziest of leads."

Kat nodded. Had their positions been reversed, she'd be doing the same. "So, what's the plan?"

"I think we need to keep your wolf on a very tight leash."

"He's not my anything, so quit it." She stirred some sugar into the second coffee, then handed it to her grandmother. "You don't have to try to set me up with every eligible male that comes within sniffing distance."

"Someone has to. You're doing an abysmal job of it yourself."

Kat rolled her eyes. "I thought gray-haired grannies were supposed to warn their granddaughters against the evils of casual sex, not devise ways of getting them into the sack."

"My dear, you're so much easier to deal with when you've been laid."

"Gran!"

Gwen's green eyes twinkled. "Well, it's the truth, isn't it?"

"Maybe," Kat muttered. A good night of sex certainly did have a way of easing the tension—but she didn't have the time for that sort of thing. Not with this case.

"My dear, there's always time if you use your imagination." Gwen patted Kat's arm, then hobbled over to the sofa.

Kat picked up the two remaining coffees and followed. "What do you mean by a tight leash?"

"Just that." Gwen eased her feet onto the coffee table and sighed. "Would you mind massaging my feet later? They're aching something fierce."

Kat nodded and placed one coffee cup on the table. The other she held on to as she walked to the door. "We can hardly hog-tie him and keep him captive."

"We won't have to. Trust your grandmother and open the door."

She did. "Welcome, detec—"

The words died, snatched away by the potency of the man approaching. In some ways, he was nothing out of the ordinary—dark hair, nut-brown eyes, a determined chin that desperately needed a razor. He wore a black leather jacket that strained across his shoulders, a white shirt pulled over the top of faded denims, and black boots. An everyday man. Except on this man, everyday was not only powerful but sexy as hell.

She inanely offered him the cup. "Coffee?"

One dark eyebrow rose as his gaze rolled languidly down her body. It was a touch that wasn't a touch, and yet one that sent lust winging through every fiber of her being. Though she wore an old T-shirt and loose sweatpants, the intensity of his gaze suggested she might well have been standing there naked. His desire burned her. Made her tremble. Ache.

"Thank you."

As he wrapped a hand around the cup, his fingers briefly caressed hers. Energy jolted her spine. Knowing werewolves were sexually magnetic during the rising of the full moon and actually experiencing the effects were two entirely different things. She resisted the urge to mop her brow and stepped back.

"Come in."

"Thanks."

He moved past, and she caught a whiff of his aftershave. It was an odd mix—the rich aroma of freshly cut wood combined with the tang of earthy spices.

"Evening, Detective Morgan." Amusement touched her grandmother's voice. "Nice of you to finally drop by and say hello."

"You were expecting me?"

"You seem surprised."

"A little." He folded onto the chair opposite Gwen. "Though Benton told me you were both psychics."

Kat sat crossed-legged on the floor and grabbed her coffee. "But you didn't believe him." It was a statement rather than a question. One that had echoed through their entire lives.

His gaze met hers. There was nothing to see in those rich depths now. No emotion, no heat. What had passed between them at the door had been carefully controlled and thrust away.

"I had no reason to. I still don't."

A werewolf who didn't believe in the supernatural? Interesting. She shared a glance with her grandmother, then said, "So what did you come here for?"

"To satisfy curiosity." He took a sip of his coffee. "Perfect. Thanks."

Kat ducked her head to hide her smile. He might not believe, but he wasn't about to query. Not when he wanted help.

It was Gwen who continued. "Ask your questions, werewolf. It's been a long night, and we both need our rest."

A raised eyebrow was the only reaction Gwen got to her calling him a werewolf. Maybe he thought ignoring the statement was better than confirming what he was. "You found the body of the second victim. How?"

His tone was deliberate. Controlled. Looking at him, you'd never guess his niece was one of the missing kids. Still, you didn't have to be psychic to see where this line of questioning would lead. Kat glanced at her grandmother. Usually Gwen didn't go too indepth with details, but she had an odd feeling it would be different with the werewolf.

"Scrying," Gwen answered.

"Which is?"

"You want the short form or the proper explanation?"

He hesitated. "Proper."

"Then it's a type of divination in which a trance is induced that allows the practitioner to see events or people—be they past, present, or future. My preferred method is via a crystal ball, but any polished surface will do in an emergency."

"Then you've tried finding the other victims?"

Absolutely nothing showed in his face. But then, he was a cop, long schooled in the art of questioning without revealing. And despite the earlier instances of sensing his emotions, right now Kat was getting zip.

"Yes, but it's not something you can turn on and off. It often takes time."

"Time those children might not have."

"We know that, Detective."

He nodded. "Does talking to the victims' families help?"

"No. It usually only muddies the psychic waters." Gwen hesitated. "You do know the chances of your niece still being alive are small, don't you?"

He didn't react, not physically. Yet his anger stepped into the room, became a presence that was almost overwhelming. "Until I see her body, I won't give up hope."

"That's as it should be."

"So will you try to find her? Now?"

Gwen pursed her lips. "I can't guarantee—"

"I'm asking you to try, not guarantee."

His voice was brusque, harsh. The voice of a man not used to asking for anything.

Gwen considered him for a long moment, then nodded. "Kat, get the crystal."

"Gran, you need to rest—"

"I feel the need to do this. Get the crystal for me."

Kat shot an annoyed look the detective's way, but he absorbed it without impact. She climbed to her feet and retrieved the small ball from the table, handing it carefully to her grandmother.

Gwen eased her feet off the coffee table, then carefully placed the crystal on it. She rolled her neck, stretched gnarled fingers until they cracked, then began to stare at the glittering surface of the ball. After a few moments, her gaze became glassy and unfocused—a sure sign it was working.

Kat walked over to the sink, grabbed a glass of water and a couple of painkillers, then sat back down. There was nothing to do now but wait.

The detective made no noise, no movement, his expression intense as he watched Gwen. He might not believe in psychics and witchcraft, but right now he was obviously desperate and willing to go to any lengths. Even if it meant relying on the unbelievable.

Kat finished her coffee and reached for the herbal pack, then lay back on the floor and placed it over her forehead. The detective's gaze swept her—something she felt rather than saw. Desire stirred deep inside. Gran was right—it had been far too long since she'd been with a man. And self-administering to ease the ache was certainly a pale substitute.

But by the same token, casual sex had lost its allure. She wanted something more. Something deeper. Something that just couldn't work, given what she did.

Lord, why did this man have to be a werewolf in the midst of moon fever? She'd been doing all right until he came along, reminding her she had needs just like everyone else.

Time ticked by. The sofa creaked as the detective leaned back. His gaze was a heated touch that began to sweep her more often. Hunger stirred between them, though it was less of a potent force than what she'd faced at the door. He could obviously control it better at some times than others, and she wondered what the deciding factor was. Inactivity, perhaps? Or the touch of the moon itself?

Gwen sighed. Kat sat up, catching the pack as it fell. Her grandmother's face was ashen, her breathing shallow. Kat scrambled to her feet and grabbed the water and painkillers.

"Here, take these."

She placed the tablets in her grandmother's mouth, then held the glass while she drank. Gwen's fingers were locked in a hooked position, and she wouldn't be able to hold anything until the rigidness had eased. It could take minutes, or it could take hours.

Gwen's gaze met Kat's. The depth of despair and horror so evident in those green depths told Kat it was another bad situation. She swallowed heavily, not sure she could stand it again so soon. She didn't have the strength—physically or mentally.

"Where?" she whispered.

"Warehouse on Tenth Avenue. First floor."

Kat rose, grabbed her coat and keys, then finally looked at the detective. His face was expressionless, but his shoulders were taut—an indication of the tension she could feel.

"You coming?"

"Yes." His gaze flicked to Gwen. "Is it her?"

Gwen sighed. "I don't know."

He rose. "I hope to God it's not."

So did Kat. Because if the violence so evident in his aura was anything to go by, they didn't want to be around him when his niece's body was discovered. She slipped on some shoes, then headed out the door.

"Detective?" Gwen called.

They both paused and looked back.

"Be prepared, because what you're about to find will not be pleasant."

"I'm a cop. I've seen humanity at its worst." His voice held an edge that was both anger and resignation.

"But humanity has nothing to do with what is happening here." Gwen's gaze flicked to Kat. "Don't go too deep. Even surface-level readings will be bad."

Kat swallowed back bile. It had been bad enough last time. What the hell had the soul-sucker done now?

THREE

THE RUMBLE OF THE MUSTANG'S ENGINE WAS THE ONLY sound to be heard. It wasn't the sort of car Ethan had expected her to drive, but nothing about Katherine Tanner was what he'd expected.

He shifted and studied her profile in the moonlight. Her features were slightly sharp, and her hair short, but thick and wavy. It tended to stick up at angles, reminding him oddly of night-colored feathers. She wasn't slender, nor was she fat. Just a woman with lots of curves she wasn't afraid to show.

He let his gaze slip to her wonderfully full breasts. She wasn't wearing a bra, and the ridiculously small T-shirt left little to the imagination. Her nipples hardened as he watched, stretching the faded cotton to its limits. The moon might be raging through his system, but he wasn't the only one who hungered tonight. He could smell her desire as clearly as he felt his own.

Perhaps he wouldn't have to go far to satisfy his needs. Maybe he'd found the perfect release right here with this woman. He certainly intended to keep an eye on both her grandmother and her anyway, if only because they seemed to have a better idea of what was going on than either he or the rest of the department.

If he wanted to find his niece and catch the bastards behind these kidnappings, these two might be the key—however unorthodox their methods.

And in many ways, he had no other choice. He didn't have the time to search for another partner, and with the full moon drawing close, it was getting harder and harder to control his hunger. If she knew what he was, she undoubtedly was aware of the effect the moon had on his system. And she was certainly outspoken enough to tell him to back off if she wasn't interested.

But right now, his needs—and hers—would have to wait until they'd searched the warehouse.

He looked out the side window. It was nearly three in the morning, and the streets in this section of Springfield were crowded with the usual mix of night-crawlers. The city had recently set up "exclusion" zones to keep the drug users, prostitutes, and other problem types out of the downtown area, which was successful in itself, but in reality had only shifted the problem to another area. And while police crack-downs usually kept the streets clean for several weeks, everything eventually drifted back. He'd long ago come to the conclusion that it was all a waste of time, and that those in the government hadn't the political will or the knowledge to truly tackle the problem.

He rubbed his eyes tiredly. He loved being a cop, but sometimes the sense of futility was almost overwhelming. No matter what he or Mark or the others did, it just didn't seem to make a difference. The pros still hawked their wares, people still got killed, and maniacs still kidnapped innocent little girls and did God knows what to them . . .

"You got a name?" Her voice was sharp, as if she'd sensed the turn of his thoughts. Given the events of the night so far, nothing would surprise him. She continued on, her voice a little softer. "Or are we keeping this strictly formal?"

He could hardly keep it formal when he intended to have sex with her. "Ethan. You?"

"Kat."

"Suits you more than Katherine."

A smile tugged her generous lips. "You're not the first to note that."

He supposed not. He let his gaze linger on her lips for several seconds, then said, "What was wrong with your grandmother's hands?"

"Arthritis. The visions make it worse."

"Then why doesn't she stop?"

She glanced at him, green eyes bright in the moonlight. "Can you stop the effects the moon has on you?"

"I can control it. Up to a point." Up until the night the moon bloomed full.

"Exactly."

"But she has a choice—"

"No, she doesn't. Neither of us does."

He frowned. "What do you mean?"

She took a deep breath, then puffed out her cheeks. "You'll see soon enough." She stopped the car. "We're here. There's a flashlight on the backseat."

He grabbed it, then climbed out. The warehouse was at least six stories high and, like the warehouse in which they'd found the last kid, had been fouled by vandals, time, and the elements. His gut clenched. He didn't want to see what he knew he'd find in there—be it Janie or the other missing kid.

Kat came around the car, her face pale as she studied the warehouse towering above them. He was half tempted to tell her to wait here, but he very much suspected she'd tell him exactly where he could shove such a suggestion. So he handed her the flashlight and said, "Keep behind me."

She didn't argue, which surprised him—especially after her stubbornness earlier. They pushed through a hole that had been cut into the chain-link fence and walked across cracked concrete littered with weeds. The wind moaned through the window's broken glass, and tin flapped. Somewhere a door creaked, creating an uneasy soundtrack that very much belonged in some B-grade horror movie.

He pressed open the door and looked inside. Though the darkness was complete, he had no trouble seeing. The moon sharpened all his senses, and his sight was wolf-keen. There was no one here.

But the metallic smell of blood hung on the air, mingled with the aroma of rotting flesh. He had to go on, had to see, but there was no reason for Kat to do either. "Why don't you go call—"

"Don't even think it." Her voice was terse. "You want to call the cops, then you go do it. Right now, I have to go up those stairs."

She pushed past him, the flashlight's bright beam dancing across the graffiti-strewn walls as she crossed the empty expanse. He caught her at the stairs.

"Damn it, woman, there's something dead up there!"

Her gaze met his, her eyes wide and haunted. "Believe me, I know."

She began to climb. He shook his head and stayed beside her. The smell was worse on the second-floor landing—sharper, fresher, and ripened by the aroma of urine and excrement. He tried breathing through his mouth, but there was no avoiding the foulness of the place. She swung left and he followed. Moonlight filtered in through the broken windows, highlighting the bottles and syringes and piles of shit lining the base of the walls. If this warehouse was some kind of refuge, where the hell were the dregs of humanity who lived in it?

When they entered the small room at the end of the hall, they found the kid. Not that anyone would have guessed the half-chewed fragments strewn over the floor had ever been a child. There was enough, however, for him to realize it was a boy, not a girl. The surge of relief was intense, but it was swiftly replaced by fury. No one deserved this sort of death, let alone an innocent little kid. His stomach rose, and it took every ounce of willpower not to lose it then and there.

There was bad, and then there was *bad*. But this was worse than either of those.

Kat made an odd sound in the back of her throat, and he quickly looked at her. She had a hand against her mouth and was shaking so hard her teeth chattered. She wasn't looking at the remains that lay scattered around them, but was staring off into space. Her eyes were wide open and filled with such horror and pain it tore at something deep inside him. He didn't know what the hell was going on, but he was sure of one thing: she couldn't stay in this room.

He swept her up into his arms and raced back down the stairs. She didn't protest, didn't say anything at all, her eyes wide and glassy. Sweat sheened her skin, but her flesh was so cold he might have been holding ice.

Once outside, he set her down on a pile of bricks and thrust her head between her knees. "Breathe deep."

She obeyed. After a few minutes the trembling eased, but she still did not raise her head. He thrust his hands in his pockets and waited. He didn't know what else to do.

At last she looked up, her cheeks stained with tears. She sniffed, then wiped a hand across her eyes. "It wasn't—"

"No," he agreed softly. "It wasn't." But it was still a kid up there—a kid who didn't deserve to die the way he had. "I have to go back up." Had to check what he thought he'd seen.

She nodded. "I'll wait here. I don't need to feel anything else right now."

Feel? That was an odd word to use. "Will you be all right here?"

A ghostly smile touched her lips, though it failed to lift the fear from her eyes. "Fine. Just don't be long, because I'll have to call your people in."

He nodded and went back. It was no better the second time around. He breathed though his mouth, but the smell still coated the back of his throat, so he swallowed death with every intake of air. He fought nausea and mounting horror as he carefully studied each of the remaining body parts. He hadn't been mistaken before. Something big had chewed through the bones. Something like a dog.

Or a wolf.

He rose and went back to Kat. She looked no better than she had twenty minutes before. "Did you call the department?"

"Yes."

"Then I'll have to go. I'm supposed to be on leave."

She didn't seem surprised. "Take my car." She handed him the keys. "I need to go to the beach after I finish here, so you can meet me down in Florence, if you like."

"What do you hope to find at the beach?"

"Cleansing." She looked past him. "You'd better go. I can hear their sirens."

So could he, and they were still a distance away. Her hearing was as good as his—and his was moon-enhanced. "How will you get there if I take your car?"

She shrugged, as if it wasn't important. And maybe it wasn't. Or maybe she simply intended to hitch a lift from someone.

"Florence is a reasonably big place," he added, "with lots of ocean frontage. How are you going to find me?"

"I'll find you, believe me."

Oddly enough, he did. "Will you be all right?"

She looked at him. Deep in the green depths of her eyes he saw a suffering so profound he had to fight the urge to reach out and comfort her.

"We both have curses we have to live with," she said softly. "And in many ways, mine is much worse than yours."

Nothing could be worse than losing your soul to an animal every full moon. "What do you mean?"

She rubbed a hand across still-damp eyes. "I'll explain later. You need to go. Right now."

What he needed was an explanation. But the sirens were drawing closer, and Benton's blood pressure would go haywire if he found Ethan here.

"I'll see you at the beach," he said, and walked away.

KAT WAITED UNTIL THE RUMBLE OF THE MUSTANG'S ENGINE had faded, then dialed the hotel. Gwen answered on the third ring.

"I'm sorry, Kat," she said. "I wish I could have warned you."

No amount of warning could have helped ease the horror of what she'd felt in that room. Bile rose and she closed her eyes, fighting the need to vomit, fighting the tears pressing past closed eyelids. "I needed to go in without any preconceptions. We both know that."

Gwen sighed. "So what did you feel?"

What *didn't* she feel? God, the room was a menagerie of the dead's emotions. "He died a lot slower than Daniel. The soul-sucker let a werewolf play around with him for a while before she sucked his essence away."

She tried not to think of the bits of humanity strewn across that room. Tried not to remember the blinding fear and agony that had savaged her mind and cut through her soul. She failed miserably at both. But it was what had followed those emotions that had sickened her most—the smells and sensations of sex. The soul-sucker had mated with the werewolf amidst all the carnage.

"Hang on," she said and hurriedly put the phone down, staggering away to the fence to lose the little she'd eaten for dinner.

She was wiping her mouth with her hand when the cops came in. Benton took one look at her and ordered an officer to go get a bottle of water.

"Where?" was all he said to her.

"Second floor, to the left."

He nodded and walked away. The water was hurriedly fetched, and she swilled some around her mouth, then spat it out. Once all the cops were inside, she went back to the bricks and picked up the phone.

"Sorry, Gran."

"The cops are there, I gather?"

"Just arrived."

"Then it'll be an hour or so before you get back here?"

"Probably more. I need to cleanse. I feel the dead right through me."

"Of course you would, after walking into that room." Gwen sighed. "Get us both some breakfast on the way back. I'll contact Seline and ask her to research what exactly this soul-sucker is. Now that we know what she looks like, it should be easier to track her down."

"It'll be nice to know what will actually kill her before we confront her."

"Yes, it would."

Kat glanced up as Benton came out of the warehouse. "Gotta go. It's question time."

"Make sure you bring your werewolf back with you."

"He's not my anything," she repeated flatly. "And why do you want him back?"

"Because we're all going to need to protect each other in the near future."

A chill ran down her spine. "Why?"

"I'll tell you later."

The phone went dead. Kat shoved it back into her pocket and looked up at Benton. And knew it was going to be a very long couple of hours before she could fly to freedom.

DAWN HAD BEGUN TO PAINT THE SKY PINK AND ORANGE BY the time Ethan sensed her. He sat halfway down a grassy knoll, watching the waves shimmer across the sand as he listened to her approaching steps.

She smelled like no one he'd ever met. Fresh and airy, like warm summer rains and crisp spring winds. It was an alluring, almost erotic combination.

She stopped several feet away on his left. The stiffening breeze tugged at her hair, throwing the dark strands across her face. Her hands were thrust deep into her pockets, but even from where he sat he could see the trembling. Tiredness, or a continuing reaction to what they'd walked into?

"I have to swim."

She *was* nuts. "That's the Pacific out there, not a sheltered cove."

"I know. And it's perfect." Her gaze met his, as remote as her voice. "Given your current state, I suggest you wait in the car."

She didn't wait for a reply, just continued toward the water. When she reached the sand she began stripping. Soon there was nothing left but flesh.

She was creamy and luscious and absolutely perfect, and he went hard just watching her. If he were any sort of gentleman, he'd go back to the car as she'd suggested, but he'd long ago given up any such pretensions. Besides, he seriously doubted whether *any* man could walk away right now.

She dove underwater, then rose a heartbeat later and rolled onto her back. Her breasts were generous white mounds with dark thrusting peaks that he suddenly ached to taste. He shifted and wished his jeans weren't so damn tight. The goddamn zipper was killing him.

It was lucky the moon had fled. At least he had control enough to simply sit there. And while he suspected she wouldn't rebuke his advances right now, he wasn't about to hit on a woman who'd been through what she'd just endured.

He watched until it became apparent she was getting ready to come out, then got up and walked stiffly to the car. His erection hadn't gone down any by the time she reappeared. Though she was fully dressed, moisture made the T-shirt almost see-through, and her sweatpants clung like a second skin.

Thank God for long shirts. "Back to the motel?"

She nodded, her teeth chattering and skin almost blue. He took off his coat and draped it across her shoulders, then settled her into the passenger's seat. After climbing into the driver's side, he started the engine and turned the heater up full blast. The car's interior quickly became a furnace. The chattering eased and her skin became a more normal color. But the T-shirt took longer to dry, and he wasn't at all sorry about that.

"Mind telling me what that was about?"

She sighed. "I'm an empath with a difference."

He glanced at her, but she still had her eyes closed. "What sort of difference?"

"Instead of sensing the emotions of the living, I soak up the feelings of the dead."

"That's not possible."

She snorted softly. "I wish."

"But . . ." He frowned. They'd known what he was from the moment he walked up to the motel door, and that was something no one could have told them. Everything else, maybe, but not that. "How?"

"I'm not really sure myself. But it seems the more emotional or violent the death, the more those feelings permeate a room."

"So when you walked into that room—"

"I felt everything that little boy had when he died."

No wonder she'd been so cold. She'd shared head space with violence and death. "How the hell do you keep sane?"

A smile touched her still pale lips. "I was under the impression you thought I wasn't."

"Well, swimming in the ocean until you're blue is pretty damn crazy."

"I had to wash myself clean," she said softly. "I could smell them. On me. In me."

A sentiment he could certainly understand. He'd done the same thing himself once or twice over the years—though admittedly, he'd chosen a hot shower rather than an icy ocean. "So what happens now?"

"Now we need to get some breakfast and take it back to the motel. You know a bakery open at this hour?"

"I'm a cop. We know the opening time of every bakery, deli, and fast-food chain in the whole damn city."

She looked at him. "Really?"

"Really," he said solemnly, glad to see her smile had finally touched her eyes.

"Then take me to your favorite, and I'll buy you breakfast." She hesitated. "Unless, of course, you'd rather go home."

He had nothing—and no one—to go home to. And he wasn't leaving this woman's side until this case was solved. Though he might not believe in psychics and witchcraft, the last few hours had certainly proven these two not only knew everything the police knew, but had an innate ability to keep one step ahead of the pack. Right now, that was exactly where he needed to be.

And if he could get into her bed as well, all the better.

GWEN WAS ASLEEP ON THE SOFA BY THE TIME THEY GOT back to the motel room. Kat dropped the bags of cinnamon rolls and pastries on the small table and walked over.

"Gran?" She kept her voice soft, not wanting to startle the older woman.

Gwen sighed and opened her eyes. "My feet feel like bricks. You'll have to massage them before you do anything else."

"I'll do that," Ethan said behind her. "You go get breakfast ready."

Kat looked up in surprise. "You sure?"

He nodded. "My mom had arthritis, too. My brother and I used to take turns massaging to ease the aches for a while."

"Well, before you touch *my* feet, you're going to have to provide a proper introduction." Gwen's eyes twinkled despite the echoes of pain. "I can't keep calling you Detective Morgan if we're going to get so friendly."

He smiled, and Kat's breath caught. She had a feeling he didn't smile much, but when he did—wow.

"It's Ethan, ma'am."

"Gwen Tanner. Pleased to meet you." She shook his offered hand. "The oil's over there by the sink."

He retrieved it, then sat on the coffee table and eased her feet onto his legs. If the relief on Gwen's face was anything to go by, he certainly knew his way around a bottle of massage oil. Maybe that was something Kat could put to good use later . . .

He chose that moment to glance at her, and for several heartbeats Kat found herself pinned by the power of his gaze. What passed between them was a recognition of fate. Of inevitability. But more than that, it was a promise of passion and satisfaction . . . and something else, something she couldn't quite define.

A tremor ran through her. She'd never felt this strong an attraction to anyone, and in some ways it was almost scary. The pull she felt had nothing to do with the allure of a werewolf in the middle of moon fever, and everything to do with the man himself. By the same token, she was positive the moon had *every-*

thing to do with his attraction to her. But that didn't matter. What *did* matter was finding time alone without jeopardizing the case.

She lowered her gaze and got down to the business of making coffee and setting out breakfast. "Gran, are you coming over to the table, or would you prefer to remain where you are?"

"I'll stay here." She patted Ethan's hands. "Thanks, pet. That feels much better."

Kat tossed him a hand towel, then brought over Gwen's coffee and cinnamon rolls. "So what's the plan today, beside rest?"

"I'll try to do another reading this afternoon. I've got a feeling this thing is not going to hang around for much longer."

"Because the police are closing in?" Ethan asked.

Gwen gave him a wry look. "The police haven't a clue. Present company included."

He raised an eyebrow. "So you don't believe we'll catch the psycho behind this?"

"No, because none of you truly know what you're up against." She glanced at Kat. "Why don't you explain it to the man?"

Kat sighed and cupped her hands around her coffee mug. "The thing that's killing these kids is what we've termed a soul-sucker. It's a vampire of sorts, but instead of blood, it feeds on souls."

His expression was blank, but she could feel his disbelief as easily as she'd felt his desire only moments before. "Vampires don't exist."

"Much as werewolves don't exist? Get real, Detective."

"Ethan," he said automatically, then added, "That

kid last night was torn apart. And the first kid was discovered drained of blood."

Kat nodded. "Neither of which was the actual cause of death."

"The coroner says otherwise."

"The coroner can't see the gaping hole this thing created when it ripped their souls from their bodies."

"How can *you* even see something like that?"

She shrugged. "I told you before, I'm empathic. I see and feel emotions. A soul being torn free is a pretty emotional event, believe me."

He stared at her for several minutes, then shook his head. "I can't. Sorry."

"Then believe this," Gwen said. "That thing is not working alone. At the very least, it still has a werewolf working with it, and I suspect there are others. It saw Kat last night, and it now knows we're on its trail. That puts us in great danger."

He glanced at Kat. "You want me to arrange police protection?"

"No," Gwen answered. "Their attempts to protect us would mean as little as their attempts to find this thing."

He flexed his fingers, then picked up his coffee. He didn't like being told his department was useless. "Then what do you want?" His voice held an edge of harshness.

"You want to find this killer fast, and you're not particularly fussy about how you do it. We need additional protection. Two very compatible needs, I should think."

His gaze flicked from Gwen to Kat, then back again, but in that brief moment Kat saw the surge of triumph. He'd had no intention of leaving anyway, she realized. He would have done all that he could—even using what was flaring between them—to keep close. It should have annoyed her, but it didn't, simply because she understood his motives.

She just had to hope she was one of the more pleasurable stones in his path.

"If Benton sees me anywhere near the two of you, I'm history."

"Then make sure you're not seen."

"Easier said than done. The captain's got a nose for this sort of stuff." He scratched his chin, the sound harsh in the silence. "If I step into this, I expect to be made a full partner. No secrets."

"Don't worry, Detective—you're going to learn a whole lot more than you bargained for on this one."

Gwen's voice was dry, and Kat shot her a quick look. If her amused expression was anything to go by, she wasn't talking about the case, but something else. Something more personal.

A thought *she* didn't like one bit. When it came to matchmaking, her grandmother was almost as bad as Seline, the Circle's head honcho. Both had been pushing Kat for years to find a man who could be a true partner—in work and out of it. Insinuating, in Kat's opinion, that the men she'd been with over the years either weren't manly enough or hadn't a hope in hell of being able to work with her, let alone live with her. And if she was being honest, the latter was certainly a half-truth. She wasn't the easiest person in the world to get along with. As Ethan would undoubtedly find out if she didn't get her regular fix of chocolate soon.

He took another pastry, then stood. "I'll go home and collect some clothes. I trust you ladies won't run off while I'm gone?"

"We'll be here," Gwen said. "You can trust that, if nothing else."

His gaze very much indicated he didn't trust either of them. But he didn't say anything, just headed out the door.

Kat looked at her grandmother. "Why?"

Gwen sighed. "I had a vision while you were gone. He's in as much danger as we are."

"Because he was part of the task force?"

"Because he was closer than he knew. Remember, he was at that warehouse before you or the soul-sucker or the vampire. I wouldn't be surprised if he has latent precognition skills."

"And the soul-sucker was heading after him because of that?"

"Yes." Gwen rubbed her eyes. "It's also after us, for much the same reason. We all stand a better chance if we stay together."

"Did you see when they'll attack?"

"You know my visions are never that specific."

Unfortunately, she did. But occasionally she hoped for a miracle. "Was that all?"

"I did see one other thing. And it's the reason I waited until Ethan left to tell you all this."

A lump settled in her stomach. There could be only one reason to wait until Ethan had left. She gulped down her coffee to ease the dryness in her throat, but it didn't seem to help much. "What?"

"His niece is still alive."

FOUR

KAT BLINKED. "WHAT?"

"She's alive. She's not dead yet."

"Then why . . . ?"

The question hung in the air, and Gwen sighed. "Can you imagine his reaction if I told him that? I don't know where she is, or what condition she's in. I just know that at this point in time, that little girl lives. It might be a different story in a few hours' time."

"And you got no image at all that could help us find her?"

Gwen shook her head. "It's not a warehouse, though. It's somewhere different."

"Why?" What sick game was the soul-sucker playing now?

"I don't know. But she seems to be working in six-day cycles, and she doesn't kill one kid until she's snatched another."

"If that's the case, then Ethan's niece has three days left."

"Maybe. Maybe not. As I said, I just don't know."

There was entirely too much on this case they just didn't know, and kids were dying because of it. She noted the slump in her grandmother's shoulders and rose. "Why don't you get some sleep?"

"I might just do that."

Kat offered a hand, then carefully pulled her grandmother upright. Gwen cursed as bones cracked, and worry stirred through Kat. The arthritis was definitely getting worse, and despite what she'd said to Ethan earlier, Gran did have a choice. Seline had recently found a way to mute both the visions and her scrying ability, so walking away was, for the first time in fifty years, a true option for her grandmother.

They had a beautiful house in San Francisco with a garden far too neglected. Over the past few months, she'd tried suggesting that maybe Gwen should stay home every other mission, but her grandmother wasn't having a bit of it. And the reason was *her.* They'd been together for close to thirty years—all her life, basically. Gwen wasn't only her grandmother, but mother, confidante, and best friend. They were so close, it always felt wrong when they were apart for more than a few days.

But that wasn't the problem. The truth was, Kat didn't have anyone else to protect her, and Gwen had no other reason for life. It was an impasse they'd obviously have to resolve soon, before the arthritis totally destroyed Gwen's quality of life.

After helping her grandmother into her nightie and then into bed, she checked the windows and locked the shutters. By that time, Gwen was asleep. Kat quietly cleaned up the breakfast mess, munching on the last cinnamon roll as she did so.

A shower and change of clothes followed. She needed sleep as well, but that wasn't an option until

Ethan got back. She wasn't about to leave the door open, and she could hardly expect him to wait outside while she and Gran snoozed. She ignored the imp slyly suggesting that wasn't her only reason and grabbed a cushion off one of the sofas.

The day outside was cool, but the sun caressed the porch with warmth. She sat on the cushion and leaned back against the wall. The view wasn't all that inspiring. Beyond her old Mustang there was only a thin expanse of concrete, then more connecting motel units—most of which were empty, which was strange, because it was awfully pretty here in winter. But maybe the news of the kidnappings was keeping the tourists away.

She closed her eyes.

She wasn't sure how long she'd slept, or how long he'd sat there, watching her. The awareness of him surfaced slowly—a tingle that rose from her toes and spread gently through every fiber, until her breath caught in her throat.

Like her, he sat on the porch, leaning back against one of the posts supporting the porch railing, his long legs stretched out in front of him. His dark hair was damp, his jaw freshly shaved, and he looked damn fine in black jeans and a dark teal shirt.

"A Christmas present from your mother, huh?" she said, eyeing the shirt with a smile.

He raised an eyebrow. "That psychic intuition?"

His voice flowed over her, as warm as cocoa on a cold night. "I don't know many men who'd walk into a store and buy a teal shirt. If you discount moms, Christmas, and birthdays, the only other options are wives or girlfriends."

"Of which I have none."

For which she was fiercely glad. "Because you're a cop, or because you haven't found the right woman?"

"Partially both, and partially neither."

"In other words, you're not saying?"

He shrugged. "What about yourself? No one waiting back in San Francisco?"

"You've been checking up on me."

"I'm a cop. It's what I do."

Yeah, right. As if the Springfield police department had the time to check the background details of everyone they came in contact with.

"I'm still waiting for a man who likes chocolate as much as I do." She hesitated, then added impishly, "So where do you stand on the chocolate debate?"

"Can't stand the stuff."

She sighed dramatically. "Another dream crumbles to dust."

Amusement touched the nut-brown depths of his eyes. "That mean we can't have sex?"

"Hell, *no*."

"Good."

Their gazes locked. Her heart began to beat in triple time, and desire burned through her veins. She wanted this man; there was no denying that. But right here and now was hardly practical—on a porch or in a motel room with her grandmother sleeping in the next bed. Gran probably wouldn't mind the noise, but the mere thought embarrassed the hell out of Kat.

"I need to sleep."

"That's a damn shame."

She wasn't exactly sure what he meant and was reluctant to ask, simply because the line between common sense and lust was thin enough. Too much more, and common sense hadn't a hope.

She stood, gathering the cushion as she did. He rose with her, and suddenly the porch seemed far too small. She licked her lips, saw his gaze drop to her mouth, and her throat went dry. He took the step that separated them, and all she could smell was freshly soaped skin and raw masculinity.

Her whole body tingled, as if brought to life by this man's presence. She'd never felt anything as powerful as this, and she so desperately wanted to make love to him. To feel his hands on her skin, his body on hers. In hers. Save for Gran being in the next bed . . .

"Gran's asleep." Her voice came out husky.

"I know."

Their bodies barely brushed, yet she was intensely aware of every part of him. From the fire burning in his eyes to the rapid rise and fall of his chest pressing against her aching nipples to the heated hardness of his erection.

"We can't. Not here."

"I know."

But he didn't retreat, and neither did she. He brushed a hand down her side to her hip, then moved his fingers across her bare stomach, searing her skin with the heat. Then his touch moved up under her T-shirt, and her breath caught in anticipation. When his thumb rubbed one aching nipple, she almost groaned in ecstasy.

She swallowed hard and tried to stay sane. "What you're doing could get us arrested."

"Sure could."

His attention moved to her other breast, and her

legs quivered. Even if she'd wanted to retreat, she very much doubted if her legs would support such an action. His other hand cupped her cheek and his thumb outlined her lips. Her heart stuttered to a stop as he slipped his hand around the back of her head, holding her still as he lowered his mouth to hers.

His kiss was like nothing she'd ever felt before. A gentle, erotic possession that gave so much and yet left her hungering for more.

"You'd better go inside," he whispered, his breath hot and unsteady against her lips. "Because I want you so bad I'm tempted to finish this right here and now."

She stepped back and suddenly remembered how to breathe again. "Thank you."

"For what?"

"For not pushing when you knew you could."

His smile was a little wry. "Trust me when I say it's little more than self-interest."

"Meaning?"

He brushed his fingers down her cheek, and she had to check the urge to step right back into his arms.

"Meaning I have every intention of making love to you as often as I can over these next few days, and if I pushed now, that wouldn't be likely to happen."

His words did little to ease her heart's unsteady pounding. "Self-preservation indeed."

He shrugged. "I'm a werewolf caught in moon fever. I need sex. But it's you I want this phase, no one else."

Then she had to thank the moon's presence, because without it she might not be standing here with this man. Might not have the promise of mind-blowing sex to warm her dreams.

"Will you be able to sleep on the sofa, or would you prefer to take the bed?"

"I'm not going to be able to sleep anywhere." His voice was ironic. "Not for a while yet."

Her gaze flicked down. "Oh. Sorry."

"I'm not." He leaned forward and brushed a kiss across her lips. "Pleasant dreams."

She had a feeling they would be beyond pleasant. As she headed inside, she thought she heard a sigh of disappointment coming from her grandmother's bed.

WARMTH CARESSED HER FACE, WARMING HER SENSES. KAT yawned and stretched, then opened her eyes. Her watch showed it was just past twelve. She hadn't slept long enough, but it was all the time she could afford.

She found a clean shirt, dug up a skirt, then headed into the bathroom. By the time she'd showered and dressed, her grandmother was awake and sitting at the table reading the paper. Ethan had come inside and was on the sofa, talking into a cell phone. But his gaze met hers and the arousal was instant. The sooner they got down and dirty, the better off they'd both be.

She turned on the kettle, then crossed her arms and leaned a hip against the small counter. "The aches better?"

Gwen grinned and said softly, "Better than yours, I'd wager."

"Don't start on me. It's likely to get unpleasant."

"This is exactly what I was talking about. Totally disagreeable when unsatisfied."

"Gran—"

Gwen held up her hand. "All I'm saying is these old ears are deafer than you think."

"Yeah, right." The woman had the hearing of an elephant. She just didn't have the floppy ears to go with it.

The kettle whistled shrilly. Kat made them all a cup of coffee, handing one each to Gwen and Ethan before sitting down at the table with her own.

"So, have you tried to do a reading yet?"

"Briefly. You know how difficult it is when I've just woken."

Kat nodded. "See anything of use?"

"One interesting point. It seems this thing knows about you and Ethan, but not yet about me, which is definitely in our favor."

"But it doesn't mean we don't have to worry about your safety any less than our own."

Gwen reached across the table and briefly squeezed Kat's hand. "But if I'm not seen with you, then its thoughts will be concentrated on you rather than me, and perhaps give me a clear field in which to see its mind and know its intentions."

They could only hope. "Even so, I want you to start using warding stones whenever we're not here."

Gwen nodded, then gave Ethan a smile as he sat down with them. "I also got a call from Seline. She thinks this thing is called a mara. It's an ancient spirit who enters houses either as a cat or as vapor to seduce men in their sleep, then steal their souls."

"It's stealing souls, but it's certainly not seducing men to do it."

"Not that we are currently aware of, anyway. But Seline's still digging around, so she might find a reason for the deviation in known behavior."

"Seline being the head of this Damask Circle you work for?" Ethan queried.

"He's a cop," Kat said with a smile. "They tend to dig."

"They do indeed." Gwen's gaze was amused as she looked at Ethan. "And yes, she is."

"Did she give you any idea how to stop this thing?"

"Not yet, but if it's some sort of vampire, then we could try all the traditional methods of killing a vampire."

Ethan's expression shut down. "I said stop, not kill. This thing has to be brought to justice and face trial."

"You don't really believe that," Gwen said. "And besides, no court or jailhouse currently built could ever hope to hold this thing."

"You know, I think white ash works against it," Kat said, remembering the soul-sucker's reaction in the warehouse. "I think I wounded it when I slashed it with the stake."

Ethan's expression was incredulous. Gwen patted his hand. "Don't worry, dear, it's going to get a lot worse." She leaned back in her chair. "I think I might try a little scrying."

Kat rose and retrieved Gwen's crystal, then nudged Ethan and nodded in the direction of the sofa. He rose and walked over. She sat down opposite him. Anything else just wasn't safe.

"So," she said, "who were you talking to on the phone?"

His gaze was doing a slow tour of her body, lingering appreciably on her bare legs. She hugged a pillow close to her chest and wondered at her sanity in choosing a skirt over jeans. This man had her hotter than hell.

"Nosy type, aren't you?" His amusement glimmered briefly at her actions.

"It's a gene all women are born with. You going to answer the question?"

"I was getting an update from my partner. Preliminary analysis confirms a large dog gnawed the bones. They believe it was only one, not a pack."

"Which is what I saw." She looked at her grandmother and saw her unfocused expression. The scrying appeared to be working again. "I don't suppose they have any indication of the time of death?"

He studied her for a moment. "Why is that important, beyond the obvious?"

She hesitated, wondering how much she should say. But it was probably better to be cautious than to give him a sliver of hope—and then have it dashed. After all, the fact that his niece might have three days was little more than guesswork on their part. "Because it would give us an idea how long this thing is keeping the kids before it kills them."

"They won't know until later today. Mark will call me as soon as he can."

She nodded. "Did you tell him you've joined us?"

"No. The less he knows in that regard, the better. If the hammer falls, I don't want to take him out as well."

"So what reason did you give for suddenly disappearing?"

His smile made her breath catch. "I said I'd met a pretty lady and intended to do nothing more than have incredible sex for the next few days."

Her pulse leaped into overdrive. "And do you?"

His smile was a wicked promise of things to come. She shifted slightly and resisted the temptation to fan her face.

"Whenever I can."

His voice was rich and husky and conjured images of those sheets again. Though even the floor would have done right now.

"And your partner didn't think this a strange deviation from a man who has no one in his life?"

"No one *permanent*. I'm a werewolf, not a monk."

"So when the moon rises, you're not overly fussy?"

He raised an eyebrow. "I've never sunk to prostitutes, if that's what you're asking."

She wasn't, and in many regards, it didn't really matter. He was here, she was horny, and if they could find the time and space, it could be damn well perfect between them. Did it matter how many different partners he'd had? She'd certainly had more than her fair share over the last ten years, despite her grandmother's recent insinuations that she was in danger of becoming a reborn virgin.

"What about yourself?" he said. "Why aren't you married and home safe with a kid or two? Why are you running around risking your life chasing madmen? Or madwomen?"

She gave him a deadpan look. "The barefoot-and-pregnant ideal went out a long time ago, Detective."

"That doesn't answer my question."

She sighed. "It comes down to the chocolate thing."

"So you're saying chocolate is better than sex?"

It was interesting he said *sex* rather than *love*. Was it some sort of werewolf thing that he kept mentioning sex without ever mentioning any form of emotion? She didn't know, but she suspected her grandmother might.

"In some cases, very definitely." She grinned and added, "Of course, I haven't had time yet to judge the offer on the table."

"So you still intend to . . . sample the offering?"

"The sooner the better."

"With that I agree wholeheartedly."

The look in his eyes smoked her insides. Gwen chose that moment to take a shuddering breath and wake from the scrying, and Kat wasn't sure whether to curse her grandmother's timing or bless it as she rose and walked over. She pried the crystal from her grandmother's fingers, then grabbed a drink and some painkillers, offering her both.

"Thanks," Gwen said, when she could.

"Get anything?"

Kat sat at the table, with Ethan next to her. She was intensely aware not only of his closeness but of his knee brushing hers. It was a promise of heaven she didn't dare react to.

Gwen nodded. "It's moving, all right. Down to Rogue River. It seems to have specific time restrictions, but I couldn't see what, exactly, it was."

Ethan frowned. "That's a tiny resort town. Why would it be going there in winter? Wouldn't summer be a better time if it wanted to prey on kids?"

"I think it's safe to say this thing has an agenda of its own, and until we uncover that agenda, we can't afford to second-guess its motives."

"So we're heading for Rogue River?" Kat said.

Gwen nodded. "But in two cars. What I saw confirms the fact that it doesn't know about me. We have to keep it that way a while yet."

"Gran, you can't drive that far in my car."

"I have no intentions of doing so. I'm going to hire myself a car and a driver, and travel in luxury."

Kat nodded. It wouldn't be the first time she had done that. The noise of the Mustang sometimes got a bit much for Gran, even if she didn't like to admit it. She glanced at Ethan. "You want to carpool?"

He nodded. "We'll take my Cadillac. You can leave your Mustang garaged at my place. It'll be safe enough."

That made sense. If, for some reason, the three of them had to travel in the one car later on, it would be more comfortable to do so in a Caddie. She looked at her grandmother again. "And after we get to Rogue River?"

"It'll be dark, but I suggest you two do a walking tour of the town and see if you can sense anything unusual."

"Then?"

"Then we fortify our defenses, sit back, and wait for their first attack."

FIVE

THEY'D BEEN DRIVING FOR A GOOD FOUR HOURS AND HAD barely exchanged a word. But the silence between them was comfortable—something Ethan found strange, considering how sexually tense they both were.

Not that he was any sort of expert when it came to knowing what it was like to spend time with a woman beyond the immediacies of sex. He satisfied his needs, made sure both parties had a good time, then he walked away. His work, his past, and what he was allowed for nothing else. And yet here he was, enjoying silence. Amazing.

"You hungry?" she asked.

"Is that a question, or are you actually saying *you're* hungry?"

"The latter." Her cheeks dimpled. "I need to eat."

So did he. But he also needed *her*. And with night encroaching, that need was becoming fiercer, harder to deny. He pointed to the Mercedes up ahead. "You want to phone your grandmother and see if she wants to stop?"

She nodded and reached for her cell phone. The conversation with Gran was short, and when she'd finished, there was heat in her cheeks.

He raised an eyebrow. "What did your grandmother say?"

"She said she's booked two adjoining cabins at the Rogue River Lodge. She said we should meet her there by ten."

That was over four hours away. Plenty of time to satisfy everyone's needs. "What else did she say?" There had to be something else to account for that flash of color in Kat's cheeks.

She met his gaze boldly. If she was embarrassed, she'd gotten over it quickly enough. "She said that werewolves are extremely fertile during the moon phase."

He didn't know what to say. Or think. The old girl certainly didn't miss a trick.

"She also said I should remember to use condoms."

Was that tacit approval? Or merely acceptance of the inevitable? "That goes without saying."

"I haven't got any."

He smiled. "I have. They're extra strong, to catch those over-fertile little rockets."

"Well . . . good." A warm smile touched her lips. "You know, of course, that the trigger to release those rockets involves food?"

"Including chocolate?"

"Chocolate will definitely earn you bonus points."

Then he was damn well going to find some chocolate. "The next town we hit is Bandon. Keep your eyes open for something to eat."

"And somewhere to have sex?"

Her voice was little more than a throaty purr and damn near shot his control to hell. He shifted slightly, but it did little to ease the sudden ache. "There's a blanket in the back, and we are near the ocean. That generally means beaches."

She raised an eyebrow, expression amused. "What is it with you and behavior that's likely to get us arrested?"

"Maybe underneath the cop there's a rebel trying to get out."

"There's certainly *something* trying to get out."

And with any sort of luck, it soon would. He pointed to the road ahead. "Concentrate. Or I won't be able to."

She grinned, and her gaze retreated to the front. But over the next ten minutes, the atmosphere became tense. He glanced at her. She still stared ahead, but her expression had become a little glazed. When he touched her arm, she jumped.

"There's trouble ahead." She picked up her phone and quickly dialed. "Gran? Did you see an attack other than the one tonight?"

She listened for a moment, her expression growing tenser. "Well, that may be the case, but I can feel something waiting ahead of us, and it's not alive."

Ethan frowned. Not alive? What the hell was she talking about?

"Yeah, I know it can't be a vampire. This is something else." She waited a few moments, then added, "No. I think you're right. I think this is aimed at us. We'll meet you at the lodge. Just make sure you set yourself a warding circle until we get there."

She hung up and looked at him. "I can feel trouble up ahead."

"What kind of trouble?" And what the hell was a warding circle?

"I don't know. But the mere fact that I'm sensing it suggests it's dead—whatever it is."

"How can something dead be a danger to us?"

"Vampires are dead. That thing we're chasing is dead." She shrugged. "Do you really think werewolves are the only supernatural beings that walk this earth?"

"I never thought about it." Which wasn't really the truth. He couldn't be what he was and *not* think about it. But it wasn't something he wasted a whole lot of brainpower over. Mostly, he just spent his time trying to either control or forget that part of himself. And generally, he succeeded.

"Well, then, you'd better start thinking and believing. Because those things are out there, and right now they're massing against us."

He bit back disbelief and glanced at his rearview mirror. There was no one behind them and no one in front of them other than the rapidly disappearing Mercedes. If they hit trouble, they'd have to face it alone, right here in the middle of nowhere.

"Any idea what we're facing?"

"No."

What good were talents that told you everything and yet nothing? "I have a gun in the back."

"Guns don't always hurt the dead."

He glanced at her, not sure whether or not she was joking. Her grim expression told him she wasn't. "So what *does* hurt them?"

"That depends on what we're facing."

He drummed his fingers against the steering wheel. "How far ahead is it?"

"Close." She hesitated. "And coming closer."

The road was long and straight. He couldn't see anything approaching. Not a truck, not a car, not an ant. Maybe her psychic senses were going a little haywire . . .

"Look out!"

From the corner of his eye he caught the flash of red. An engine growled, then a truck surged out of the trees and across the road. He planted his foot on the gas pedal, but it was already too late. The truck hit the back of the Cadillac and slewed them around. He fought the wheel for control, but the trees loomed fast. They hit with a sickening crunch that jarred every bone in his body. Through the creaking of metal and slight hiss of air came the sound of an engine—and not his. Whoever it was wasn't finished with them yet.

He undid his seat belt, then reached across and undid Kat's. "You all right?"

She nodded. There was blood on the side of her face, and her hands were trembling as she pushed back her hair. Her gaze met his, then went past him and widened. "It's coming again."

"Get out." He reached past her and thrust open the door. Then he did the same on his side and dove out, tasting dirt as he rolled and rose. And not a second too soon. The truck crashed into his Caddie, buckling the door and pushing in the entire side of the car.

He ran around and wrenched open the truck's door. The stink that hit him was almost overwhelming, and he gagged. God, hadn't this madman showered in the last twenty years? He reached in, grabbed the idiot by the arm, and pulled him out of the cab.

The driver hit the dirt and didn't move—though if the wild gyrations of his arms and legs were anything to go by, he was certainly trying. It looked for all the world like there was an invisible weight sitting on his chest, holding him down.

"It's a zombie." Kat stopped beside him, a bead of perspiration running down her cheek and an odd look of concentration on her face.

"As in *Night of the Living Dead*?"

"Yep."

He kicked the idiot's foot. "He doesn't feel dead. And he's certainly not acting dead."

The look she gave him suggested frustration. Or annoyance. "Well, no, and that's because he's the living dead and not the *dead* dead."

He swallowed the urge to argue the point. "We'll tie this moron up, then I'll call Mark and ask him to take care of the problem."

"The zombie won't be here by the time your partner gets the cops here."

"I tie a pretty mean knot, lady, and I have no intention of leaving the keys here."

"That doesn't matter. He's a zombie. He has more strength than you or I, and being tied with rope won't slow him down."

He took a deep breath and tried to remain calm. "So what do you suggest I do?"

"Kill it."

He stared at her. "You and your grandmother really do have this thing about killing, don't you?"

She indicated the squirming, stinking mass at their feet. "When you're dealing with the likes of this, you have no choice."

"I'm a cop and, despite common belief, we do not go around shooting people just for the fun of it."

"I'm not for a moment suggesting you shoot anything for fun. However, unless you want this thing coming after us, you need to either shoot its brains out or break its neck."

"I may be a werewolf, but I'm not a monster." He was beginning to wonder, however, if she was. But that certainly didn't kill his desire for her. Not in the least. "Go fetch the rope from the trunk."

She glared at him, then spun on her heel and did as he asked. Several seconds later she tossed the rope at him. "You'll regret this, you know."

"I'd regret killing him even more." He quickly tied the stinking mass, then tossed it in the back of the truck. The aroma of death seemed to cling to him as he stepped away. "I'll drive this thing off the road, then we'll continue on."

"Will the Caddie be drivable?"

"I think so." However, it certainly looked as if he'd be climbing in and out from the passenger side for the next few days. He leaped into the pickup and reversed it off the road, out of everyone's way. Then he checked to make sure the idiot was still trussed tight and tossed the keys deep into the trees.

When he turned around, Kat had her hands thrust onto her hips, one foot tapping and eyes narrowed. She looked as if she was up to something, but he wasn't sure what. He crossed the road, and her expression suddenly cleared.

"All done now?" Annoyance and amusement combined in her voice and made him just a little uneasy.

"Not yet." He walked past her and inspected the

damage to his car. As he suspected, the driver's door had been punched in too far to open. Both driver's-side door panels had sustained severe damage, but nothing that would affect the car's overall drivability. He hoped. It would be a cow to handle, though.

"Let's go." He dug a handkerchief out of his pocket and offered it to her, then climbed into the car and started the engine.

She got in after him, then flipped down the sun visor and began cleaning her wound with the aid of the vanity mirror. "Not deep."

"No."

He took off slowly. The Caddie shuddered and groaned, the rear end making a variety of noises he just didn't like. He gradually built up speed, but he had to ease up on the accelerator as they neared forty. The vibrations were too drastic to tempt fate by going any faster.

Silence fell between him and Kat, but it was nowhere near as easy as it originally had been.

"You have to trust me," she said eventually. "I really do know what I'm talking about."

"I have no real reason to believe that." Sure, her background checked out okay, but that didn't mean she and her grandmother weren't pulling some stunt.

And while his instincts said he *could* trust her, his instincts had been proven wrong before. Not often, but sometimes when it really counted.

"You don't have a lot of faith in women, do you?"

Her comment surprised him, and he looked at her. There was hurt in her green eyes, and while he regretted that, he had to wonder why. They might be sexually attracted to each other, but they were still strangers, after all. He had no more reason to trust her than he did any possible witness to a crime. "What's that got to do with anything?"

She crossed her arms. "Do you often sleep with women you don't trust?"

"All the time." Because he didn't trust *any* woman. Not nowadays.

"So women really are just a form of release to you?"

"Yes." He looked at her again. "But you knew that. You've known from the start that I was a werewolf."

She pulled her gaze from his and stared ahead. He had a sudden feeling it was going to take an awful lot of chocolate to get back into her good graces.

They cruised on. The terrain passed by, interesting but endless, and the vibrations coming through the steering wheel gradually got worse. Obviously, more damage had been done to the vehicle than he'd originally thought.

"What do you want to eat?" he asked as they rattled into Bandon.

She shrugged. "Something hot and hearty. I need to rebuild some energy."

He cruised around, and they eventually settled for a classy-looking restaurant that was close to the beach. He stopped the car and watched her climb out, enjoying the flash of her honey-colored thighs. "Get us a table. I'll take the Caddie to the service station just down the road, and be back as soon I can."

She nodded and slammed the door shut. He watched until she entered the building, then headed to the service station. Thankfully, it had a mechanic who seemed to know what he was talking about, and after a quick few minutes under the car, the mechanic came up with the news he'd feared.

"The accident has broken the rear axle. I usually have replacements, but I've just used up my last."

"How long will it take to get the parts in?"

"I've got them on order already. It shouldn't be more than a day or so."

They couldn't wait that long, so he plucked a business card from his wallet. "Fix it as quickly as you can. Is there a place nearby where I can rent another?"

The mechanic took a quick glance at the card, then shoved it into a greasy pocket. "There sure is. Just down the road. Tell Jim I sent you, and he'll give you a good deal."

"Thanks. Call me when the car's fixed?"

"Sure thing."

He collected their bags, the condoms, and his gun out of the car, but by the time he'd arranged a rental and got back to the restaurant, an hour had passed. He glanced at his watch. They still had a two-hour drive to Rogue River. Time was slipping away too fast. Kat wasn't eating when he arrived, which surprised him. She just sat at a table, sipping wine and staring out the window.

He slid into the chair opposite her. Things could have happened a whole lot quicker if he'd sat beside her and let the aura of the werewolf do its stuff, but as much as he wanted her, he also wanted her truly willing—a need that was a little disturbing and certainly something he'd never worried about before when in the midst of moon heat.

She glanced at him. There were smudges under her eyes, and her skin looked a little pale. "All set?"

"I had to rent a car. The Caddie's out of action for a couple of days."

"The Circle will reimburse all your expenses." Her voice still held a touch of coolness.

He waved the comment away. He'd spend his entire savings if that was what it took to bring Janie home and this killer to justice.

A waitress came over and handed them both menus. After some consideration, Kat ordered a steak, and he chose the salmon. The woman gave them a cheery nod and disappeared into the kitchen.

Kat picked up the bottle of wine. "You want a glass?"

He nodded and held his glass out. He would have preferred a beer, but he couldn't be bothered calling the waitress out again. He sipped the cool liquid carefully. A little sweet for his taste, but drinkable.

"Did you call your grandmother and tell her we're okay?"

She nodded. "She said it's important we get there by nine."

He frowned. "Why? What difference is a few minutes going to make?"

She studied him for a minute, then glanced out the window. "If we don't make our presence felt, another kid will be kidnapped."

Then they'd definitely be getting there by nine. "So, basically, we're bait."

She nodded. "If they're worrying about us, they're not stealing little kids."

"Won't that just force them to run again?"

"Gran doesn't think so. She thinks it'll all end in Rogue River, one way or another."

"You put a damn lot of faith in your grandmother's visions, don't you?"

Her gaze flicked to his. "I have no reason *not* to."

And therein lay the cause of her remoteness. Trust. Or more precisely, *his* lack of it. "I'm a cop," he said softly. "We tend not to trust anyone."

She leaned back and studied him for several moments. "That's just an excuse."

Yes, and she was reading him better than anyone ever had. "It's nothing personal."

Her look suggested it was *very* personal. She took another sip of her wine, then said, "Why?"

He shrugged. "The nature of the beast, I think." And an easy scapegoat in situations like this.

"The beast being the werewolf rather than the cop?"

"Yeah." He hesitated, but he knew he owed her at least some honesty. "I can't help the way I am. I don't need or want any complications in my life. All I'm after is a good time while the moon is full. After that, it's thanks for the sex, but bye-bye, sister."

"So there's never been anyone you've felt the slightest bit emotional about?"

"No." The lie slipped easily off his tongue. "And there won't ever be. As I said, it's the nature of the beast."

"So what lies between you and me—"

"Could be mind-blowing. But I won't allow it to be anything more."

She studied him for a moment, eyes bright and judgmental. Then she nodded. He wondered if that meant she accepted his terms. He hoped so, because he had nothing else he was willing to offer. The waitress approached with their meals, and silence fell as they began to eat.

When she'd finished, Kat leaned back in the chair. Her legs brushed his, charging his skin with electricity and sending a flash flood of heat to his groin.

"That was wonderful. All I need now is chocolate and my life would be complete."

Hopefully not *too* complete. He drew out the chocolate bar he'd bought earlier and offered it to her.

Her eyebrows rose. "And you think *that* trumps the chocolate cake I was eyeing for dessert?"

He glanced at his watch. They had only half an hour of free time left, and he needed her so fiercely it was becoming painful. "That rather depends. If we're to be at Rogue River by nine, we either have time for the chocolate cake here or a . . . walk on the beach, and a chocolate bar later. Lady's choice." He hoped to hell he hadn't misjudged her intentions.

Her cheeks dimpled. "Walk and lackluster chocolate bar it is, then. Want to ask for the check?"

"Most definitely."

She put the chocolate on the table, then picked up her purse and stood. "Then I'll be back in a moment."

His gaze slid down her back to her legs as she walked away. He fervently hoped she kept wearing overly tight tops and short, swirly skirts while he was around. A figure as good as hers shouldn't be hidden under layers of clothing. He glanced up as the waitress approached.

"Coffee?" she asked.

He shook his head and asked for the check instead. When Kat came back, he glanced out the window.

"Would you like me to go get your coat from the car? The wind can be pretty brisk around these parts, and it will be worse down near the waves."

A smile touched her full lips. "I'll be fine. Thanks."

When the check arrived, Kat took it out of his hands. "I'll get this," she said, and dropped cash on the plate.

They headed outside and found the steps down to the sand. Kat took off her shoes, dangling them from her fingers as she strolled barefoot along the damp golden sand. Waves teased her toes and splashed up her bare legs, and suddenly he found himself fighting the desire to lick the salt from her skin.

He scrubbed a hand across his jaw and studied the long stretch ahead. The beach curved around to the right and disappeared. Once they walked beyond that point, they'd be beyond the sight of those in the restaurant and, hopefully, alone.

They continued on slowly. Heat pounded through his veins and surged to his groin. He was hard and aching like hell. Dusk was beginning to shadow the horizon, and darkness would only bring the fever into full focus. He had to ease his needs before then, or there could be real trouble. He'd never tested his will like this before. He didn't know what would truly happen if the moon fever took over. But he could imagine, and he didn't want to do that to Kat. Or any other female, for that matter.

They rounded the corner. The sea stretched before them, dotted by huge outcrops of rocks, and the sand was a long stretch of emptiness. He gave a mental sigh of relief. One problem down.

She moved up the beach toward the grass-topped

dunes, then stopped, staring at the horizon as she rubbed her arms. He stopped behind her, close enough to smell her fresh fragrance, close enough that the scent of her desire washed over him. But not touching her. Not quite.

"Cold?"

She nodded. "You were right. I should have gotten my jacket."

If things went the way he hoped, she wouldn't really need it. The heat they'd raise between them would keep her warm enough. "Do you want to go back?"

She tilted her head back, one eyebrow arched as she met his gaze boldly. "Do you?"

In answer, he slid his hand around the cool skin of her bare waist and drew her close. She wriggled her bottom against him, sending heat flashing through his veins, then she sighed. "So much nicer."

It certainly was. He slid his hand under her shirt. A tremor ran through her, and her breath caught as he brushed one taut nipple. He hoped it was a sign she was ready for him, because there wasn't much chance of slowness once he started down the path of seduction. Not this first time, with the night coming on and the moon pounding so fiercely through his veins.

He pressed a kiss into her neck, then ran his tongue up to her ear. She tasted like she smelled—fresh and sunshiny. He took the lobe in his mouth, gently nibbling. Her soft groan ran across him, tearing at his control. He slid his other hand under her shirt and cupped her lush breasts. Teased and caressed her nipples until her breathing was as rapid as his own.

"Turn around," he whispered.

His hands slid around her waist as she complied, and he pulled her close. He claimed her lips, exploring her mouth with his tongue, tasting her leisurely but deeply. She made a needy sound deep in her throat and ran a hand down his side until she touched him. He shuddered and pulled away.

"Don't," he said, fighting the surge, "or I'll lose it."

Her smile was pure cheek. "Isn't that what you want?"

"Not yet." Because as much as he wanted her, he wanted to at least give her some pleasure this first time. Or there might not be a second.

Always look after your own interests, his father had once told him. It was a lesson he'd learned all too well.

He took possession of her lips again and slid his hands under the hem of her skirt to caress the silk of her thigh. Then continued up the cool, smooth skin to discover heaven had no restrictions.

"When?" He slid his finger past her curls and into her moistness, gently caressing.

She pressed into his touch, forcing it deeper. "When I went to the restroom."

"Clever girl."

"Horny girl would be more accurate."

"Suits me."

Her grin was saucy. "Thought it might."

He kissed her again, this time more urgently. His veins burned with heat, and every muscle trembled with the effort of restraint. She grabbed his shirt, her hands cold on his skin as she began undoing the buttons. He didn't stop her, just enjoyed the sensations trembling through him. She kissed his neck, his chest, her lips feather-light on his skin yet burning deep.

Her touch moved to his waist, and she slowly undid the button on his jeans. “Condom?” she whispered against his lips.

He took a shuddering breath, then whispered hoarsely, “Right pocket.”

She pulled out the foil packet, then pushed his jeans down. He skimmed his hand down her waist and hips, then caught the end of her skirt and bunched it up between them.

“Beautiful,” he said, running his hands down her glorious rump.

“Definitely,” she agreed, echoing his movements with gentle hands.

He kissed her fiercely, drinking in her essence, exploring every inch of her mouth until both of them were panting for breath. He trailed his tongue down the long line of her neck, then pushed up her shirt and circled the pebbled points of her breasts. She shuddered, arching her back, as if offering them to him. It was an invitation too good to refuse. He took one nipple in his mouth, sucking hard as he slid a hand down the flat of her stomach and into her moistness. Her moan shuddered through him, testing his strength, his will.

He delved deeper, sliding through her slickness, until her muscles pulsed around his fingers. She pressed against him, riding his hand with increasing urgency. Her skin was feverish, flushed with desire and need.

A need he understood only too well.

She grabbed his shoulders, fingers trembling, nails digging deep.

"Oh . . . God." Her voice little more than a fractured whisper. "Please . . ."

Her plea raged across his senses, almost destroying his restraint. He shuddered and pulled his touch away, knowing if she came right now it would shatter what little control he still had left.

Her groan almost shot it to hell anyway.

"Condom," he said, voice harsh with the urgency pounding through his body.

She tore open the packet with her teeth and rolled it on with an ease that spoke of practice. Not that he cared. He pulled her close again and began to stroke her. Her soft cries urged him on, her body trembling against his, her skin glossy with perspiration. He kissed her ear, ran his tongue down her neck. She tasted like no woman he'd ever had, and right at this moment, he wanted to keep on sampling her forever.

Her shuddering reached a crescendo, her movements urgent against his hand. Her strangled cry of pleasure echoed through him and smashed any remaining restraint. He cupped her buttocks and lifted her up. She wrapped her legs around him, then pushed him deep inside. He groaned at the sheer glory of it. She felt so good, so hot and firm.

She captured his lips, her kiss passionate. Demanding. She rode him harder, enveloping him in sweet, sweet heat. Hot flesh slapped against hot flesh, and there was nothing gentle about it. It was almost as if the urgency of the moon were driving her as fiercely as it did him. She claimed every inch of him, her taut muscles quivering with rising urgency against him.

The red tide rose, becoming a wall of pleasure he could not deny. Her movements quickened, her desire and need matching his own. Her gasps reached a second crescendo, and her cries echoed as her body bucked against his. He came—hot, glorious release that locked his body in pleasure.

They stood there for what seemed like forever, and he didn't really care because it felt so good. The sea breeze cooled the sweat on their skin, and the rich aroma of sex mingled with Kat's warm, sunshiny scent, stirring his senses anew. Only the fact that they had to get to Rogue River kept him from instigating a second, much slower, seduction.

When she began to shiver, he lowered her gently to the grassy sand, kissing her nose. After they'd both straightened their clothing, she picked up her purse and chocolate bar from the sand. Her pupils were still dilated, evidence of the satisfaction that touched her lips. "That sure beat the chocolate cake."

He cupped her cheek with his hand and brushed his thumb across her kiss-swollen lips. "Sorry it was so fast."

She raised an eyebrow, her amusement deepening. "In case you didn't notice, I was more than a little fast myself."

Thankfully. He certainly couldn't have held off much longer than he had. She'd felt too damn good.

"Next time," he said, "we'll try someplace more comfortable."

"And warmer." She rubbed her arms, then glanced past him. "We'd better get moving. Dusk is closing in."

He knew that without looking. The fever stirred in his veins, despite the fact that his body was momentarily sated. Or maybe it was just the scent of her lingering on his skin that stirred his blood.

They walked back to the rental car and continued on to Rogue River. Kat fell asleep fairly quickly, and he half wished he could join her. It would be nice to be in bed at this moment, holding her lush, warm body against his as he drifted off to sleep. Then he frowned at the thought and thrust it away. No matter how good it promised to be between them, it could never be anything more than just sex.

He'd learned that lesson long ago.

KAT WOKE WHEN THE CAR STOPPED. SHE YAWNED AND stretched, then glanced out the window. Warm lights shone through the trees, providing enough light to see the two log cabins just ahead.

She glanced at Ethan. "What time is it?"

"Eight forty-five."

His reply was a little terse, and she frowned, wondering why. Then she shook her head at her own stupidity. It had been a long day, and he'd done most of the driving. He was probably tired as hell.

She climbed out of the car and grabbed her bag from the trunk. He collected his, then locked the car and motioned for her to lead. She picked her way through the heavy darkness, shivering a little as the cool breeze caressed her bare skin. She was definitely going to have to change into something warmer before they did their tour tonight. Wearing this skirt and shirt had been nothing short of stupidity—though she certainly didn't regret it. Heat flushed through her at the memory. The chill she was feeling now was worth every minute. And if *that* had been rushed, she could hardly wait to feel what it was like when he took his time.

Her grandmother opened the door as they approached. Her gaze went from her to Ethan and back again, and her smile stretched.

"About time," she said, and Kat knew she wasn't referring to their arrival.

"There are some things that can't be rushed." Even though Ethan seemed to think they had.

"I guess not." Gwen stepped back, waving them in.

The cabin was basic but comfortable. Kat dropped her bag on the sofa and headed for the open fire, holding her hands out to the flames.

"I've put you two in the bigger cabin next door." Gwen indicated a side door. "And I lit the fire, so it'll be nice and warm when you come back after your walk."

Kat glanced at Ethan to see what reaction he had to this presumption, but he had his cop face on. She looked back at Gwen and said, "Have you tried scrying yet?"

"No. And I won't until you come back."

"What about this attack you mentioned earlier?" Ethan dropped his bag on the floor, then joined her by the fire. His shoulder brushed Kat's, warming her faster than any flames. "Shouldn't we be getting ready for that?"

"Until we know what is attacking us, it's useless trying to build a defense. But I've taken basic measures."

"Locked the doors, checked the windows?"

"Placed warding stones around my bed, as ordered." Her gaze met Kat's. "But not yours, so be warned."

She nodded. The magic of these particular stones

extended only so far, and a queen-sized bed wasn't within those limitations. There were stones that *could* guard the bed—and even a whole town, if needed—but they tended to be larger, and therefore were harder to carry around. Of course, her grandmother was also presuming she and Ethan were actually going to share a bed. Looking at him now, she had an unsettling feeling that wasn't likely.

He'd said nothing more than sex, and that's what she'd agreed to. Did that "nothing more" include not sleeping together?

She crossed her arms and hoped that wasn't the case. She'd like to think there was something between them other than the immediate need for release. That it wasn't just the moon and the fever rushing through his veins that made him want her. That he actually liked her.

"I'll go change, then we can get our walk over with." She picked up her bag and walked into the other cabin. It was a mirror image of Gwen's, only a little bigger. She continued into the bedroom. The bed was luxurious, covered with a comforter thick enough to lose fingers in. Across from it was another open fire, smaller than the one in the living room but just as warm. She dumped her bag on the bed and checked out the bathroom. It was basic, but there was a big old claw-foot tub. Just the thing she needed to take the chills from her spine later.

She went back to the bedroom and changed into warmer clothes, then grabbed her coat and the chocolate bar and headed back to the other cabin. Gran was sitting on the sofa, a bemused expression on her face. Ethan was nowhere to be seen.

"What have you done with him?"

Gwen snorted. "He's outside, pacing."

"Why on earth is he pacing?"

"At a guess, I'd say he's angry. Not sure why, though." She paused, eyebrows raised and eyes twinkling. "What on earth did you do to him?"

Heat touched her cheeks. "Me? Nothing." Nothing except make love to him, and surely he couldn't be angry at that. He'd wanted her as badly as she'd wanted him.

"Well, something's got him all worked up, so tread warily." Gwen glanced at her watch. "And be careful when you're walking around out there. It's always possible I was wrong about the timing of the attack."

Kat nodded. "Are you retreating to the stones?"

"Right after I finish my coffee. Ethan's got the key to your cabin, but if my light is on, come in and give me a report."

Something she'd be doing anyway, just to make sure Gwen was okay. She shoved on her coat, then went out to find Ethan.

He'd stopped his pacing and was standing in the middle of the driveway, staring up at the cold silver moon. She stopped beside him and thrust her hands in her pockets. "It must be horrible," she said softly.

She could feel his gaze on her but didn't meet it.

"What must be horrible?"

"Being forced through the change every full moon." She loved shifting shape, but then, she was able to pick and choose. A werewolf had no such choice, not when it came to the full moon.

"It's just the *actual* change that happens with the

full moon. The true change begins five days before, when the base urges begin to rise."

She smiled. "I wouldn't have thought that part of it would be much of a problem to most men. Doesn't the allure of the werewolf guarantee a satisfied outcome?"

"Mostly."

"Then surely it's only the forced change that presents any real problem."

"Losing your soul to a beast is never pleasant."

She did look at him then, a little surprised by the acerbity in his voice. "But the werewolf *is* your soul. It's you."

"It's not me. It's a beast I'm forced to live with once a month."

Good lord, he couldn't mean that! "Are you saying you don't shift shape at any other time except when the moon is full?"

"I'm human, not an animal." He thrust his hands into his pockets and walked away. "Let's get this over with."

"But . . ." Her voice died. This was the first time she'd ever met a shifter who didn't accept his heritage, and she wasn't entirely sure what to say.

And what would he think of *her*, if he ever discovered she could shift shape as well?

"But," she repeated, running after him, "you're not an animal, because you control the werewolf, not him you. Even on the night of the full moon when the change is forced on you."

"It's not something I want, regardless."

Why? Had he always felt this way, or had something happened in the past, with this bitterness the end result?

"But if you don't accept it, how in hell are your kids ever going to understand and control—"

"I won't ever have kids," he broke in, voice harsh. "So that's not going to be a problem."

She blinked. His fury spun around her, so deep and raw it snatched her breath away. "You don't like kids?"

"No." His voice was flat. Dead. "If we're going to play twenty questions, why don't you try answering a few?"

She gave him a sideways glance. His face was still expressionless, but the way he moved, the set of his shoulders, all suggested anger. At her. "What?" she said warily.

"Why did you kill the driver that rammed us?"

It certainly wasn't the question she'd been expecting, and though she schooled the surprise from her face, she knew he'd probably seen it anyway. "What do you mean?"

He stopped and grabbed her arm, spinning her around to face him. His eyes were dark puddles of rage, his fingers hot and tight through the thick layers of clothing.

"Mark arranged for a cruiser to go out and pick up the suspect. But he was dead when they got there."

She cursed internally. Trust the damn cops to get there before the thing had disintegrated properly. "I have no idea—"

He shook her so hard her teeth rattled. Energy surged, and she clenched her fists, fighting the desire to slap his angry butt across to the other side of the road.

"Don't lie to me," he said. "You killed the driver. I don't know how, but I intend to find out why."

She narrowed her eyes and glared at him. "I've told you why already. If you don't want to listen, it's your problem, not mine. Now let me go before I do something I may regret."

"You killed a suspect in a murder case—"

"You're going to have a hard time proving that, buddy. First, I didn't go anywhere near the suspect, and second, by morning that body is going to be nothing more than a few scraps of bone and hair."

He stared at her, anger so evident in his eyes they practically glowed. He didn't believe her. She wondered what in hell it was going to take before he did.

"What do you mean?"

"I told you, it's a zombie. Now that it really *is* dead, it'll undergo an accelerated decomposition process. Now get your hand off me."

"Not until you tell me how you killed it."

She hit him with kinetic power instead, wrenching his fingers from her arm and thrusting him across the road. He hit a pine with enough force to shake some cones loose and slithered down its trunk to the ground.

"That's how," she said loudly, then spun and walked away.

It was a few minutes before she heard him move, longer until he began following her. His anger was a cloud that practically reached out and suffocated her. She had no idea why she was sensing his emotions so clearly, but she really wished it would stop. Right now, she'd rather not deal with any of it. Maybe if she put some distance between them, it would give them both time to cool down.

She swung onto a side street and shifted shape, taking to the skies on night-dark wings. The air was crisp and cool, and the sheer freedom of it felt so good. It had been too long since she'd flown for the pleasure of it. For several minutes she simply drifted, enjoying the caress of moonlight and the play of air through her feathers. She soared a little higher, circling as she watched Ethan's progress. He reached the side street and came to a halt, and even from above she could feel his surprise. A laugh bubbled through her, but it came out the harsh and raucous cry of a raven.

He glanced up. She flicked her wings and swept away, flying across the small town until she was on the opposite side. This section was in the foothills, and streetlights and houses were few and far between. Not an ideal place to be alone in the dark of night—unless you were trawling for the dead. In a town the size of Rogue River, the lonely outskirts were the only place they could hide with any degree of safety. The hearts of such towns were usually too full of gossips who didn't miss a trick. Even dead ones.

She spiraled downward, shifting shape as she neared the ground. The minute her feet hit dirt, she felt it.

Death, headed her way.

ETHAN STARED AT THE EMPTY STREET AND WONDERED IF HIS eyes were playing games. No one could move that fast. Not even him in wolf form.

High above a bird squawked, the sound oddly reminiscent of a laugh. He glanced up, catching sight of a black form before it flew off. Odd to find a raven this close to the coast—not that he was any sort of expert when it came to birdlife around these parts.

He let his gaze sweep the street again. She definitely wasn't here. Her scent stopped at this spot and became something else, something far more ethereal. He walked on, but the night air gave no clue as to where she'd gone. He cursed under his breath, then got his cell phone out and dialed Mark.

"Hey," his partner said. "I thought you were supposed to be screwing yourself silly right about now."

"I was." And had it not been for this case and one infuriating woman, he probably still would have been.

He glanced skyward again. This afternoon's lovemaking had eased the pressure, but as the moon rose, so, too, did the fever. It worried him. He had no wish to find another partner right now, but if Kat wasn't accommodating, he just might have to. When the moon ran to fullness, desire gave way to base-level need. He had no wish to test the breaking point of his control.

"I want you to do me a favor," he said.

"Sure. What?"

"Go check out that body they found in the back of the truck."

"They wouldn't have had time to do an autopsy yet."

"I know. Call in some favors if you have to, but get down there tonight and check it out for me."

"Why the urgency?"

"Because there may not be much of a body left in the morning to check out."

Mark hesitated. "Have you been drinking?"

"No." Though he wouldn't have minded a beer or two right now, if only to ease the stiffness in his bruised back muscles. "Just trust me on this and do as I ask."

Mark grunted. "Anything else?"

"Yeah. Do another background check on Katherine Tanner. I want to know all there is to know about her."

The phone line was silent for several seconds, then Mark said, "Don't tell me she's the pretty girl you're bedding, partner, because the captain will hit the roof."

"My sex life has nothing to do with Benton."

"It does when the woman you're involved with is a major player in a case you've been warned off."

"I started this case, and I have every intention of finishing it. And neither the department nor the captain is going to stop me."

"This could get you into very deep trouble, my friend."

"If we catch this killer, I don't really care."

Mark grunted. "So where the hell are the three of you now? The captain went off his tree when he discovered they'd left the hotel with no word."

"We're in Rogue River. The killer's apparently on the move, so I can't say how long we'll stay."

"You want me to inform the local sheriff you're there?"

No, he didn't, but if things went pear-shaped, it

was better to have their butts covered. "You'd better. I guess you'd better tell the captain, too."

"I will. And keep me posted. If you find anything—and I mean *anything*—you report in. I don't want to be going through the hassle of breaking in a new partner. I just got you trained properly."

"Yeah, right," Ethan said dryly. "Just do the checks for me, will you?"

"I'll see what I can do and call you back."

"Thanks."

He hung up and stopped at the end of the street. There was no sign of movement to the left or the right. It was as if Kat had disappeared into thin air. But then, someone who could throw him across the road with sheer energy probably had another trick or two up her sleeve.

He sniffed the air, sorting through the odors of the night, and detected the faintest hint of sunshine to his right. He turned that way, but he had barely gone three steps when pain hit him so hard he stumbled.

Kat. In trouble.

He didn't question his certainty, just ran like hell in her direction.

KAT DUCKED THE ZOMBIE'S CLENCHED FIST AND LASHED out with a booted foot. Her blow hit the creature's knee with a satisfying crack, but if she'd done any damage it certainly didn't show. The creature swung around, fists a blur. She leaned back and felt the rush of stinking air past her chin. She hit the zombie kinetically, thrusting it backward. It tumbled over a roadside barrier and disappeared from sight.

Two more emerged from the night. She swore softly. Three against one was decidedly unfair. Time for a strategic retreat, perhaps. She reached for her alternate shape, but in that instant, she felt the breeze of a fourth approach. She dove away, but something hit her arm, sliding through her jacket and sweater and deep into her flesh.

White fire burned through her veins and pain engulfed her. *White ash. They had white ash.* Holy hell, she was in trouble now! She gulped down air, fighting the blackness. Ignoring the sweat beading her face, she pivoted, smacking the zombie hard in the nose. Bone crushed and bits of flesh and God knows what else flew, but he didn't seem to care. He grabbed her foot, twisting hard, and she screamed. Energy bubbled through her and she flung it his way, twisting it around his neck and snapping it taut. He was dead before he knew what hit him. She thrust his limp body into the other two. They went down like bowling pins but just as quickly righted themselves.

She turned and ran. She had no other choice. The white ash pinned her to the one form, and if she didn't get it out quickly it could very well kill her.

Their footsteps thudded behind her, drawing ever closer. Zombies might be dead, but they weren't slow. Even without turning, she could feel their fingers reaching for her.

She flung kinetic energy at the nearest tree, ripping free a heavy tree limb and tossing it behind her. Bodies thumped, and the stink of their presence disappeared. She stopped, spun, and hit another one kinetically, breaking its neck. Two down. But her whole body was shaking, and it wasn't just a reaction to the white ash in her arm. She was pushing her abilities to the limit. If she wasn't very careful, she'd have no energy left with which to defend herself.

But she couldn't run much farther, either. The movements were driving the white ash deeper into her flesh.

The zombies tossed the tree limb aside like so much rubbish. She took a deep breath, raised kinetic energy from God knows where, and hit them both, drawing a tight leash of energy around their necks. She stood her ground as they ran at her, waiting until they were close enough to smell before she snapped the leash tight. They dropped as one at her feet and didn't move.

She took another shuddering breath, then looked at the warm glow of lights below her. She couldn't make it that far by herself. Not with the white ash in her arm. But she couldn't stay here, either. It would be just her luck that the local sheriff would decide to drive by, and she wasn't up to explaining the bodies of the zombies right now. If the man who'd shared a moment of bliss with her didn't believe her story, why in hell would a complete stranger?

She continued on down the hill. The white ash burned deep, until it felt as if her whole body was being consumed. She wished she could wrench it free from her flesh, but she didn't dare even touch it in her weakened condition—not even kinetically. Blood dripped from her fingers, splashing in big, fat drops near her feet. The shaking grew worse, until she was staggering like a drunkard all over the road. She couldn't go on. She had to sit.

She found a signpost and leaned back against it,

closed her eyes, and took a deep breath in the hope it would stop the spinning. It didn't seem to help.

But it didn't matter. Help was on the way. She reached into her pocket and dragged out the chocolate bar. Tearing it open with her teeth, she began to munch on it as she waited for Ethan to arrive.

ETHAN SLOWED AS HE NEARED THE CREST OF THE ROAD, HIS breath ragged gasps that tore at his lungs. The smell of death and blood tainted the night air, and for the briefest of moments, he was afraid to go on. Afraid of what he might find.

An odd reaction, given all he'd seen over his years as a cop.

He flexed his fingers and walked on slowly. The metallic tang of blood got sharper and mingled with the warm scent of summer he'd come to associate with Kat. He glanced to his right. There in the shadows, leaning against a signpost and surrounded by discarded pieces of chocolate wrapper, sat Kat.

Relief surged through him, but it just as quickly disappeared. Blood soaked her left hand and dripped steadily into a small puddle near her fingers. He knelt next to her, noting there was a stake of some sort sticking out of her arm. If it hadn't been for the smell of death, it was possible to think she'd had an accident, maybe fallen and stabbed herself with a tree branch. But that smell was an echo of the driver who'd rammed them, and he didn't think it was a coincidence.

"Kat?" He touched her face. She was trembling and, though her skin was cold, sweating profusely.

She looked at him. The pain in her green eyes seemed to echo right through him.

"You need to take out the stake."

"You need to get to a hospital." He reached for his phone, but she stopped him. The strength of her hold was surprising, given that she looked like hell.

"Just take the stake out, then wrap the arm and take me back to Gran. It's really not as bad as it looks."

"I've been a cop long enough to know a bad wound when I see one, and this—"

"Is not what you think. Just take the goddamn stake out and stop arguing."

"If that stake has hit an artery—"

"Look, will you just pretend I know what I'm talking about for five minutes and take the stake out?"

Her voice rose and cracked, and the desperation and pain in her eyes grew. He swore under his breath but turned his attention to her wound. The stake appeared to have pierced the fleshy part of her upper arm and had gone right through. The section visible near her breast was barbed.

"I'm going to have to thrust it right through," he said. "Otherwise the barbs are going to take half your arm as they come out."

She nodded and closed her eyes. "Just do it."

"It's going to hurt."

"Imagine that," she muttered.

If she could manage to be sarcastic, she obviously wasn't as bad as she looked. He took off his coat and ripped off a shirtsleeve to use as a tourniquet. Then he lifted her arm and carefully gripped the end of the stake. "Ready?"

She bit her lip and nodded. Sweat dribbled down her cheeks and fear touched her eyes.

"One. Two. Three." He ripped the wood from her skin, and she screamed—a sound of pain that tore right through his soul. Blood poured from the wound, but it didn't pulse, indicating that at least he hadn't ruptured an artery. He grabbed the sleeve and wrapped it tightly around her arm. Somehow, she stayed conscious through the whole thing, though her breath was shallow gasps and her skin was pasty.

"Back to Gran," she said between clenched teeth.

"This needs stitching at least, and—"

"Trust me. Just this once," she muttered and fell sideways.

He caught her before she could whack her head on the ground, gently lowering her the last few inches. He took a deep breath, then got out his phone and, against his better judgment, dialed Gwen.

"What's happened?" she asked immediately.

"Kat's been injured. She's had some sort of stake thrust through her arm and—"

The old bird's swearing cut him off. He raised his eyebrows and wondered if she'd been in the navy. She was using words that would make old sea dogs proud.

"Where are you?" she asked eventually.

He glanced at the signpost and gave her directions. "But you'll have to catch a cab, because the keys to the rental car are in my pocket."

"I have a rental, remember, though in this particular case, the driver can stay in his bed," she said. "Be there in five."

She hung up. He checked the tourniquet on Kat's

arm, and then her pulse. It was a little thready but reasonably strong. He rose and walked a little farther up the road. The source of the smell was easy enough to find. There were three bodies that he could see, and at least one other farther up the road he could smell. Somehow, she'd beaten four of them.

Shaking his head in amazement, he squatted beside the first two. She'd called them zombies, the walking dead, and that was exactly what they looked and smelled like. Bodies that had been dead for some time. As he watched, the skin on their faces seemed to be sucked closer to the bone, giving them a gaunt, skeletal appearance. An advanced rate of decomposition is what she'd said they'd go through. It looked like she wasn't kidding.

Lights swept across the trees, approaching fast. He rose and walked back to Kat. The car skidded to a halt and Gwen climbed out.

"Did you take the stake from her arm?"

He nodded. "But she's bleeding pretty heavily—"

"That doesn't matter." Gwen lowered herself beside Kat and checked her pulse, then her arm. "Good job, lad. Pick her up, and we'll get her back to the cabin and tend that arm."

"But shouldn't we—"

"No. Believe me, we know what we're doing."

He bit down on his annoyance, but knew he had to trust that both Kat and her grandmother *did* know what they were talking about. If only because they might be his only chance of getting Janie back safely.

As Gwen turned the rental around and sped back to the cabin, he cradled Kat's head on his lap. She looked absurdly young, innocent almost—which she very obviously wasn't. He brushed the dark strands of hair from her eyes and wondered why someone like her was still single. Granted, she had an attitude she wasn't afraid to use, but she was a stunning-looking woman. A good catch, by anyone's standards.

Except his, because he didn't have standards. And had no intention of ever being caught.

When they got back to the cabins, he carried her inside. Gwen pushed him gently toward the second cabin. "You strip her and put her into bed, and I'll go fetch my medicines."

"I don't think she'd appreciate—"

"Don't go getting shy on me, Ethan. You've seen all there is to see anyway, haven't you?"

He stared at her, at a loss for words. He'd never met anyone as forthright and open about sex as these two seemed to be. Maybe he just had to get to the big cities more often. "This is different than sex." It was more personal.

"Rubbish. And watch that arm doesn't bleed all over the sheets."

She walked away, leaving him with no option but to obey. He carried Kat into the other cabin, stripped back the comforter, and laid her down. He grabbed a couple of towels from the bathroom, placing them under her arm before he began removing the tourniquet. Amazingly enough, the wound didn't seem to be bleeding anymore. He stripped off her clothes, trying to ignore her warm scent, trying to ignore his own reaction to the sight of her naked body.

Gwen came in and sat down on the bed. "Here," she said, thrusting a bowl of what looked like dried herbs at him. "Hold this."

He did as ordered, watching as she washed down the wound with a soft wet cloth. When the wound was clean, she grabbed the bowl and began packing the herbs in it. He couldn't ever remember seeing this step in any of the first-aid manuals he'd read over the years.

"What is that you're using?"

"My magic mix. Kat heals fast naturally, but this will ensure no infection gets into the wound over the next couple of hours."

"Hours? It's going to take a week, if not more, to heal a wound like that."

Gwen smiled. "By the morning this will be nothing more than an annoyance. Hand me that bandage, will you?"

Werewolves could heal that fast, but he'd never known a human to do so. Maybe it *was* simply a matter of magic—something he would never have even half believed before meeting these two.

Still, time would tell which of them was right. He grabbed the white roll off the side table and handed it to her. She quickly bandaged the wound, her movements deft and fast despite her gnarled hands.

"There," she said, rising a little stiffly. "That should do. Make sure she takes it easy for the next couple of hours, but after that, you both should be all right."

He chose to ignore the twinkle in her eye. "Are you going to be okay alone in the other cabin?"

"Safer than you are, Detective."

"Because of the stones?"

She nodded. "To satisfy your curiosity, when the stones are placed in certain sequences they can provide protection against either magic or evil."

"Oh."

She patted his arm. "Don't worry, my boy. By the time this week is over, you're going to believe in a whole range of things you never have before."

He didn't trust the sparkle in her eyes. He watched her leave, then grabbed the comforter and drew it over Kat. She stirred, murmuring something he couldn't quite catch. He let his fingers brush her cheeks, then ran them down to the lips he wanted to kiss and keep on kissing.

He snatched his fingers away and walked into the next room. It was going to be another long night without sleep.

KAT STIRRED. THE NIGHT WAS STILL, AND THE ACHE IN HER arm was little more than a twinge—one that shouldn't have been strong enough to wake her. She didn't move, just opened her eyes. She was in the cabin. In bed. Alone—although that in itself didn't surprise her.

What did surprise her were the condoms scattered on the bedside table. Ethan had obviously had intentions of doing *something* during the night.

She could hear no sound, and yet awareness stirred. But not an awareness of evil. It was an awareness of longing. Need.

She reached for one of the foil packets, then looked

around. Ethan stood near the window, his arms crossed as he leaned against the frame and stared out. He wore black silk boxers but little else, and his hair looked rumpled, as if he'd spent the last few hours tossing and turning rather than sleeping. But if the pristine sheets on the other side of the bed were any indication, he certainly hadn't tossed and turned with *her*.

She took a moment to simply enjoy the sight of all that firm, hard flesh, then threw off the comforter and padded across the room to him. He didn't move, didn't say anything, but his shoulders tensed.

"What's wrong?"

"Nothing. Everything."

She touched his shoulder, and he flinched. She ignored it and ran her fingers lightly down his spine. "Tell me."

He took a shuddering breath. "My niece is out there. Maybe alive. Maybe dead. And all I can think about is how badly I need to sate my lust."

"You can't do anything more about your niece than what you're doing."

She slipped her hand around his waist and took a step closer, pressing her breasts against his tense back. His skin quivered, as if touched by fire. And that was what raged through his system right now. A cold, moon-spun fire that needed to be quenched before things got out of control. She knew enough about werewolves to know she didn't want to face the consequences of *that*.

"That doesn't stop the feeling that I should be doing something," he replied. "That I should be looking, or going through the files again, or going over her room—"

"If you didn't find any clues the first few times, what makes you think you'd find them now?" She slipped her hand down the flat of his stomach and under the waist of his boxers.

He sucked in air. "Hope. Desperation."

She ran her fingers down the length of him and pressed feather-light kisses across his back. Still he didn't move, though his whole body shook with the effort of control.

"Don't," he said softly.

But she continued to caress him. He needed the pressure released, and she was more than willing. While she had no doubt this first time would be hard and fast—more so than at the beach—they still had hours left until daylight. There would be time enough for her.

"Kat, stop," he all but groaned.

"Why?" She ran her tongue across his neck and shoulders, tasting him as he'd tasted her earlier.

"Because you're injured. And because my need is so great I might just hurt you."

"Your need is a bigger danger than my wound."

She touched his face, forcing him to look at her. His eyes were almost otherworldly. The moon fever truly had him in its grip, and once he was released there would be no going back until the fever was sated. It was a wonder he'd had enough control to resist her this long.

She kissed him gently, then said against his lips, "Take me, werewolf. Take me now."

He groaned and grabbed her, pulling her so close

his heat nearly melted her skin. His mouth claimed hers with such ferocity that her head swam. He forced her back, not to the bed but to the rug in front of the fireplace, and lay down beside her. He kissed her lips, her throat, her shoulders as his hands set her alight with an urgency as great as his own. She was more than ready when he thrust inside her, and she groaned at the sheer pleasure of it. His powerful strokes drove deep, promising satisfaction, but they were too fast, too soon. He came with a roar that flushed heat through her body and left her trembling with unfulfilled desire.

When his shuddering stopped he kissed her again, gentler this time but no less urgently. The fever still raged in his eyes, and she knew that at this moment she was just a body on which he sated his needs. He didn't actually see *her*. Yet.

But this wasn't about her. For the moment, it was about him.

He continued to kiss her, and after a while he grew hard again. He replaced the condom, then slipped inside of her, stroking slow and deep, until it felt as if there wasn't an inch he hadn't delved. Pleasure rippled across her skin, became a pulsing need that grew more urgent as his stroking quickened. He kissed her neck, burned a trail with his tongue down to her breasts, then took one nipple in his mouth and sucked hard. She groaned, arching against him, wanting it faster, harder. He complied. When he came a second time she went with him, her whole body shaking with the force of it.

But the moon fever wasn't finished yet.

He pulled her to her feet, picked her up, and carried

her to the bed, where he continued to make love to her until the flush of dawn touched the skies and the pile of condoms was severely depleted. But the fever finally left his eyes, and the last time they made love it was her he saw. Her he made love to. Then he left her and went to sleep out on the sofa.

SEVEN

KAT PULLED ON HER SWEATER AS SHE WALKED THROUGH the living room. Ethan still slept on the sofa, the blanket tangled around his hips, revealing the lean planes of the body she now knew so well. She let her gaze linger on him for a moment, her pulse stirring as she remembered the feel of his skin against hers, the heat of his touch—the way he'd claimed her, at first with such ferocity, then later with such tenderness and passion. She swallowed to ease the sudden dryness in her throat and walked on.

It was barely eight and, after his efforts last night, she really didn't expect him to surface for another couple of hours. Which was a good thing, because she wasn't entirely sure what she was going to say to the man who could create such magic with his touch and yet refused to allow the slightest bit of intimacy afterward.

Gwen was in the process of carrying a large tray of food over to the table when Kat entered the second cabin. She took the tray from her grandmother's hands and placed it on the table, then walked over to the small coffeemaker and poured them both a cup of coffee.

"You feeding an army?" She sat down and surveyed the platters of bacon, eggs, Danishes, and fruit.

Gwen's eyes twinkled. "Thought you two might need some sustenance after last night."

Kat grinned despite the slight flush of heat to her cheeks. Last night the walls could have been thinner than air, and she wouldn't have cared. "The man does have stamina, I'll give him that."

"He's a werewolf and the moon is rising. That's a given." Gwen plucked a Danish from the plate and began eating it. "As long as you were careful, that's all that matters."

Kat gave her a long look. "We're not sex-mad teenagers. Both of us are able to contain our hormones long enough to take care of *that*."

"Maybe, but listen to an old woman who knows what she's talking about and make sure you keep your wits about you, because as the moon gets closer, he won't."

She stared at her grandmother for several seconds. She'd lived with this woman all her life, and still there seemed something new to discover almost every week.

"You had a werewolf lover?"

"Oh, yes." Gwen's reply was more a sigh. "And a most enjoyable six months it was, too. They're very athletic lovers."

She could vouch for the stamina, but the athletic part was still to be discovered. But then, Gran had always been more adventurous than she was, and even now thought nothing of making love someplace horribly awkward or public. "Are they all . . . wary of intimacy, or is it just mine?"

Gwen frowned. "Werewolves can be strange beasties. Did you know that they mate for life?"

Kat blinked. "How can that be possible if they screw themselves silly every full moon and aren't particularly fussy about with whom?"

"That's sex. Most men separate sex from love, but in a werewolf's case, that line is more defined. But when he—or she, for that matter—gives his heart, it's given forever."

Kat swallowed a lump of suddenly tasteless bacon. "So the lack of intimacy might very well mean—"

"He's already given his heart, and all that is left is sex." Gwen reached across the table and squeezed Kat's hand. "But don't take that as gospel. Not until you've asked Ethan."

"He doesn't have a girlfriend or wife. I did check that before I got involved." She grimaced slightly. "I'm not a home-wrecker."

Although it sounded as if it didn't really matter if she was, especially if werewolves considered sex and love to be two entirely different things. While she wasn't sure she would ever understand the differences, it really didn't matter. She wasn't a werewolf. And she wouldn't ever be anything more to him than a means of release.

Which was kind of sad, given the level of intimacy and understanding they'd reached during their lovemaking last night.

"What's in his past?" Gwen asked.

She shrugged. "Something, I'm sure. He views women in a somewhat harsh light, and he certainly doesn't trust us."

"Us? As in you and me, or women in general?"

Kat grinned. "Both."

"Someone's hurt him in the past."

"Obviously." The question was, had he given his heart to that someone?

And why did she even care? It wasn't as if there could ever be anything more between them than there now was. Because of their jobs. Because his instinctive hate for his werewolf half would undoubtedly extend to shifters like herself. And because he hated kids and, above all else, she wanted them.

Gwen patted her hand again. "Just enjoy your time with him. Werewolves can give you that, if nothing else."

Maybe, but she was getting a little tired of being nothing more than a good time. She wanted something else. But she wasn't going to find that with Ethan. Wasn't likely to find it with anyone in the near future, either.

She finished the rest of her meal, then picked up her coffee and leaned back in the chair. "What's on the agenda for today?"

"I think you should fly around those hills this morning and have a look around. Those zombies didn't spring from nowhere. They must have a nest up there somewhere."

She nodded. "This soul-sucker has vampires, werewolves, and zombies at its beck and call. That's a little unusual, isn't it? I mean, both vamps and werewolves are fairly strong-willed. I can't imagine them being yoked to another for long, so they've got to be getting something out of this situation."

"More than likely. But until we have some idea

what this thing is up to and just what exactly it can do, we won't know."

"Well, it can obviously raise the dead." Not that *that* in any way benefited either a wolf or a vampire. And even vamps had more sense than to feed on a zombie.

"And if it's ancient, it might have a lot of dead it can raise, so be very careful out there."

"You tried to scry yet this morning?"

Gwen sighed. "Yes, but I couldn't see a damn thing. I get the feeling they're waiting to see what we do next before they decide their next move."

"Which would mean they consider us a threat."

"This thing is not stupid."

"I never thought it was. Anything else?"

"Just be careful when you're up there. This thing knows you're a shifter, so it might have set traps."

She nodded and pushed away from the table. "I'll bring back lunch."

"Do that. And get yourself another box of condoms while you're at it. You must have used most of his supply last night."

Heat touched her cheeks again. She might have grown up in a sexually liberated household, but her grandmother still had the power to embarrass her. Though after thirty years, she really should be used to it. "I thought you said you were deaf?"

"Not *that* deaf." Gwen's eyes twinkled. "You'd better get going before your wolf begins to stir."

She left. Clouds crowded the sky, and the breeze was cool and steady. An almost perfect day for flying. She shoved her hands into her pockets and walked down through the trees toward the road. When she was sure she couldn't be seen from any of the cabins, she shifted shape and flew skyward.

She drifted toward the sea, watching the waves roll in and wishing it were summer so she could go for a swim—though a good soaking in icy water might be just what her tired muscles needed to revive them. But later, when she had more time. She flicked her wings and soared sideways, flying toward the mountains.

They looked different in daylight. Less threatening. She circled until she found the signpost and looked around. There were half a dozen small farms in the immediate vicinity. The zombies must have come from one of them, because they'd been on her almost as soon as she'd sensed them. They could run fast, but not *that* fast.

She dipped her wing and drifted down to inspect the first farmhouse.

AN INSISTENT RINGING WOKE ETHAN. HE GLANCED AT HIS watch and cursed when he saw it was well after nine, then reached blindly for his cell phone on the nearby coffee table.

"Yeah?" His voice came out as little more than a gruff croak.

"Partner, you sound like shit."

"Just tired, that's all." He rubbed a hand across his eyes and glanced around. Kat wasn't in the cabin, though her lingering scent told him she hadn't been gone long. Perhaps she was next door.

Mark grunted. "Aren't we all. I went to the morgue

like you asked. Seems like you weren't as crazy as I thought you were."

"Body gone to mush?"

"Completely. They managed to freeze a couple of fingers so we can get some prints, but other than that, it's gone."

"You searching through the database for a fingerprint match?"

"Yeah, but we both know it's going to take a long time. And if the guy doesn't have a record, hasn't been in the military or had a government job, or didn't volunteer his fingerprints when he got his driver's license, we'll be out of luck."

Ethan had a suspicion they'd be out of luck anyway. "Anything else happening with the case?"

Mark hesitated. "Your brother has posted a reward for information that leads to Janie's return."

Ethan closed his eyes. "How's he holding up?"

"Why don't you find out yourself and call him?"

He really should call Luke, but he didn't know what to say to him any more than he knew what to say to Kat. He wasn't comfortable with intimacy of *any* kind. Hadn't been for a long, long time. Luke understood his reasons, but he had a feeling Kat never would.

No, he wouldn't call his brother. Not until he had something to say. "How's Benton taking my being in Rogue River?"

"Badly. You're dead meat if he catches up with you before he calms down."

Then he'd just have to ensure he wasn't caught. "The autopsy on the second kid come through yet?"

"Yeah. They've estimated the time of death to be between seven and eight yesterday evening."

"So the kid had been kept alive five days before they killed him?" If that was the case, there was still hope for Janie.

"He was drugged and pretty much starved, though."

"No indication of any other abuse?"

"Nothing, other than starvation. They found traces of dirt in his fingernails. They're still analyzing that to see if they can discover anything unusual."

He frowned and scratched his chin. Something about this case didn't make sense, though he couldn't exactly put his finger on what was bugging him. But if the beings behind these kidnapping *were* vampires of one sort or another, why were they snatching these kids and keeping them for nearly a week before killing them? Granted, he didn't know much about vampires, let alone truly believe in them, but if they did exist, that just didn't make sense. Unless they were taking the kids for something other than feeding . . .

"Look, just on a hunch, will you check to see if there were other disappearances reported in the same area as each of these kids? Take it a few days either way."

"You suspect this could be bigger than just the kids?"

"I don't know what I suspect. I could be just reaching for straws."

"Even so, given your record with straws, I'll get it checked out immediately."

"Give me a call if you find anything."

"Will do."

Ethan hung up and walked into the bedroom. Kat's

scent was stronger here, and as he glanced at the bed, his blood stirred. He couldn't remember much of last night, not until the end, but he'd certainly never felt this satisfied before in his life. And yet he knew she only had to walk into the room and he'd want her again. It was odd how attracted he was to her. Normally, he only sought out his chosen mate as the evening fell.

He cleaned up the room, picking up a still-wrapped condom near the window and discarded wrappers off the floor, then got rid of all the rubbish and made the bed. After showering and changing, he headed into the other cabin.

He knew without looking that Kat wasn't there. "Where's she gone?" he asked when Gwen looked up from the paper she was reading.

"Out." She patted the chair next to her. "Grab yourself something to eat and drink, then come sit beside me. We need to chat."

He studied her warily. "Why?"

She sighed. "Always questions from a cop. I promise it's nothing personal, so just relax and get something to eat."

He didn't relax, but he did get something to eat. Once he'd warmed up some bacon, eggs, and a couple of Danishes, he sat down at the table opposite her.

"What do you need to know?"

"How old is your niece?"

It wasn't the question he'd been expecting. "Five. But you know that. You must have seen the files."

She nodded. "But files only give bare facts. Sometimes it helps if I get a more intimate idea of what the people are like."

"You said the opposite yesterday."

A smile touched her lips. "Kat tells me you hate kids, so you're not likely to blind me with emotional vibes like the child's parents would."

"I don't hate—" He hesitated. He'd given Kat one story, so he'd better stick to it. "Don't get me wrong. I love Janie, and I'd do anything to get her back. But she's as close to having a kid as I ever want to get."

"Why?"

He could feel himself shut down, but tried to shrug nonchalantly. "I like my freedom. I like being able to walk away once the moon fever has passed by."

"So you've never lost your heart to anyone?"

"You weren't going to get personal, remember?"

She shrugged. "So I lied."

"Kat understands what lies between us can never be anything more than just a moon dance."

"I'm not asking this for Kat's sake. She's happy enough cruising along as she is for the moment."

He raised an eyebrow, not sure how to take that bit of information. "Then why are you asking?"

"Just trying to figure you out, werewolf."

"Then stop trying, because once this case is solved, I'm out of here."

A smile touched her lips, a smile he didn't trust. "Maybe." She studied him for a moment. "Does Janie come from a line of werewolves?"

He hesitated. "It runs in the family, but not everyone is afflicted by it."

She raised an eyebrow. "That's a rather odd way of putting it."

"But nevertheless true," he bit back. "Can we drop it now?"

Her smile grew. "For now. In the meantime, tell me what Janie's like. What does she like to do?"

He rambled on about his niece as he ate his breakfast. Gwen didn't say anything, just leaned back in her chair and watched him. He had an uneasy feeling she was still trying to figure him out.

And that she might just succeed where many had failed.

"You must see this kid pretty often to know her that well," Gwen commented eventually. "Odd for a man who's a professed kid hater."

He finished his breakfast and leaned back in his chair with his coffee. He kept his face carefully blank, even though the old woman's line of questioning was beginning to annoy the hell out of him. "She's my brother's kid. That's different."

"Can't see how."

He drank some coffee, then said, "I was talking to my partner earlier. It appears these kids are being kept alive for up to five or six days before they're killed. They'd been drugged, but other than that, there didn't appear to be any other form of abuse."

Gwen frowned. "Were they dehydrated as well?"

"Mark made no mention of it." And if it was in the autopsy report, he would have.

"Interesting."

"Why?"

"Because starvation is often used as a form of cleansing when preparing for many forms of rituals. That they *aren't* being starved suggests she's using them for something else."

He stared at her for several seconds, not really sure

he wanted to hear anything more. "As in magical-type rituals?"

She nodded absently. "The question is, what else would she be using them for?"

"And if she does need them, why allow a werewolf to tear apart one kid, and a vampire to drain the other, after keeping them alive for five days?"

"Maybe she needs specific emotions for whatever it is she's actually doing." Gwen rose hastily. "I think I'd better go talk to Seline. If you want to meet Kat, she'll be at the bakery down the road in another hour."

She hobbled into the other room, and a few seconds later he heard her dialing the phone. He finished his coffee, then glanced at his watch and decided to go for a walk before he met Kat.

At the fourth farm, Kat hit pay dirt. She circled lower, trying to ignore the overwhelming sense of death as she looked for any signs of life. Or *un*life.

An old Ford sat in the circular drive, but the cobwebs hanging between the steering wheel and the sun visor suggested it hadn't been driven for at least a week.

The old farmhouse itself looked abandoned. Tin rattled on the ancient roof, shutters banged, and the strengthening wind whistled through a broken window on the back porch. Nothing moved, not even a mouse. The smell was coming from the barn, so she dipped lower and headed that way.

The haunting cry of the wind was sharper here, thanks to the decayed state of the barn. She touched down on a tree and moseyed out along the limb that reached toward the window. The barn was filled with dusky shadows, making it hard to see anything. She couldn't see any movement, but that didn't mean the zombies weren't there. The reeking stench indicated *something* dead was near, even if she couldn't see it.

She hopped skyward again and flew to the roof. It was in worse condition than the house, and there were plenty of gaps where a raven could squeeze through. She chose the largest of them and landed on a rafter.

The stench almost knocked her off the perch. It was ten times worse inside the barn than outside. She walked along the rafter, trying to see past the shadows gathering in the corners. There were no man-shaped lumps to indicate life. No rattle to indicate death drawing breath. Nothing but that awful smell.

She spread her wings and drifted through the barn. It was filled with all sorts of machinery, and might have once housed horses, but not in a very long time from what she could see. The smell was coming from the end stall. She set down on another rafter and peered into the darkness. And discovered death, but not the form she'd expected.

He was a dry old stick of a man who looked to have been in his mid-sixties. The smile frozen on what was left of his face, and the fact that his overalls and boxers hung over the old stall door, suggested he'd been having sex with someone when he died. As did the lingering remnants of ecstasy she could feel in the air.

And though he must have been dead for at least a week, there was no rat or maggot activity to be seen on his body. Unusual, especially given the fact that he lay in a barn.

But the cause of death was easy to see—like the kids, his soul had been sucked free. Yet given that he was in the midst of orgasm at the time, he probably didn't even feel death hit him.

She headed out through the roof and back to the house. The old man obviously hadn't been too proud, because the place looked abandoned from the outside. And just as obviously, he didn't go into town much, which would explain the cobwebs in his car and the fact that he could lie there dead for a week without anyone coming up to check on him. Small towns were usually far more aware of things like that than city folk.

But why had the soul-sucker killed him? Had she simply wanted to feed, or was there something more sinister behind her actions? Like using his house—a place obviously few people visited—as a base?

She arrowed in through the smashed glass and did a circuit around the house. Evil had been here, as recently as a day or so ago. The air still recoiled from its presence.

The house was in bad shape, many rooms filled with boxes of junk and yellowing newspapers. Dust was inches thick everywhere except in the bedroom and kitchen. Obviously these were the two rooms the old man had used most. She shifted shape in the bedroom, drawn by a scent that wasn't age and decay and death. Hands on her hips, she studied the double bed and tried to ignore the room's almost overwhelming sense of sadness and loss. But it was almost impossible when everywhere she looked there were photos of a smiling, gray-haired woman.

The sheets were surprisingly clean, the creases barely disturbed. Perhaps he'd changed them in expectation. Light sparked off something close to the pillow, and she reached for it. It was a delicate gold chain and cross. Not the sort of thing an old man would wear, but certainly something a little girl would.

Janie had been here. Kat had obviously been closer than she'd thought last night. Maybe even close enough to rescue that little girl.

She closed her eyes and took a deep breath. It didn't do a whole lot to ease the frustration running through her. Damn it, why couldn't they catch a break in this case? Her gaze swept the room again, looking for something she might have missed the first time. Nothing. But given that the farmer had been dead for about a week, and Janie had been taken only three days ago, someone else had obviously been caring for the little girl. She couldn't imagine zombies doing it, so either the soul-sucker had undertaken the task or someone else was helping her. The werewolf, perhaps? Though what would a wolf—or a vamp, for that matter—be gaining from such a situation? It surely couldn't be sex, given that they had to be aware of the danger of getting their soul sucked during such an act.

She clenched her fingers around the cross and turned away from the bed. The kid wasn't here now, but neither were the soul-sucker or the zombies. And she very much suspected they wouldn't be found at the last remaining farmhouse. Still, she had to check. Then she had to go back and face Ethan.

And she had a feeling it would be easier facing a

dozen zombies than telling Ethan they'd missed rescuing his niece by the slenderest of margins.

She shoved the chain in her pocket, then shifted shape and flew back out the window.

ETHAN LEANED AGAINST THE QUAINT, WHITE PICKET FENCE that bordered part of the bakery and watched the traffic roll by. Not that there was much, and not that they rolled by very fast. In fact, most of them slowed down to give him a good, long look. Small-townsfolk didn't miss much. By later today, he'd no doubt be the subject of much speculation.

If it weren't for the fact he was officially off the kidnapping case, he would have started asking some questions himself. If the kidnappers were here, then surely someone in this town would have seen something. But the minute he started nosing about, the sheriff would be informed. While Benton now knew he was here, he at least needed to keep up the pretense of *not* investigating. Otherwise his boss *would* come down hard on him.

Kat strolled down the street about ten minutes later, wearing a dark red cashmere sweater and a short black skirt that swirled around her thighs. Though she looked good enough to stop traffic, his gaze was drawn to the shadows under her eyes. To the shadows *in* her eyes.

He caught her hand and drew her in between his legs, wrapping his arms around her waist. He kissed her, enjoying the sweetness of her warm lips but resisting the urge to taste deeper, and asked, "What's wrong?"

She hesitated, her gaze searching his. Something in his gut clenched tight.

"Does your niece wear a necklace?"

The restriction moved up from his gut to his chest. "A cross. Why?" His voice was harsh, flat.

She reached into her pocket. "This cross?"

The sun caught the cross as she pulled it free, sparking fire across the gold surface. He reached for it slowly. He'd given Janie the cross last Christmas. He closed his eyes for a moment, fighting the turmoil, fighting the fear. "Where did you find it?"

"At a farmhouse. She's not there, Ethan. I looked."

She reached out as if to comfort him, but he jerked away and pushed her to one side. He took several steps before he could force himself to stop.

"Where is this farmhouse?" He had to see, had to check himself. Had to know if there was a scent to follow.

"You can't go there."

He swung around, fists clenched against fury rising inside. "Like hell I can't!"

Her green eyes were full of understanding, full of compassion. It only seemed to fire his anger more, though he couldn't say why.

"The soul-sucker killed the farm's owner. Benton will have to be called in, as will the sheriff."

"You call them before I get up there, and we may lose her scent."

"There's no scent to follow. It lingers in the bedroom where they kept her, but that's it."

"You don't have a wolf's nose," he retorted. "I may find what you couldn't."

She crossed her arms, as if to contain the anger he

could see forming in her eyes. "You don't have a wolf's nose, either, unless you shift shape."

He took a deep breath. It didn't help the anger or vague sense of desperation boiling through his blood. "You have no idea what a wolf is and isn't capable of."

"I know more about werewolves than you probably do, especially since you've spent a major part of your life denying your heritage." She shook her head, then brushed past him. "You want to go look for her, then go. See of you can find her without my help. I'm going back to Gran."

He reached out to stop her, but she slapped his hand away, her strength and speed surprising him. "Don't think last night gave you the right to try to order me around, wolf man. I've got a job to do, and I intend to do it right."

"This is my niece we're talking about," he ground out.

"And at this point in time your niece appears to still be alive." She flung the words over her shoulder as she continued marching up the street. "You go rushing in blindly, and you just might be the trigger that kills her."

What she said was common sense. He knew that. But it went against every instinct he had to stand here and do nothing while the unthinkable could be happening to one very precious little girl. He thrust a hand through his hair and glanced in the direction from which Kat had come, then took another deep breath and followed her back to the cabins.

And wondered if he could still become a wolf after all the years of denying that part of himself.

* * *

KAT CROSSED HER ARMS AND WATCHED ETHAN PACE. HE didn't say anything, but he didn't really need to. His anger, frustration, and perhaps even fear filled the room, as sharp as the wind outside.

"It's not that easy," he said eventually. "I can't just become a wolf."

"It *is* that easy," she replied, keeping her voice calm. Anything else would only inflame him further. "And it's not a case of can't. It's more *won't*."

He glared at her, his fists clenched by his side. Controlling the anger rather than any desire to lash out, she knew.

"You have no idea what you're talking about," he growled. "Not this time."

"And that's where you're wrong. Again."

He snorted and resumed his pacing. "What, are you trying to tell me you're also a werewolf? Because, *trust* me, I'd know if that were true."

"Of course that's not what I'm saying," she bit back. So much for calmness. "I am, however, a shifter."

He stopped abruptly, his expression a mix of surprise and disbelief. "What?"

"I'm a shifter. I can take on the form of a raven."

"No."

"God save me from obstinate men," she muttered. She pushed away from the wall. "Watch and learn."

With that, she called to the shifting magic and felt it surge through her, with eager fierceness. In a matter of seconds, she was a raven rather than a woman.

And the look on his face was priceless.

She shifted back, adjusted her clothing, and said,

"It's that easy, Ethan. You just have to go with the flow."

He stared at her for a moment, then shook his head. "I really have lived a sheltered life, haven't I?"

"Apparently so." But *why* was the question—though one she knew he wouldn't answer right now.

He walked across to the window and shoved his hands deep into his pockets. "I don't know—"

"Look," she said, "if you want to come to the cabin I found that cross in, you have two choices. Face the wrath of your captain in human form, or avoid it altogether by becoming a wolf. Your choice, as I said, but decide quickly. We need to get up there."

He took a deep breath, then released it slowly. "I don't know *how* to take wolf form willingly. The only time I tried—" He stopped and shrugged, but she felt the flash of pain nevertheless. Obviously, something had gone seriously wrong that one and only time.

"I can guide you, Ethan. It really *is* easy enough to do. In the end, the magic is a part of you. You just have to be willing to release it."

"Something I've spent a lifetime avoiding." He swung around to face her, his expression resolute. "What do I do?"

"First off, relax. Breathe deep and release the anger, the fear, and the tension."

"Easier said than done," he muttered.

But he did as she bade and, after a few minutes, a sense of calm fell around him.

"Now," she said. "Imagine there's a well deep down in your soul. Imagine it filled with warm and eager light. Feel its welcoming caress surround your fingers, your hands, your arms, as you reach for it."

Soft golden light began to dance around his fingertips, reaching upward toward his torso.

"Imagine that light surrounding you, embracing you. Feel in it every fiber, every muscle. Let it become you, and you it."

The golden light swept up and across his body, until it encased him entirely. He was close, so close, to changing.

"Now, imagine the wolf. Welcome him into being."

Doubt rose. She could see it in his face, feel it in the air.

"The wolf will never hurt you," she said quickly. "Nor can it hurt anyone else unless you desire it. You control it, Ethan, not the other way around."

Still he doubted. The magic pulsated, reflecting Ethan's uncertainty.

"Become the wolf, Ethan," she said softly. "Because Janie's life might well depend on it."

Which wasn't a fair thing to say at this point, even if it was the truth. But it was also the one thing that might break his deadlock.

And that's exactly what happened. The magic surged, and a few seconds later, a wolf stood before her. She smiled. "That wasn't so hard now, was it?"

Annoyance glittered in his brown eyes. Her smile grew. "You know, as werewolves go, you're not badlooking. Shall we go?"

He walked to the door. She grabbed her keys and purse, and they headed out.

* * *

"DON'T SUPPOSE YOU CAN CONTROL THAT DAMN DOG OF yours?" The sheriff's voice was gruff and edged with frustration. "He's starting to give the team the creeps."

Kat grinned. Ethan—in wolf form, and complete with a bright pink scarf tied around his neck to indicate her ownership—had spent most of the afternoon following the coroner's men around, listening and watching all that was going on.

"Believe me, that dog does exactly what he wants to do."

"Looks too much like a wolf for my liking." The sheriff took off his hat and wiped a hand across his bald head. "This place feels like a sauna."

She hadn't noticed the heat when she'd come in here earlier, but the sheriff was right. The place felt hotter than hell. Frowning, she glanced around. They were standing in the living room, surrounded by the old man's memorabilia and lots of papers. As she stared at one stack, she noted the edges were beginning to curl up and go dark.

And it was getting hotter with every passing second.

Goose bumps raced across her skin. Only the two of them were in the house. Nearly everyone else was in the barn or searching the grounds. What better time for evil to kill a pest?

"Sheriff, I think we should leave."

He gave her the sort of look she'd seen half her life. The look that queried sanity. "Why?"

The sense of wrongness grew, until it felt like her skin crawled with it. She grabbed his arm and pushed him toward the back door. "Because I have a very bad feeling about this heat, and my bad feelings have a habit of coming true."

"I think—"

She never did get to know what he thought, because at that moment the house blew apart, and a fist of air lifted them off their feet and out the windows.

EIGHT

ETHAN CAUGHT A FAMILIAR SCENT AS HE WAS SNIFFING through the rotting pile of old straw dumped on the far side of the barn. Baby powder. He nosed around a bit more and found a footprint. A child-sized footprint. Hope surged, and he felt like howling in joy. She'd stood here, and not all that long ago.

The baby-fresh smell led away from the barn, toward the dark trees ringing the farm's boundary. But there were other prints here—a man's prints, if the shoe size was anything to go by. They'd led Janie away from both the barn and the house, to God knows where. But why make her walk? Why not carry her?

He followed the prints for several yards, then hesitated, glancing over his shoulder. Something felt wrong. He couldn't pinpoint what it was—just a feeling in the air, a vibration of power that somehow tasted foul.

And whatever it was, it was headed for the house. Kat was inside. He had to warn her.

He took a step, but in that moment, the house literally blew apart. It wasn't an explosion—there was no heat, no noise. One minute the house was there, the next it was in a million deadly splinters.

Ethan froze, and for one horrible moment it felt as if something had grabbed his gut and his throat and his heart and twisted hard.

Then he ran, past the scrambling deputies, out into a yard suddenly filled with smoke and dust and deadly wooden missiles. He sniffed the air, caught Kat's scent, and ran as quickly as four legs could carry him to what was left of the rear of the house.

And saw her. Bloodied, and not moving, but definitely breathing. A weight lifted off his chest, and suddenly *he* could breathe again.

She lay on the ground in a ball. Her arms were scratched, her skirt rucked up and torn, her calf cut and bleeding. But she was alive, she was relatively unhurt, and that was surely a miracle.

He pulled down her skirt with his teeth, protecting her modesty even though he wasn't really sure if she'd care, then nudged her with his nose several times. When that got little response, he licked the side of her face, his tongue rasping against the sooty silk of her skin. She finally stirred, muttering a curse under her breath before she pushed him away.

"Yuck, Ethan." Though her voice was a little husky, it was strong. She uncurled, wincing a little as she stretched out her cut leg. "Now I smell like dog breath."

He couldn't reply, as much as he wanted to. Couldn't ask if she was okay. So he licked her again, this time across her lips.

She spluttered and finally opened her eyes. "I'm okay. Will you quit it?"

He sat back on his haunches and eyed the overeager deputy who came rushing over.

"You okay, Miss?"

The jerk knelt beside her, all but pawing her in his eagerness to help her into a sitting position. A growl rumbled up Ethan's throat, and the deputy jumped back.

"Bad dog," she said, green eyes twinkling as she looked at him. "He's only trying to help."

Yeah, and his hands just *happened* to brush her breasts in the process. He continued to glare at the offending deputy, and the kid swallowed. Hard.

"Emergency services have been called. They won't be long, Miss."

The deputy half rose, but she put a hand on his shoulder, stopping him. "How's the sheriff?"

"He's conscious, like yourself, Miss." The deputy gave Ethan another look, then pulled away from Kat's hand and stood. "But I'll just go double-check."

"That was uncalled for," she said softly, glancing at Ethan as the deputy walked away. "Especially since you're the one who said there's nothing between us but sex."

There *was* nothing between them but sex. But while he was with her, he was going to make damn sure no one else was. The thought stopped him. That sounded territorial. Perhaps wolf instincts were stronger in this form. He couldn't honestly say, because he hadn't willingly worn this form for close to fourteen years.

But by the same token, he *didn't* want to share her. Not with anyone. Not even the slightest caress. But he couldn't tell her that. Couldn't tell her anything in this guise. And he couldn't risk shifting shape just yet. Benton had apparently asked the sheriff if he could send a team down to see if there were any similarities to their kidnapping case. They were due any minute, and he just couldn't afford to be seen.

Kat rose stiffly, dusted off her hands, then limped over to the sheriff. Ethan followed close on her heels, and the men hovering near the sheriff seemed to sidle away, giving them space. The sheriff was up on his feet, and other than a bloody cut on his cheek and a ripped shirt, he looked none the worse for his ordeal.

"You okay?" His voice, like Kat's, was still a little croaky.

She nodded. "I'm going to head back to the cabins and clean up, if you don't mind."

"You don't want those cuts checked first?"

She waved a hand. "They're only minor. You know where I'm staying if you want to talk to me."

The sheriff nodded, and she walked away. The car was parked halfway down the long driveway. Ethan shifted shape as they neared it, flowing from wolf to human form in several smooth steps that belied his lack of practice. He touched her arm and stopped her.

"What the hell are you doing?" Her gaze went past him, studying the farm behind them.

"There's no one near to see us. Are you okay?"

"I told you that already." Irritation touched her voice. "And how do you know they can't see you? You got eyes in the back of your head now?"

"I can smell them." As he could smell her. Taste her. On his skin. In his mouth. His gaze dropped to her lips. "Can you drive?"

"I've only cut my leg. Shift shape before someone sees you. If you want to talk, wait till we get back to the cabins."

"I'm not going back just yet."

And neither was she—not until he'd tasted her more fully. His lips claimed hers, his kiss hard, demanding. Though she made a small sound of protest at the back of her throat, her lips yielded to his. His tongue savored the sweetness of her mouth as he pressed her back against the car. Her body trembled against him, her nipples hard against his chest. He slid his hand under her soft sweater, caressing their peaks as he pressed his groin against her. Wanting, needing, to get inside.

She felt so good, so right, that he wanted to keep on tasting and touching her forever. But now was not the time, because there were scents that would not wait. He pulled back. Her breathing was as harsh as his, her pupils wide and dilated. He touched her cheek, thumbing the thin trickle of blood away.

"Sorry."

She took a shuddering breath. "You should be. It's not like you can finish anything right now."

"No." But he certainly wanted to, and that in itself was somewhat surprising, given the number of condoms he'd thrown out this morning. The fever should have been well sated until this evening. "Perhaps tonight."

"Perhaps." Her tone suggested he shouldn't count on it.

Though he certainly did. He took off the ridiculous pink scarf she'd forced him to wear and handed it to her. "I have to go. I found a spoor I have to follow." He shifted shape before she could argue and leaped away.

* * *

For two seconds, Kat thought about following him. But if she didn't drive the car away, the deputies would wonder why it was still there and perhaps begin a search. They couldn't afford that, not right now, and not when the zombies and God knows what else might still be in the area.

She took a deep breath that did little to ease the ache of desire as she climbed into the car and headed for the cabins.

Her grandmother was asleep when she arrived. Kat headed into the bathroom and cleaned up the cuts on her face and leg, then made two cups of coffee and carried them into the bedroom. Gwen stirred as she sat down on the edge of the bed.

"You're back," she said, yawning as she sat up. "Did you find anything?"

"A necklace belonging to Janie, and another soul-sucker victim." She handed her grandmother the coffee, then leaned against the wall. "This one was an old man, though."

Gwen frowned. "New or old death?"

"Newish. He's been dead for about a week."

"So the mara is still taking its victims in a traditional manner. Wonder what it needs the kids for, then?"

Kat rubbed her arms. "I have a bad feeling that we don't want to know the answer to that."

"Me, too." Gwen's frown deepened. "I'll have to call Seline and see if she's discovered anything on rituals that need specific emotions for completion. Where's that wolf of yours?"

"He ran off to follow a scent." And she hoped he was careful. Those zombies were still out there, as was the soul-sucker. And he didn't stand a chance against them—not when he didn't believe he had to kill rather than arrest.

"Damn fool. Hope he has more sense than to charge in if he finds anything."

"He's a cop. He knows better than that."

Gwen snorted. "He's also a werewolf in the midst of moon heat, so sense is not playing a major role in his thought processes at the moment."

"You want me to go look for him?"

Gwen hesitated. "No. You need to head over to this restaurant." She grabbed a slip of paper from the dressing table and handed it to Kat. "With the moon high, that other werewolf is going to be trolling for victims tonight. You've got to stop him."

"So this time he's not hunting children for the mara?"

"No." Gwen frowned. "I'd love to know what he's getting out of the relationship with her, though."

"Maybe we need to ask him when we stop him." She glanced at the address, noting that the restaurant was the one Ethan and she had stopped at yesterday. "We don't have any silver bullets."

"The silver daggers will work just as well." Gwen hesitated. "But be careful. This wolf is one of the bitten, and they're usually mean. By all means try to question him about his role in all this is, but make it fast, or you could be in trouble."

Kat nodded and tried to ignore the fear of what might happen. Finishing her coffee, she rose. "I'll mix up some truth herbs and see if I can slip them into his drink."

Gwen nodded. "Just don't push too hard, even if

you do get them into him. If you make him suspicious, you'll be in danger."

She'd be in danger anyway, and they both knew it. "What about Ethan?"

"The moon fever has him feeling a might territorial, and that could prove disastrous in this situation."

Because he'd attack rather than question. And as much as this werewolf deserved to die, they needed the answers he might provide. "So what are you going to tell him when he gets back?"

"That what you do on your own free time is none of his damn business."

She gave her grandmother a long look. "What possible good is telling him that going to do?"

"Nothing at all. I just want to see his reaction."

"You're a bad woman, you know that?"

"And enjoying every moment of it." Gwen grinned, but there was a seriousness in her green eyes as she said, "He needs to be shaken, Kat. Or this could end very badly."

"This case, or him and me?"

"Both."

She had a feeling it would end badly between Ethan and her no matter how much stirring her grandmother did. His actions made it all too clear that he really only wanted sex from her. Which was a damn shame, because there were definitely signs that there could be a whole lot more.

She glanced at her watch. It wouldn't take long to fly down to the restaurant, but even so, she had to get moving. It was past four, and dusk was closing in fast. "I'll change and get going."

"Just be careful. And don't let the aura of the wolf overwhelm you."

"I won't." She knew her voice sounded as uncertain as she felt.

ETHAN SAT ON HIS HAUNCHES AND STUDIED THE SMALL cabin in the clearing below. The baby-fresh scent had faded a good ten minutes back, but he'd continued to hunt around, desperate to find it again.

The only thing he *had* found was this cabin. It looked like nothing out of the ordinary. Just a rundown old shack that appeared to have been abandoned for years.

Yet the smell of death hung so heavily in the air it almost choked him.

He sniffed the breeze, trying to discern if there were any other scents layering the air. Nothing beyond decay and the faint tang of balsam.

He rose and padded through the trees. There was no life, no movement to be seen anywhere. Even the quiet songs of the birds had faded away. Keeping to the deepening shadows as much as possible, he headed down to the cabin. Still no sound, no sign that anything living had been near this place in the last few months. Not even spiders—though there were plenty of webs to prove they'd once been here. He shifted shape, pressing his back against the rough-hewn walls as he edged toward the grimy rear window. And discovered the cause for the smell.

Dead men. *Living* dead men.

There had to be at least ten of them sleeping on the floor. He shifted position, trying to see into the shadows filling the corners. Janie wasn't there. He couldn't see her, couldn't smell her. But if these things were working for the woman snatching the kids, then maybe all he had to do was sit here and wait for either the killer to show up or these things to lead him to the mara. And Janie.

He had nothing to lose by trying.

Nothing except time spent with Kat. Unease stirred, and the sudden desire to race back to her caught him by surprise. Because it wasn't motivated by the moon fever, but rather a surge of fear for her safety. And though he had the bruises to prove she was more than able to take care of herself, the certainty that she was flying into trouble settled like a weight in his gut and refused to budge.

He frowned and shifted shape, making his way back to the trees. But as the shadows mottling the clearing became one and the sky drifted toward night, the feeling that Kat needed help became a certainty he could not ignore.

He rose and ran for their cabin. Night had settled in by the time he arrived, and the wind was as cold as his heart. He entered their rooms, but knew from the lingering scents that Kat hadn't been there for at least two hours. He walked into the other cabin.

"Where's Kat?" he said the minute he saw Gwen.

The old woman lowered the newspaper and raised an eyebrow. "Out chasing a lead."

"Where?" His voice was brusque, but right then he didn't care.

Gwen crossed her arms, her expression amused. "She's working, wolf, and you have no right—"

"She's in trouble."

Amusement fled from the old woman's face. "What do you mean?"

"I mean she needs help. That without it she could be seriously hurt." Perhaps even killed. The thought twisted something deep inside him, and for a minute he couldn't even breathe.

Gwen studied him, her green eyes intense, almost otherworldly. As if she were seeing things those of the mortal world never could. Then she blinked and rose, hobbling into her bedroom. "How do you know this?" she asked over her shoulder.

He hesitated, but if anyone would understand his certainty, it would be this strange old woman. "I don't really know. It's just a feeling—a conviction—I have."

"Precognition," Gwen said. "I thought you might have that. She's at the restaurant you stopped at yesterday."

He felt like cursing. A two-hour drive was going to stretch his nerves to the limits. He swung to leave, then stopped. "Why is she there?"

"Because the werewolf that tore apart the kid will be there trolling for victims to slake his lust on. She's going to stop him."

The ice in his gut grew. "You sent her out alone after that thing?"

"She's hunted far worse than werewolves."

"When the moon is high, there *is* nothing worse than a berserk werewolf." He knew that for a fact, having seen it back home as a cub. He briefly closed his eyes, forcing away the images of the woman who'd been attacked, and tried not to imagine Kat in her place.

Gwen snorted as she came back out and handed him a small first-aid kit. "Werewolf, you have no idea of the world we walk in."

Maybe not. But he knew werewolves, and despite all their experience, these two obviously had no idea just how dangerous a berserker could be. And Kat was out there, facing one alone. He picked up his car keys and walked out the door.

And knew with certainty as he jumped into the car that he was not going to be in time to stop her from getting hurt.

KAT GLANCED AT HER WATCH FOR THE UMPTEENTH TIME. It was close to eight, and still she had no sense of the werewolf's presence in the crowded room.

She sipped her champagne and let her gaze drift across the dance floor. There were plenty of women here, and plenty of men. All of them dancing and flirting and generally having a good time. She had no doubt that, to a sensitive nose, the smell of lust would hang heavily in the air. And maybe that was the reason the werewolf intended to hunt here tonight. The pickings would probably be easy for a wolf in the midst of moon heat.

A chill raced a warning across her skin. She looked toward the door as it opened, and her stomach dropped to the vicinity of her toes.

The man who entered was tall and powerfully built, with chiseled features and dark blond hair. The sheer sexual energy radiating off him told her this was the werewolf she sought. But he was not the reason for the sudden rush of fear. That honor went to the petite Asian woman who stopped beside him. The soul-sucker.

The woman scanned the room, and Kat dropped her gaze. Though she now wore a blond wig and colored contact lenses, she wasn't about to risk the mara recognizing her. The heat of the soul-sucker's gaze lingered for a moment, then moved on.

Relief surged through her and she looked up again. The mara headed left, the werewolf to the right. Kat hesitated, half thinking about going after the soul-sucker. But in reality, she knew that was a move best kept until they knew more about what would kill it. For now, it was better to chip away at the mara's defenses by getting rid of her lieutenants.

She finished her drink in one gulp, then walked to the bar and ordered two more. Once back in the shadows, she slipped the herbs into one glass and watched the werewolf prowl around the room. The force of his aura rolled before him like a wave, hitting men and women alike. Obviously, this particular wolf wasn't too choosy as to what sex he mated with. Their sighs and stares followed in his wake, but he didn't stop, his gaze continuing to hunt the room.

Her stomach began to churn. She checked to make sure the herbs had disintegrated, and then she walked toward him.

The heat of his aura hit her like a punch to the stomach. It left her breathless, hot, and yet oddly uneasy. Because while *this* werewolf's aura was every bit as powerful as Ethan's, there was an undercurrent of violence in his energy that shook her to the core. Sex with this man would not be pleasant . . . maybe not even survivable.

She stepped in front of him, forcing him to stop. His gaze collided with hers, and deep in the blue depths she saw madness and hunger. A chill ran down her spine, but she forced a smile and offered him a glass. "You look like a man in search of a drink."

His smile was high wattage, sexy, yet one that left her cold.

"Thank you." His voice, like his smile, was designed to seduce.

He took the drink, the brief touch of his fingers hot and somehow needy. She resisted the urge to wipe her hand and raised her glass, taking a sip. The sweet liquid only succeeded in further agitating her stomach. "Do you come here often?" she said.

"Yes. And I haven't seen you here before."

His gaze slid casually down her body, then rose to meet hers again. The desire so evident in his eyes made her throat go dry. Heat surged between them, caressing her skin with its intensity. Yet while she reacted physically, it left her numb deep inside. Which was odd, given how susceptible she was to Ethan the minute he came within arm's reach.

"No," she murmured. "I'm just passing through."

Something surged in his eyes. Relief. Perhaps even triumph. He swallowed the last of his champagne, then placed the glass on the nearby table. "Shall we dance?"

She hesitated briefly, but knew she had no choice. She had to let him think his aura was doing its job, that she was indeed struck with desire for him. She downed her drink in a gulp that left her head buzzing and placed her glass beside his. He pressed a hand against her back as he guided her down to the dance floor, his fingers caressing her spine, sending chills skating across her skin. The music swirled around them, its beat heavy, languid. The floor was crowded with sweating, needy people, and she could almost smell their lust. He pulled her close, his body hard and smelling faintly of pine and death. His touch slid down to caress her rear. Had it been Ethan, she would have ached. With this wolf, the only true sensation she had was fear.

She lifted her gaze to his again. "Doesn't your girlfriend mind you dancing this . . . intimately . . . with others?"

Tension flowed briefly through his limbs, and the hand holding her side dug deep. Pain slithered through her, and she bit down on a yelp.

He raised a pale eyebrow, his gaze all cold heat. "Girlfriend?"

She nodded. "I saw you come in and was disappointed to see you weren't alone."

His grip relaxed a little. "Ah, you mean Ming. She's my employer."

"But not your lover?"

"Our arrangement does sometimes include sex." He gave her a half-smile that made her stomach flip-flop—and not in a good way. "Does that worry you?"

"That very much depends on just what sort of business you're both in."

"You could say my part in our venture is taking care of the young."

His touch slipped from her rear to her thigh and moved under her skirt, caressing bare skin. The tremor that ran through her had nothing to do with desire.

She fought the flash of kinetic energy and raised an eyebrow. "Charity work?"

"No. Not unless you consider self-interest a charity." His other hand slid under her breast. She couldn't help trembling again, and he chuckled softly. "Is this what you want?"

He caught a nipple between his thumb and finger and squeezed hard. Her moan was one of pain rather than ecstasy, but he didn't seem to care. He brushed a kiss across her cheek, his breath hot and foul as it fanned her skin. His mouth moved down to hers, but at the last moment she turned away, pressing the slightest kiss to his neck instead. Even that brief contact had her stomach squirming in distaste.

The waves of his aura were blasting her with heated desire. Her nipples hardened in response, and her breathing became more rapid. Yet they were both outward signs of a response she didn't feel inside.

She swallowed to ease the dryness in her throat and said, "Have you lived around these parts long?"

He shrugged and cupped her breast, kneading it hard through the gauzy material of her shirt. "Not at all. Only a few weeks, in fact. I actually tend to move between Springfield and here."

Energy prickled across her fingertips. She clenched her hand behind him, fighting the desire to smack him across the room. "Is it your work that makes you divide your time between the two?"

"Yes. Although we're only here until her kids are old enough—" He stopped, suspicion darkening his expression.

Fear stirred. She ran a hand down his body and pressed her palm against the hardness so visible under his jeans. "Perhaps we should do something about this before we continue our chat."

His suspicion fled, replaced by avid hunger. "We could go somewhere more secluded," he whispered into her neck. "And dance a little more intimately."

She shivered. There was no way in hell she was going to be caught alone outside with this man. She didn't like the edge of violence so evident in his aura—and besides, there was the soul-sucker to consider. She might be able to cope with one mad creature, but two was pushing her limits.

"It's too cold outside," she murmured, running a finger back up his chest and undoing the top button of his shirt. "But I noticed earlier that the ladies' room has a lock."

Amused anticipation gleamed in his eyes. His hand slid up her thigh and settled on her rear, but his touch was so hot it felt as if he were branding her.

"I like your thinking."

So did she. At least help was within yelling distance if she got into trouble. "Then let's go."

She stepped away and caught his hand, leading the way through the crowded dance floor. When they neared the restroom she released him, her smile teasing as she looked up. "I'll just go check to make sure we're alone."

"Don't be long." His voice was brusque and edged with hunger.

The urge to run all but swamped her. She forced her smile and entered the restroom. It was empty. She checked the stalls anyway, then reached up to close the window.

A warning tingled across the back of her neck, telling her she was no longer alone. She ignored the urge to turn and face him, knowing she had to lock the window just to make sure no one else could join them. Especially the soul-sucker—though a locked window wasn't going to delay her long if she decided to join the party.

He kicked the door shut, then slammed the bolt home. Her heart began a double-time dance that had nothing to do with desire. She slid her hand into her bag and clenched her fingers around one of the two silver knives she carried.

"Getting a might anxious, aren't—" Metal slithered across her throat, cutting off her words. She reacted instinctively, thrusting a hand up to her neck as the wire snapped taut. A ribbon of fire began to burn around her throat and cut into her fingers. It wasn't ordinary wire. It was silver, which meant she couldn't shift shape to escape the garrote.

"Did you think a wig would fool us?" he whispered, his breath hot and unsteady against her ear.

She didn't answer. *Couldn't* answer. The wire was growing tighter, cutting into her fingers and neck. Moisture pulsed down her palm, and her chest burned as air suddenly became scarce.

Energy blistered through every fiber, but she fought desperately against the urge to release it. She didn't dare when he held the garrote so tight. She might just end up cutting her own throat.

"Scream for me," he whispered. "Beg for your life."

He slammed her face-first against the wall and began rubbing himself against her rump. He was thick and hard, his breathing fast and hot against her ear.

Bile rose in her throat, threatening to finish what the garrote had begun. She closed her eyes, battling panic. Remembered the knife still clenched in her hand.

She lifted it free and stabbed backward. The blade sliced through flesh as easily as butter, sinking hilt-deep. He howled, and the noose around her neck cut deeper. She fought for breath, her lungs burning and heart pounding so fast it felt ready to leap from her chest.

The smell of burning flesh tore at the air, then metal clattered against the tiles. "You will pay for that." His voice was little more than a husky growl. "I shall tear your limbs from your body, then drown you with my seed as your blood pulses around you."

Magic shimmered around her. He was changing shape . . . but the garrote didn't loosen. He must have tied it. Lights danced crazily before her eyes, and the whole world seemed to be roaring at her. Her heart thumped in her ears, and the burning in her lungs had spread throughout her body. Every muscle seemed to scream with the need to breathe.

She thrust a hand into her bag and felt desperately for the second knife. Heard the rumbling growl behind her and spun, stabbing blindly.

If she hit anything, she didn't feel it.

She cursed, but the words seemed to lodge somewhere in her throat, the effort to speak choking her. She felt the breeze of movement and lashed out kinetically. Wildly. Something hit the far wall and anger rumbled around her. Her fingers twitched against the knife. She glanced down, surprised that she still held it, but couldn't see anything through the darkness rushing into her mind. She closed her eyes, imagining the knife burying itself so deep into the werewolf's heart that it pinned him to the wall. Felt energy burn through every fiber, as if in response. Then the darkness took hold, and she knew no more.

ETHAN THRUST OPEN THE RESTAURANT DOOR AND WALKED inside. His gaze swept the room, taking in the crowd gyrating on the dance floor and the overflowing tables and booths. Kat wasn't anywhere near, yet she was still in the building. Her fresh scent teased his nostrils, drawing him on. As did the sensation of her pain.

He clenched his fists and headed left. Beneath the faint smell of sweat and alcohol, desire roamed. Given the full moon was closer tonight, that smell should have stirred his senses, made him hunger. Yet he felt dead inside. Dead and cold.

He didn't stop to wonder at that. Didn't dare.

A woman stepped in front of him. She was a pretty Asian, her face full, her body luscious. "Care for a drink, stranger?"

The invitation in her dark eyes suggested she was offering far more than a drink. At any other time he might have accepted both the drink and the sex, but right now he had something far more important to do. Someone far more important to find.

"Sorry, I haven't the time to play." He tried to walk around her, but she stepped in front of him again.

"What will a drink cost you?" she murmured, her voice a smoky promise of heat.

"Plenty." Especially if Kat died. He picked the woman up and placed her to one side. "Sorry, but I'm in a hurry."

He continued on. Up ahead, a crowd had gathered around the restroom. A security guard thumped the door, but he didn't appear to be getting any response. The ice in Ethan's stomach rose, settling across his chest, making it difficult to breathe.

"Police," he said, pushing his way through the crowd. He reached the guard and flashed his badge, then said, "What's the problem?"

"One of the ladies reported hearing fighting, but whoever is in there has locked the door and doesn't appear to be responding."

Ethan nodded as he put his ID away. "Clear this area for me, and don't let anyone come past that last table. I'll take care of it."

The guard began pushing people back. Ethan waited until there was no possible chance of anyone seeing inside, then stepped back and kicked the door open.

The werewolf lay at the base of one of the stalls, a glittering silver knife lodged deep in his heart. He'd been caught early in the change, so that he looked like a malformed human who hadn't shaved in years. At least it meant he didn't have to explain the existence of werewolves to anyone—though he suspected Mark might know more than what he was saying on *that* subject.

Kat lay on the floor under the window, blood pooling around her face. A face that was mottled, and lips that were blue. For an instant everything seemed to freeze—his heart, his mind, his body—but then he was beside her, quickly feeling for a pulse.

It was there—rapid, weak, but there. Relief surged through him but just as swiftly fled when he saw the silver garrote still around her neck. He swore and released the wire's tension, easing it away from her burned and bloodied flesh.

She coughed, then sucked in air, her whole body shaking with the urgency to breathe. He pinched her cheeks, trying to gain her attention. The danger was far from over yet.

"Kat, did he bite you?"

She rolled onto her back and continued to suck in air. Blood poured from the vicious wounds on her right hand, and her neck was burned and swollen around the paper-thin cut. He couldn't see any bite marks, but that didn't mean there weren't any, especially seeing as the werewolf was partway through the change. Even a bite from a berserker in human form could be deadly.

He grabbed her shoulders and shook her gently. "Katherine, did he bite you?"

She shook her head and opened her eyes. They were brown rather than green.

"Don't think—" The rest of her words were lost to a bout of coughing that left her shaking.

He swore under his breath and did a quick but careful check. He couldn't see anything resembling a bite and relaxed a little. But she was still cut and bleeding, and he had to treat both wounds as soon as possible. He stripped off his jacket and wrapped it around her. "Let's get you out of here."

"Soul-sucker," she gasped. "Outside."

"Kat, you can't go after it like this—"

"No. But it may—" She stopped and coughed so hard her face went red.

"Attack?" he finished, and she nodded.

Given the commotion they'd raised in the last ten minutes, he very much doubted it. This thing, whether it was human or something else entirely, was smart, and hanging around in a place about to be invaded by cops wasn't smart. With any luck, by now it was halfway back to the hell that had spawned it. He just had to hope it wasn't taking Janie with it.

He took a business card from his wallet, scrawled the cabin's address on the back, then slipped his arms under her and carefully picked her up.

"Tell me if you sense it," he said.

She nodded and closed her eyes, leaning her head against his shoulder. Coarse blond hair scratched at his nose. The wig didn't suit her. It made her look brassy and cheap, and she was neither of those. But at least it might prevent her from being recognized by anyone later. He wasn't going to be so lucky.

And Benton was going to be furious.

He carried her out of the restroom and stopped near the security guard. "Call the sheriff, then call this number." He handed the man the card and pointed to the department's phone number. "Get hold of Detective Fairfield and tell him Detective Morgan has found another suspect." The sheriff and Benton weren't going to be happy about his interference, but right now, Ethan didn't care.

"Is the lady all right?"

"Yeah. If they want to talk to me, I'm staying at the address on the back."

The guard flicked the card over and nodded. "And the lady?"

"Will be with me."

He headed for the door. The night outside was cool, unfettered by the odors of sweat and lust and curiosity. He took a deep breath, clearing his head as he walked toward the car. Kat's sweet scent surrounded him, stirring his blood once more. Even bloody and bruised, she still smelled good. Still felt good.

He unlocked the car and placed her upright on the backseat. She stirred, blinking rapidly. Her breathing had evened out, but her mouth was still pinched with pain.

He squatted down next to her and opened up the small first-aid kit. Inside there was antiseptic, swabs, bandages, and a small pouch of dried herbs. Obviously, Kat and her grandmother considered the herbs to be a cure-all for all manner of wounds. And while it went against every instinct to use such unconventional healing methods, they'd worked almost miraculously on the wound in her arm. He wasn't about to gainsay their benefits when she was bleeding all over the seat and he had nothing else.

He touched a hand to her cheek, and she opened her eyes. He hated the contact lenses. On her, green was far prettier. "I'm going to have to take off your shirt to clean the wound properly." The collar was brushing the thin line around her neck, irritating the wound and making it bleed again.

"Don't need excuses." Her voice was little more than a husky whisper. "Just ask."

A mischievous smile played about her mouth, and heat shot to his groin. "I'm afraid even the *thought* of asking is out of the question tonight." It was just as well he'd sated the worst of his desires last night, otherwise restraint would not be so easily offered.

"Tomorrow," she said, closing her eyes again.

"Maybe."

"Definitely."

He eased the jacket off, then undid the buttons of her shirt and peeled it away. Her creamy breasts were smeared with blood and showed signs of heavy-handed bruising. Anger rose inside him, swift and sharp. He swallowed it. The berserker was dead, and as much as he wanted to go back and kick the bastard's body, it wouldn't achieve anything.

After soaking a swab in antiseptic, he carefully cleaned her wounds, then applied the herbs and bandaged them. She bore it all without comment, even though he saw her wince. She was undoubtedly braver than he was—straight antiseptic would have had him screaming. He put his jacket back on her and zipped it up as far as he could to keep her warm.

"Home, James," she murmured as he did up her seat belt.

He smiled and brushed a kiss across her lips, then rose before he gave in to the desire to taste her more fully. Once they were on the road, he called Gwen to let her know everything was okay. Even so, she was waiting outside when they got back to the cabins.

She hobbled across to the car and flung open the

door. "Nice job of bandaging," she said after a few seconds. "And you used the herbs."

"Why wouldn't I? I've seen them work, remember."

"That you did." She patted his arm. "Put her in my bed for the time being, Detective, because your boss isn't that far behind you."

He raised an eyebrow as he lifted Kat. "How?"

"I called him after you left. I thought you might have needed some backup."

Then they must have *just* missed each other, and for that he was grateful. Benton would have insisted on sending Kat to a hospital. She was far better here, under her grandmother's care, though only a day ago he wouldn't have admitted that.

He carried her into the cabin and placed her into bed, stripping off her shoes but leaving on his jacket. She was asleep, and he didn't want to disturb her any more than necessary. He ran his fingers down her cheek to her lips, then bent and kissed them. Lightly, gently.

She stirred, murmuring something he couldn't quite catch. "Sleep," he murmured against her lips. "I'll be here if you want me."

She didn't respond, and he spun, leaving the room before he could give in to the urge to do anything more.

"I'll wait for Benton in the other cabin," he said to Gwen. And hide any evidence that Kat and he had shared a bed. Mark might know the truth, but there was no need for Benton or anyone else to know what was going on between them.

Gwen nodded. "I'll be in after he arrives. Then you can fill us all in on what happened."

He snorted softly. "Benton is not going to believe anything you or I say."

"Wouldn't he have seen the werewolf?"

"Yeah, but Kat caught him early in the change. He looked more like a deformed and hairy man rather than a wolf." And that was a good thing—he had no real wish for Benton to start believing in werewolves.

"A man whose tooth measurements will probably fit the marks left on the last victim's bones."

"Which will make him think the wolf killed the kid, and Kat says that's not true."

"And it isn't, as you know." Gwen patted his hand again. "Go clean up and rest while you can. It's going to be a long night once your boss gets here."

A long and *noisy* night, Ethan thought sourly, and headed into the other cabin.

"GODDAMN IT, MORGAN, I DISTINCTLY REMEMBER TELLING you to keep away from this case!"

"Keep your voice down." Ethan crossed his arms and leaned a shoulder against the wall. "Katherine's asleep in the other cabin."

Benton threw a hand out as he continued to pace. "I don't *care* who's asleep. I want to know what's going on."

"You won't believe what's going on." Nor did he want the captain to believe. But he had a suspicion Gwen planned otherwise.

"What *was* that thing we found in the restaurant's restroom?" Unlike Benton, Mark kept his voice low. He was sitting on the sofa and looked as tired as Ethan felt. "It sure as hell didn't look entirely human."

Ethan shrugged. "I think he was some kind of mutant."

"So how is a mutant connected to the case?" Benton stopped his pacing and glared at Ethan for a moment. "And why did it attack Miss Tanner?"

"He was apparently working with the woman behind all the kidnappings and murders." He paused, then added, "I think if you check the bite marks on the last victim, you'll find they match the mutant's."

They both stared at him for several seconds, then Benton swore and resumed his pacing. "So Tanner was tracking it?"

He nodded. "It must have spotted her, because it attacked her in the restroom."

"And she killed it." The captain shook his head. "I should have her head on the block. We needed that man for questioning."

Ethan realized he was clenching his fists only when he saw Mark studying him. He flexed his fingers and tried to relax. "You almost did have her neck on a block," he reminded Benton shortly. "And it's hard to be precise with a knife when someone is strangling you from behind."

The captain sniffed. "You know we found a second body at the restaurant."

Ethan glanced at Mark. "Where?"

"In one of the booths," his partner supplied. "We discovered it after everyone had been questioned and released. Looks like he died the same way as that old man in the barn."

In the middle of a crowded restaurant? This woman was obviously bold when she took them—sexually and spiritually—or had some sort of magic happening that prevented other patrons from seeing what she was doing. "Did you run that other check for me?"

Mark nodded. "And your straw-clutching guess was right. In each case, there were reports of disappearances over a three-night span before the kids were taken."

"All men?"

"Yep. And the body of one was recently discovered. The report says cause of death unknown."

"But I'm guessing he was found in a somewhat compromising position?"

"Naked and obviously in the middle of sex when he died." Mark shook his head. "By all accounts, it looks like we have some sort of black widow at work."

It was something a whole lot worse than a black widow, Ethan thought grimly, though he doubted Benton would actually believe it. Hell, there was a part of *him* that still wasn't believing, despite everything he'd seen. "The question is, how are those murders connected to the kidnappings?"

Because they were; Ethan was sure of it. He glanced at the door separating the two cabins. Though he'd heard no sound, the hint of summer touching the air told him Kat was awake.

"No one knows how any of these men died," Benton exploded, "and to add to the confusion, there have also been reports of a number of men going missing around the same time frame. Whether they're connected or not, we're not sure, but I have a damn *bad* feeling about it all."

So did Ethan. The door opened, but it was Gwen who stepped through. "They're connected," she said, voice sharp. "But the trouble is, you seek answers that lie in the ordinary, and this case has nothing to do with the ordinary."

Kat followed her grandmother through the door. She no longer wore the wig and her eyes were once again green. But they were haunted with exhaustion and pain, and her face was pale. She should have been asleep, and probably would have been had it not been for Benton's booming voice.

She no longer wore Ethan's jacket, and her low-cut shirt revealed a tantalizing glimpse of her breasts. Her black skirt swirled around her thighs as she headed for the second sofa, showcasing long, wonderful legs. He wasn't the only one who silently admired them as she sat.

Her gaze rose to his and, for an instant, there might well have been no one else in the room. Though she was tired and still in pain, the need in her eyes was every bit as strong as the one that pounded through his veins. The momentary smile that touched her lips did strange things to his breathing. *Tomorrow,* she'd whispered. He suddenly wasn't sure he could wait that long.

"What do you mean?" Benton's voice cracked the brief silence. "If you two are withholding information—"

Gwen's snort was contemptuous. "The only thing we're withholding is knowledge you're not likely to believe."

"Right now, I'm desperate enough to listen to even the most outlandish theory."

"Then I've got one that'll blow your socks off." Gwen perched on the arm of the sofa beside Kat. "The thing that is taking these kids is called a mara. It's an ancient spirit that can enter houses by taking the form of a cat or vapor. It seduces men and eats their souls while they're in the midst of passion."

Benton stared at her for a second. "This thing is human." His voice was harsh. "Your granddaughter saw it."

"The fact that it can take human form doesn't make it human," Gwen said dryly. "As yet, we have no idea why it is taking these kids, but it *is* stealing their souls. And doing so while they are in great pain."

"The first was drained of blood," Mark said. "Six days later, the second kid was torn apart. How's that related to this soul-stealer?"

There was very little doubt in Mark's voice, Ethan noted. But then, Mark had seen the disintegration of the zombie firsthand. That would be enough to make anyone believe that something beyond the norm was going on in this case.

"The first kid was drained by a vampire who was working with the soul-sucker," Gwen elaborated. "Kat killed it in the warehouse. You probably would have found a man-shaped black stain on the concrete."

That explained the bits of humanity found among the soot. Ethan looked at Kat. "Is that why you were attacking him with stakes?"

She nodded. "White ash."

Her voice was little more than a croak, and he raised an eyebrow, glancing at Gwen for explanation.

"Most stakes will damage a vampire," she said. "But to ensure a kill, it's best to use white ash."

"And the mutant in the restroom this evening?"

Though Benton asked the question, his expression suggested he really didn't want to know. "How is that connected?"

"Ethan has already told you it was working for the soul-sucker. And it was a werewolf," Gwen said, meeting Ethan's gaze for a moment. "Not a mutant. Not a freak of nature."

He had a sudden, unsettling feeling the old woman was beginning to figure him out.

The captain scrubbed a hand across his mottled cheeks. He looked sick, Ethan thought. Heartsick.

"You're seriously expecting me to swallow this?" the captain said, voice flat.

"You have the werewolf, and I guarantee his bite will match those on the second kid's remains. You have the residue of the zombie who tried to force Kat and Ethan off the road. You have the charcoaled remnants of humanity from the warehouse." Gwen crossed her arms and studied Benton coldly. "What further evidence do you need that something beyond normal is going on with this case?"

"More than that," he bit back. He glared at Gwen a moment longer, then resumed his pacing. "We know this . . . woman . . . is taking these kids. We don't know the reason." He glared at Gwen again, as if daring her to contradict him. "Why, then, is it killing the men?"

"Like all things, it needs to eat to exist," Gwen said. Mark swore softly and she gave him an amused look. "Amen to that, Detective."

"So the next question we have to answer is, how did it become involved with the werewolf and the vampire?" Ethan said.

"Kids," Kat croaked. "The werewolf said part of his job was taking care of the kids."

Ethan frowned. "The ones they kidnapped?"

She hesitated. "No, he said *her* kids."

"Good God," Gwen said. "If this thing is *breeding,* then that could certainly explain both why she's taking the kids and why she's killing the men."

"How?" Benton growled. "What has one got to do with the other?"

"Breeding takes a great deal of strength. To produce young, she has to be at optimal levels herself."

"But she's not killing the young," Ethan noted. "Her henchmen are. So why take the kids?"

"I don't know," Gwen said, her expression one of frustration. "We're still trying to uncover more information about maras."

Ethan glanced at Kat. "Did the werewolf say anything else?"

She nodded. "He said he'd been moving between Springfield and here for a couple of weeks. He also said they couldn't leave until the kids were old enough."

"If that's true, why is it taking the children to warehouses to kill them? Why not kill them wherever it's keeping its own kids?"

Kat shrugged. It was Gwen who answered. "Maybe it needs these children for something more than feeding. Or maybe it simply kills them elsewhere in an effort to throw police off the trail. Which it did, until we came along."

"If this thing is supposed to be a spirit, how the hell can it have kids?" Mark asked.

"It *does* have a physical presence. It wasn't a spirit

who seduced and killed those men." Gwen pushed to her feet. "I feel the need to scry. Kat?"

Kat rose and followed her grandmother into the other cabin. Benton and Mark looked at Ethan.

"She can sometimes see future events," he explained. "Through a crystal ball."

Benton snorted. "You really believe that rubbish?"

Until he'd met these two, he hadn't really believed in anything supernatural—despite the fact that *he* was a werewolf. He'd been born and raised in a small farming community, and his family had very carefully shielded the townsfolk from the knowledge of what they were. He'd grown up feeling like a freak—a dangerous freak who needed to be locked up one night every month. But the last couple of days had certainly opened his eyes to just what else was out there. "I thought you were willing to use anyone who helps solve this case?"

"Doesn't mean I have to believe it."

"Believe in them. They're the real deal."

Mark's blue eyes glimmered with amusement. "You've changed your tune over the last few days. Wonder what the reason for that is?"

"I've seen things—"

"I just bet you have."

Benton's gaze wavered between the both of them. "Am I missing something here?"

"Nothing important," Ethan muttered, shooting an annoyed look his partner's way. "Did you come up with any ID matches for the driver that attacked us?"

Mark shook his head. "Not yet. And it's a long shot, at best."

Everything about this damn case seemed to be a long shot. Including finding Janie alive. He scrubbed a hand across his jaw. He couldn't think like that. He had to find her. Anything else was simply unacceptable. "The lab boys find anything unusual when examining the second kid?"

Mark frowned. "Maybe. They found some dirt under a couple of his fingernails."

"Most kids have dirt under their fingernails."

"Yeah, but this stuff was slightly phosphorous. It didn't come from that warehouse in Springfield, that's for sure."

It was a clue. Maybe their first. "Are they trying to place it?"

"It's going to be a long task, so don't expect miracles."

He didn't expect miracles. He only expected answers. "Nothing else?"

"The kid's clothing and shoes were still damp. He'd been immersed in water a couple of hours before his death."

"No telling whether it was bath, river, or sea, I suppose?"

"It wasn't seawater, but that's the only thing they are sure of."

Another possible clue that led them nowhere. He glanced at Benton. "What about the old man? Any clues there?"

"No—" A shrill ring interrupted him. The captain swore and dug his cell phone out of his pocket. "Benton here."

It was bad news. That was obvious from the captain's expression. After listening for a few moments, Benton said, "Where?"

He scrawled down an address, then hung up. "Another kid's gone missing," he said grimly. "And this time, the mother was killed in the process."

TEN

"I'M COMING WITH YOU."

Ethan's response was almost automatic. There was nothing he could do that Mark and Benton couldn't, beyond finding scents. And this thing left as little in odors as it did other clues.

But it was better than standing here. Better than wondering if the soul-sucker would follow the pattern it had set so far. Wondering if, in three days' time, they'd find Janie's body, sucked dry or mutilated.

Benton stabbed a finger his way. "You take one step toward that house, and your ass is in the nearest jail cell."

"Captain—"

"I'm serious, Morgan. Keep your nose clean." Benton glanced at Mark. "Let's go."

Ethan looked at his partner, and Mark nodded at the unspoken request. The two men walked out the door. For several minutes, Ethan stood there, weighing his need to follow them against the wisdom of staying put for the moment. He swore and locked the door, then headed into Gwen's cabin.

Gwen was at the small table, staring into her crystal ball. He sat beside Kat on the sofa and gently touched her neck. "How are you feeling?"

"Tired. Sore." She shrugged. "It's to be expected."

At least most of the bruising and swelling had gone down. Those herbs were definitely miraculous—either that or Kat had supernatural self-healing abilities, which he'd seen in werewolves, but never before in a human. He blinked. But she *wasn't* human. She was a shifter, a raven.

"Where's your boss headed?" she continued.

"Another kid has gone missing."

Her hand caressed his and squeezed gently. "We'll find her. Before the three days are up, we'll find her."

His smile was grim. "I wish I shared your certainty." Wished he could share it with Luke. But he'd learned the hard way that some promises were never meant to be, and he wasn't about to inflict false hope on his brother. Not when they both knew the reality.

She touched his face, forcing him to meet her gaze. "Believe it," she said softly, "because it's the truth."

He stared into the green depths of her eyes and for a moment was totally convinced. Then his gaze flicked down to her lips, and before he knew it he was kissing her. Urgently. Hungrily. She responded in kind, her fingers so warm against his cheeks it felt like she was branding his soul with her touch. He released himself to the simple pleasure of being close to her. Of kissing her without caressing her, of feeling the closeness of her body, smelling the sweet aroma of heated desire that was both his and hers.

"Wow," she murmured at last, her pupils dilated and body trembling.

"Wow, indeed." He leaned his forehead against

hers for a second and wondered what the hell was going on. He'd never felt anything like this before, not even during the moon fever.

Maybe it was just this case—and the stress of Janie's disappearance—coming out in the most natural form for a werewolf. Especially with the moon rising. Yet he had a sneaking suspicion the answer was not so simple. And *that* was something he had no intention of exploring. Not now. Not ever.

He rose and walked over to the window. He felt the flash of her confusion and anger, and thrust his hands into his pockets. "How long is your grandmother likely to be scrying?"

"However long it takes." Kat's voice was calm, despite the turmoil he could feel within her.

He frowned, wondering why he was catching her emotions so clearly. While that particular gift ran in his family, it was never one in which he'd shown any ability. No, all he'd gotten was the damn curse. A curse that had first come into his family after his grandfather was bitten. While his father had escaped it, his uncle had not, and neither had Ethan or his brother. Which was why he would never have any kids of his own—he had no desire to pass this thing on. Luke had, but then, Luke had always been more accepting of the curse than Ethan had been. "If another kid has gone missing, why didn't she see it?"

She shrugged, something he felt rather than saw. "Scrying is not a perfect science. It shows some possibilities, not all of them."

"Has this Seline of yours come up with any answers about the soul-sucker?"

"No, but it's obviously an extremely ancient spirit

we're chasing, which means the Circle have to go through all the old texts that have not yet been transcribed to computer. It takes time."

"Time we haven't got."

"I know that. Gran knows that. Even Seline knows that." She hesitated and he tensed, knowing her question even before she asked. "Why do you keep running, Ethan? What are you afraid of?"

"I'm not running. I'm not doing anything more than simply enjoying a moment."

"And that's all we are? A moment?"

He closed his eyes. "Yes."

"Are you sure of that?"

"Yes."

The swirl of emotions that had surrounded him died abruptly. It was as if some door he couldn't see had slammed shut. The sudden stillness felt cold. Lonely.

"You're wrong, you know." Her voice was soft, detached. With the emotive eddy locked down, he couldn't read what she was feeling, but in many respects, he didn't need to.

"No, I'm not." Because he'd given his heart long ago, and there was nothing left to him now *but* moments. "I warned you before we started this that I wanted nothing more than a good time. Nothing we share is going to change my mind."

No matter how good it felt. No matter how right.

She shifted, her movements full of controlled anger. If he had any sense, he'd walk away now, before this got messy. But he couldn't. He needed these two to find Janie. They were his best hope—he was sure of that. And he couldn't deny his need for Kat. The moon's spell was far from over, but he had no desire to find another partner right now. He wanted her. Only her.

"So, who is the woman who captured your heart and left you unable to love?"

Surprise rippled through him. Had she read his mind, or did she know a lot more about werewolves than what she'd admitted? Not that he knew a whole lot about them himself—it wasn't as if he'd grown up in a pack or anything. He'd had only his small family unit, and all they could impart were truths as they saw it.

And he was beginning to suspect many of their truths were not the reality. "It doesn't really matter, does it?"

"It does to me, especially if she's still around."

"I didn't lie to you, Kat." His voice was grim as he stared out into the star-bright night and tried not to remember. But pain rose regardless. The pain of betrayal. Hurt. "And she's definitely not still around."

"Did she die?"

He snorted softly. "No." She was living in Denver with her very normal husband and three kids, and probably didn't even remember the lives she'd destroyed when they were both still teenagers.

"Then why—"

Gwen groaned, and he'd never been so grateful for an interruption in his life. He didn't want to relive that moment of his past, not even briefly. Whoever it was that said time heals all wounds was wrong. Time only made them more unforgivable.

He turned and watched Kat tend to her grandmother. The older woman was pale and shaking, her hands locked into a clawlike position. He grabbed the oil off the coffee table and sat down next to her.

"Let me massage these for you." He poured the oil into his hands and began to rub hers gently.

Gwen's smile was tremulous. "Thanks."

He nodded. "Did you see anything of use?"

Kat sat down opposite him. He was aware of her gaze but didn't meet it, keeping his focus on easing the tension from Gwen's knotted hands. Right now, he didn't have the energy or desire to answer Kat's questions.

"I saw a couple of things," Gwen said. "First off, your boss is chasing a wild goose. That murder has nothing to do with this case. It's a custody battle gone wrong."

Just as well he hadn't followed instinct and gone after them, then. "You sure of that?"

She nodded. "It doesn't follow the pattern. They'll discover that as soon as they get there."

"Do we need to rescue the kid anyway?"

Gwen shook her head. "No. The cops will get the father soon enough, and the little boy is safe. But there is another kid you have to worry about."

His gut clenched. *Not Janie,* he thought. *Not this soon. Please . . .*

"The soul-sucker?" Kat rose and moved over to the phone table.

"Yes," Gwen said, rubbing her temple with her free hand. "Here, in this town, sometime tonight."

Kat retrieved the local street directory and plopped it down on the table. "Where?"

"Forest Road. Some place called The Pines."

"Out of town," Kat said after a few minutes. "And

not all that far from where the soul-sucker killed the old man."

"I found a cabin full of zombies up that way," he said, suddenly remembering them. "About a twenty-minute run north from the old farm."

Kat gave him a long look. "And you didn't think to mention it before now? Or were you simply planning to do a little solo exploring later on tonight?"

"Neither," he said, ignoring the sarcasm in her voice. "I didn't remember because I had more important things to worry about."

He held her gaze. After a few seconds, heat touched her cheeks, and she dropped her gaze to the directory again.

Gwen pulled her hand free of his and flexed it lightly. "You have a nice touch, wolf. And you didn't tell us you were empathic."

He put the lid back on the oil bottle. "I'm not."

Gwen raised an eyebrow. "Really? Then why do you seem to be catching Kat's emotions?"

He kept his face expressionless and raised an eyebrow. "What makes you think I'm catching Kat's emotions?"

Her cheeks dimpled. "Because I'm a nosy old witch who can sense these things."

"Well, in this case, the nosy old witch is way off course." He rose to put the oil back on the coffee table. "We going to call in the sheriff on this one?"

Gwen studied him a second longer, her expression a mix of amusement and concern. Still trying to figure him out, obviously. He had a feeling he'd better be long gone before she did.

"No," she answered. "We won't need to if we can

stop the mara before it gets to the kid." She looked at Kat and added, "Did you manage to make those charms earlier?"

Kat nodded and disappeared into the bedroom. Gwen grabbed his hand, her strength surprising him. "Be honest with her, wolf," she whispered, her voice as fierce as her expression, "or I'll make damn sure you regret it."

She was half his size and half his weight, but he had a sudden feeling this fierce old woman could take on a hundred men his size and still come out on top. "I've been nothing *but* honest with her."

"Then be honest with yourself, or it's going to cause problems."

"I have no idea—"

"You have every idea," she said angrily. "Don't you lie to me."

Anger rose, a tide so strong the effort to control it left him shaking. "I haven't lied to anyone," he said, his voice surprisingly calm. "And Kat's a big girl who doesn't need her grandmother's protection."

Gwen snorted and released his hand. He resisted the urge to flex his fingers as she leaned back in the chair.

"Who says I'm trying to protect her? You're the one who's going to regret it if you don't wake up to yourself."

"You can't hurt what you haven't got," he said bitterly.

"Oh, you have it, wolf. You're just too blinded by the perceived hurts of the past to realize it."

He clenched his fists and took a step toward her, then realized what he was doing and walked across to the window. "You have no idea what you're talking about."

"Don't I?"

Gwen's voice, though soft, still reached him easily. And though his hearing was naturally better than any human's, he had a vague suspicion there was something supernatural—or magical—in the fact that he was hearing her now. And that Kat obviously wasn't.

"In the meantime," she continued in that same soft but angry tone, "I'll just leave you with a warning. If what is freely given is rejected, it is never offered again. We Tanners tend not to forgive nor forget."

"What the hell is going on in here?"

Ethan glanced around sharply. Kat stood in the doorway, her gaze jumping between him and Gwen.

He took a deep breath and released it slowly. "Nothing. We were just talking."

"Yeah. Right. Tell that to someone who can't feel the tension."

His gaze slid to Gwen's. The older woman only raised her eyebrows, as if daring him to deny the possibility. He turned away from them both and stared out the window again. He couldn't explain why the old woman seemed to be catching his emotions any more than he could explain him catching hers.

"Are we going to go save this kid or not?" he said without looking around.

"We will as soon as you put this on," Kat replied. He heard the air stir and raised his hand, instinctively catching what she'd thrown. It turned out to be a leather thong threaded with three stones. He turned around. "What's this?"

"It's a necklace. You put it around your neck." She

didn't even glance at him as she began tying an identical strip around hers.

Two of the stones felt warm against his palm; the third felt colder than the Arctic. "I mean, what is it meant to do?"

"Protect you."

"How are three stones supposed to do that?" He tied the necklace on regardless, then grabbed his shoulder harness and strapped it on. He'd left it in here earlier, and it was just as well. If the captain had realized he still had his gun, he would have been in real trouble.

"The red stone will stop the mara from sensing your presence unless she's looking right at you. The green stone provides a shield that'll help stop her from entering your mind to take control."

"And the blue stone?" he asked when she hesitated.

Heat touched her cheeks, but her gaze met his defiantly. "It's a last-minute warning that the mara is about to steal your soul."

Anger stirred through him again. "She's never going to get that close."

Her eyes mocked him. "But the moon is full, and you're a werewolf in heat. Who knows what'll happen if push comes to shove?"

He knew. No matter how much the fever raged in his blood, he would never lie with the mara. No matter what form she took. "Are we going or not?"

"As soon as I change into jeans." She disappeared into their cabin and did that, then grabbed her coat from off the sofa and went over to kiss her grandmother's cheek. "Be careful. Use the warding stones until we get back."

"It doesn't know about me yet. Its attention is still caught by you two." Gwen's gaze ran past Kat and met Ethan's. "Concentrate out there, or it could be fatal."

"The wolf doesn't rule me yet," he said grimly and walked out the door.

KAT TOOK A CANDY BAR OUT OF HER POCKET AND UNwrapped it. The wind was almost unbearably cold, and the smell of rain touched the air. The bright light of the moon had long ago been blanketed by a heavy layer of clouds, and the night seemed unnaturally dark. But lightning flashed in the distance—an indicator of the storm she could feel approaching.

She bit down on the candy and wished she had something more substantial to eat. Chocolate might be one of the five essential food groups, but right now she could have done with something a whole lot more warming. Like a good, thick stew. Or even a meatloaf.

As she munched, she studied the house that sat in the small clearing below. It was a big, old ramshackle building that had seen recent renovations and was absolutely beautiful. What wasn't so beautiful were the two Dobermans who roamed the confines of the main house's fenced yard—a fact they'd found out the hard way when they'd first tried to get near the house. Both she and Ethan had barely gotten back over the fence in time when the ruckus the dogs raised had brought out the weapon-bearing homeowner.

But dogs certainly wouldn't stop the mara, which

meant *they* had to stop it before it got anywhere near the house and the dogs.

She moved her gaze on, studying the line of trees to her right. Ethan was in there somewhere, padding through shadows as restlessly as the dogs in the yard. He'd barely said two words all night, and she'd long ago decided she was going to have a long talk with her grandmother when they got back. Gwen didn't usually interfere in her relationships, be they casual or not, so to do so now meant Ethan must have said or done something that had raised her protective hackles. And Kat had a feeling that any interference from her grandmother could prove deadly to any hopes she had of a relationship with him.

She frowned at the thought. He'd made it clear from the beginning he didn't *want* any relationship beyond sex, so why did she keep thinking of them in terms of something more permanent?

She didn't know. All she knew was that she liked him. A lot. And while they were dynamite together sexually, it was more than that. There was an empathy between them—just beginning, but there nonetheless. She'd never felt anything like that before, and she had a feeling it could be a whole lot deeper, a whole lot stronger, if only he'd let it.

And that was the problem. He was never going to let it be anything more—because of the woman who'd stolen his heart long ago.

The chocolate lost its taste, and she shoved the half-finished candy bar back into her jacket pocket. Rising, she brushed the dirt from her jeans, then headed through the trees. Lightning flashed, closer than before, caressing the air with electricity. Underneath her jacket, the hairs along her arms rose on end, then the aroma of evil hit her so strongly that it snatched her breath and left her gasping.

She pulled a white ash stake from her jeans pocket and ducked behind the nearest tree. The wind was coming from the right, blowing the sounds of heavy footsteps toward her. Zombies. At least five of them, if those steps were anything to go by. She crouched down and studied the barely visible sweep of trees. Ethan was down there, moving away from the sounds. Obviously, the wind was snatching away the scent of death long before it reached his nose. She couldn't call to him, couldn't warn him, and in some respects, didn't want to. If the mara knew he was here, she might go after him rather than the kid. And while they were here to save the child, she wasn't about to risk Ethan's life to do so. Because if Gran and she failed, he might be Janie's only hope.

The heavy steps drew closer. She closed her eyes for a minute, gathering strength, then rose and stepped from the cover of the tree.

The dead stopped, surprise flitting across their decaying features. The mara was in the lead, her gown as flimsy as smoke and revealing more of the woman than Kat ever wanted to see. Obviously, it wasn't only the child the soul-sucker hunted tonight.

"Sorry, folks," Kat said, raising the stake, "but kid and soul are off the menu for tonight."

The mara screamed—a sound that sliced through the night. Her form began to melt into air as the zombies crowded forward. Kat hit them with a wide beam of kinetic energy, thrusting them on their bony backsides as she ran at the soul-sucker.

Smoke condensed and began to slither away. Kat slashed it, and the soul-sucker screamed in pain. She raised the stake to strike again, but was hit from behind and thrust face-first into the ground.

She grunted, battling for breath and spitting out dirt as bony knees pressed into her back. The zombie chuckled, his breath washing dead things past her cheek. Bile rose. She swallowed heavily and hit him kinetically. Before she could rise, something else grabbed her and dragged her upright. Kinetic energy surged again, but a second before she released it she realized that the smell had changed, had become the scent of freshly cut wood combined with the tang of earthy spices. Ethan, not one of the zombies.

"Go," he said, his face grim as he pushed her toward the house. "Stop the mara."

She didn't argue, just ran hell-bent for leather down the path toward the house. The dogs were barking furiously, and the owner was outside, gun in hand, yelling at the dogs to shut up.

She skirted the fence line and climbed into the yard on the opposite side of the house. The mara was at the window and beginning to seep inside. Kat lunged forward, slashing the smoke with the stake. The soul-sucker screamed, and blood as black as the night sprayed across the glass.

Out of the corner of her eye, Kat saw movement. She spun and raised the stake, then saw it was the dogs, not a zombie. She hit them kinetically, tossing them across the picket fence. It wouldn't stop them long, but her only other option was hurting them, and she wasn't about to do that.

The mara had seeped through the window. Kat

swore and hit it kinetically, drawing the glass backward rather than pushing it forward and spraying the room. Inside, a child began screaming—a terror-filled sound that was quickly cut off.

Because the soul-sucker had her.

"Don't you be moving, little lady." The harsh warning was overridden by the sound of a rifle being cocked.

Kat swore again and hit the man kinetically, thrusting him onto his ass. The gun went off, the shot blasting the house dangerously close to her head. Wood splintered, tearing past her cheeks. She dove through the window, hit the carpet, and rolled to her feet in one smooth movement.

Neither the child nor the mara was in the bedroom, and the trail of evil led into the hall. A nightie-clad woman was hurrying toward the bedroom, but she froze, eyes widening in fear when she saw Kat.

Kat threw out her hands to show she held no weapons. "Did you see anyone run past here?"

The woman's gaze flickered. In that instant, Kat realized someone was behind her. She spun, but it was too late.

Something smashed into her head, and the lights went out.

ELEVEN

"THE LEAST YOU COULD DO IS GET ME A WET CLOTH TO clean her face with." Ethan's tone was brusque, and it seemed to be coming from a great distance.

"No one is doing anything until the sheriff gets here." The second voice was harsh and low and filled with so much anger it quivered. But it was a voice Kat recognized. It was the homeowner who'd tried to shoot her. The father of the little girl the soul-sucker had taken.

She opened her eyes and blinked several times, trying to get her bearings. She was still lying on the floor, but she was no longer in the hall. Her head was cradled on muscular thighs, and warm fingers touched her cheek, gently caressing. There was so much pain in her head it felt like her brain was about to explode, and the same could be said for the air, which was sharp with anger and tension.

She tilted her head and met Ethan's gaze. "You're here." She hadn't expected him to be. She'd thought he'd be chasing the soul-sucker.

"I am." There was concern in his voice, but the fury she could feel in the air was visible in his nut-brown eyes. "How are you feeling?"

"Like shit. What about the mara?"

"Gone with the kid."

She struggled to rise. "We have to go after them—"

Ethan put a hand on her shoulder, but it was the sound of a rifle being loaded that made her freeze.

"We're being held at gunpoint in the living room by the father and the oldest son," he explained, voice clipped. "They called the sheriff."

Her gaze met his again. "Have you told them you're a cop?"

"Yeah," he said dryly. "They aren't buying it."

"You showed them your badge?"

"They're not buying that, either. And they took my gun."

She raised an eyebrow. "And you let them?"

He hesitated. Something flashed in his eyes. "They had a gun to your head. I had no choice."

"Ah." She was tempted to ask why that had stopped him, but she knew the answer would be anything other than an admission of caring. "Is there a football swelling on the side of my head? It feels like it."

A smile touched his mouth and did strange things to her pulse. "It's more like a golf ball." His fingers moved from her cheek to her head, gently probing her scalp just above the temple. "Nasty-looking, but there's no cut."

"Good." She'd had more than her fair share of cuts already on this case. She raised a hand, touching his stubble-lined cheek. "We'll find her. Before the three days are up, we'll find her."

Just for a moment, his anger and fear and torment surrounded her, strong enough to almost taste. Then it shut down, as he shut down emotionally, until all that was left was his cop face. "Don't promise." His voice, though soft, was harsh. "Because promises like that are almost never kept."

"Mine will be."

"Don't." The sound of sirens touched the air, and he asked, "Are you up to trying to track down the mara's scent once the sheriff releases us?"

She nodded but couldn't help wincing in pain. "Don't suppose anyone would give me a painkiller?"

Silence greeted her request. If it weren't for the heavy breathing, she might have thought Ethan and she were alone in the room. She certainly couldn't see anyone else from where she was lying.

The sheriff and his men arrived about five minutes later. The big man's gaze swept the room, hesitated on them briefly, then moved on. "Jesus, Frank, put the gun down. What in hell do you think you're doing?"

"Karen's gone." The homeowner's voice was defiant but shaky. "And these two know about it. They broke into my house—"

"These two are part of a special task force trying to *stop* the kidnappings. Deputies, grab those damn rifles." The sheriff strode toward them. "You two okay?"

Kat nodded and sat up with Ethan's help. "Do you mind if we look around? There's still a chance we can find the kidnapper's trail."

"Sure. Just come back and give me a full report. I particularly want to know why you didn't call for help."

She nodded again and tried to ignore the pounding ache in her head. She needed painkillers and rest, but she wasn't likely to get either of those anytime soon.

Ethan helped her rise and kept hold of one hand as he led her past the white-faced trio near the hall door. His fingers felt good against hers, warm and strong.

He stopped near the little girl's bedroom. "Is this where you were knocked unconscious?"

She nodded, then took a deep breath and completely lowered her shields, seeking whatever emotions might lie in the hall. Death was a slither of darkness staining the air. She couldn't feel anything from the little girl, but then, she wouldn't. Not until Karen was dying.

"This way," she said, untangling her fingers from his.

She followed the trail through the kitchen and out the back door. The dogs barked, but someone had chained them, and they were no longer a threat.

Rain began to fall, big, fat drops that hit with the intensity of hail. Overhead, thunder rumbled. If the heavens opened up, she'd lose the scent completely. She hurried across the yard and leaped the fence. The storm hit as they entered the trees, and within minutes, the thread of evil had evaporated. She stopped, cursing long and loud.

"I'm gathering you've lost it," Ethan said, amusement momentarily warming the frustrated anger still evident in his voice.

She nodded and rubbed her arms as she studied the trees above them. "Where exactly was that cabin you found?"

"To the north."

He took off his coat and placed it over hers. Heat rushed through her, as if the warmth of his body had infused his coat and now transferred it to her. Or maybe it was just the scent of him lingering on the thick leather that warmed her senses.

"You think that's where they might be headed?" he continued, catching the ends of the coat and tugging her closer.

She was too aware of his nearness, too aware of the fingers brushing her stomach as he zipped up the coat, to do anything but nod.

"How safe is it to be investigating that cabin at night?" His gaze met hers, and deep in the brown depths, hunger stirred.

It echoed through her. She might be angry at his continuing insistence that they could be nothing more than a moment, but right now, she was more than ready to enjoy one of those moments—pounding headache, aching cold, and all.

She licked the rain from her lips and saw his gaze leap down. "Not very. It's better to wait until dawn, when they're less active."

"Then we wait." He lowered his mouth to hers, his kiss a gentle explosion of heat that ended far too soon. "But for now, let's get out of this rain."

The promises in his eyes made her every nerve ending tingle, and for a moment, she found it difficult to even breathe. "The sheriff wants an explanation," she somehow said.

He touched a hand to her cheek. Desire slithered through her and pooled deep in her abdomen.

"The sheriff is going to get the shortest explanation in history." His voice was a smoky whisper that made her body thrum. "You need to get back to the cabin and tend to that headache."

She raised her eyebrows. "How do you know I've got a headache?"

"I can see it in your eyes." He kissed her forehead, then twined his fingers in hers. The grin that touched his lips was sexy enough to curl her toes. "Of course, once we've tended to the headache and got you warm again, we just might be able to do something about that other ache."

"I hope so," she said. "I certainly hope so."

HOWEVER MUCH THEY MIGHT HAVE WANTED TO PROVIDE THE shortest explanation in history, the sheriff certainly wasn't about to let them get away with it. It was nearly an hour before they made their escape. Kat closed her eyes and leaned back against the headrest. They'd given her some painkillers, and her headache had eased to a muted thumping. Bearable, but still not pleasant.

She had a suspicion, however, that a decent cup of coffee, something to eat, and a good hour or so of loving might take away the rest of the ache.

The storm raged, making conversation almost impossible as they drove back to the cabin. Not that she minded. There was a certain intimacy in sitting here, cocooned in warmth, the sound of rain pounding on the car's roof mingling with the swish of wipers. And Ethan caressing her thigh as he drove, warming her more thoroughly than any car heater ever could.

She was almost disappointed when the car slowed and he moved his hand to change gears. She opened her eyes to discover they were back at the cabins.

"If those lights are anything to go by, your grandmother's still awake," he said. "You want to go in and give her an update?"

"We'd better." If they didn't, she'd just come in to see them. "Besides, she might have heard from Seline while we were out."

They got out of the car and raced for the door. Gwen opened it as they neared, and heat and warmth rushed out at them.

"I lit the fire in your cabin, too," she said. "Thought you might appreciate it."

"Thanks." Kat took off the two jackets and hung them over the chair to dry. "You heard anything from Seline yet?"

"They found some text that looks promising. She hopes to have it transcribed by morning." Gwen's gaze narrowed slightly. "I'm gathering the mara got away again?"

Kat nodded and held out her hands to the fire. "With the kid, unfortunately. The farmer's son took me out before I had a chance to follow it."

Gwen looked at Ethan. "And you had no chance of following it?"

He shook his head. "I couldn't even smell it, let alone see it."

"So the mara is invisible even when it's holding the kid?"

Kat turned and warmed her rear end. "The kid was invisible, too. I didn't feel any sort of psychic shield, so it has to be some form of magic."

"Psychic shield?" Ethan asked as he stripped off his wet shirt.

Kat tried not to stare at all the lean muscle on show, then gave it up when she realized her grandmother was openly enjoying the view and Ethan didn't seem to care.

"Many vampires have the ability to touch your mind and make you think they disappear into shadow," she said. "But the reality is, your brain simply stops seeing them."

"So is this mara a vampire, or a spirit?"

"It might be both, for all we know. It just takes souls to survive rather than blood." Gwen disappeared into the bathroom and came back with towels she tossed to both of them. "So, we—or you—try to hunt down this thing in the morning."

Kat nodded. "We'll start with that cabin Ethan found. The zombies have to be guarding something."

"It could just be a trap," Ethan said.

"The only way to know if it's a trap is to spring it." Gwen's voice was grim. "You two had better go get something to eat, then grab some sleep. I've got a feeling it's going to be a long day tomorrow."

But hopefully, in the end, a more successful one than today, Kat thought. "Have you eaten?"

"Yep. I'll stay here and work on zombie deterrents." She hesitated, her eyes twinkling mischievously as she added, "With all the noise of the storm and such, I'm not going to be getting much sleep anyway, am I?"

"I guess not," Kat said blandly. She could feel Ethan's gaze on her. Feel his sudden amusement. "Just make sure you set the warding stones again."

"I have. Stop fussing and go get warm."

Kat walked into the other cabin and discovered two pizzas waiting for them in the fridge, and the coffee machine on and ready. She zapped the meals in the microwave and poured two cups of coffee as Ethan squatted near the old record player.

"What do you prefer?" he said. "Elvis Presley or Frank Sinatra?"

"There isn't anything more modern?"

"It's them or jazz, and personally I'm not a big fan of jazz."

Neither was she, though Gwen was, so she'd certainly heard enough of it over the years. "What Elvis albums we got?"

"Compilations. Ballads, mainly."

"That'll do." Right now, Frank singing *I did it my way* was not what she needed. Especially since the man she was with had every intention of doing just that and to hell with what might be happening between them. The microwave beeped. She gathered the cutlery and put everything on the table. "Dinner's ready."

"Nothing like soggy pizza after midnight," he said, smiling ruefully as he sat down opposite her.

"I didn't think cops were overly fussy about when and what they ate." She picked up her coffee, savoring its bittersweet taste.

"We're not, which is why most of us develop ulcers later in life."

"I would think job stress would have something to do with that."

He shrugged. "It doesn't help."

She cut her pizza into four, then picked up a piece and dug in. "Did you always want to be a cop?"

"Not especially."

"So why did you become one?"

"Had to do something once I left home."

She studied him for a minute, noting his closed expression, and said, "You don't want to speak about the past?"

His gaze met hers. Pain briefly lit the nut-brown depths. "Not especially."

"Why not?"

"Because it doesn't matter anymore."

"It matters to *me*." Because she needed to know, needed to understand, what was going on in his head, if not his heart.

"Then it shouldn't." His gaze hardened a little, became more wolf than man. "Don't look for what isn't there. Don't expect me to give anything more than what I already have."

"I know, I know—it's just sex for you." And she didn't believe it any more now than she had originally. She pushed away her half-finished pizza. "So, what are you waiting for? Let's get down to it."

He studied her for a minute, then sighed and looked away. "Don't do that."

"Why not?" She rose and stripped, throwing her clothes in a pile beside the table. The warm air caressed her skin, but it was the hunger suddenly visible in his eyes that made her hot. "This is what you want, isn't it? A willing partner? Sex when you need it?"

His gaze skimmed her, then leaped away. His need intensified, burning the air. "Don't push, Kat. Not like this."

Pushing him sexually was *exactly* what she had to do. He needed to see there was a difference between what he wanted and what they actually had. Even if he never admitted there *was* a difference, even if he still walked away when this case was over, she needed to do this.

"Why not?" She walked around the table and stood in front of him. "You want sex. I want sex. What's the problem?"

His mouth was a slash of anger, his body tense. But his eyes glowed, and the scent of his desire was so strong she could smell it. The wolf was very close to gaining control. While she suspected that might not be pleasant, she trusted him not to hurt her.

Desperation glinted briefly in his eyes, only to drown in the hunger. "I will not—"

She snagged him with kinetic energy and dragged him to his feet. Then she pressed herself close and kissed him. With a growl deep in his throat, he wrapped a hand around the back of her neck and held her still and hard against him. He tasted her deeply, thoroughly, and she fought the need to return it in kind. If he wanted nothing but sex, she was going to make damn sure that was all he got.

His touch became demanding, almost forceful. She quivered, fighting the sensations coursing through her, fighting to remain passive. He clasped her rear, pressing her closer still, so that all she could feel was the hammering of his heart and the pulsing heat of his erection.

A heat she ached to feel deep inside.

He kicked aside the chair and pushed her back against the wall. Pinning her with his weight, he rubbed his hardness against her. It felt so good she had to bite back a groan. She reached for kinetic energy and undid his zipper, thrusting his pants and boxers down to his ankles. There was very little gentleness in the way he entered her, his thrusts hard and deep and almost angry. But it didn't matter. Right now she wanted him any way she could get him.

Maybe there was wolf in her, as well. Given what her mother had been, it was certainly more than possible.

He made another sound deep in his throat, then abruptly pushed away from her. His chest heaved as he sucked in air, and his eyes were wild with anger and passion combined.

"Not like that." His voice was little more than a growl. "Never like that. Not with you."

Though she felt like dancing, all she did was raise her eyebrows. "But it's what you want, isn't it?"

"There's a difference—"

"Yes," she cut in. "There is. And why do you think that is?"

He didn't answer. Maybe he never would. Maybe all this was for nothing, and she was nothing more than a fool to even be worried about it. Maybe she should do as her grandmother had suggested and just enjoy the time they had together.

Except she wanted the chance to explore the promises he made with his touch and his body and his eyes. Even if, in the end, all it amounted to was nothing more than a semi-serious moment.

But such exploration required two willing participants, and right now, there was still only one.

She sighed and stepped past him. "I'm going for a shower." And a cold one at that.

He didn't reply and he didn't stop her, though his gaze burned a hole into her back as she walked away.

* * *

ETHAN GRABBED THE DOOR KEY AND STRODE INTO THE night. He needed to put distance between him and Kat. Needed to cool the thrumming desire to take what she had so readily offered. To finish in anger what she'd started in anger.

The rain lashing his skin was icy, but it did little to cool the ardor pounding through his blood. He'd come as close as he'd ever come to losing control tonight, and it was an experience he didn't want to complete. Not with Kat. Not with anyone. He'd spent most of his adult life fighting that part of him, keeping it fully leashed, and he had no intention of letting all that slip—especially now, when Janie's life was at stake.

He strode across the road and onto the beach. Waves pounded the shoreline, seething whitely in the storm-swept darkness. He thrust his hands deep in his pockets and stopped on the edge of the foam-kissed sand.

He felt like those waves—tossed a hundred different ways and unable to do anything about it. The past couldn't be altered. Nor could the effect it had had on him. Change was impossible. Because of what he was. Because of the curse that was his heritage.

Kat, with all her knowledge of the supernatural, should have been the one person in the world who could truly understand that.

So why didn't she? Why did she keep on insisting there was more to them than there ever could possibly be?

He raised his face to the sky, letting the stinging

rain numb his skin. Wished it could do the same to his mind. His blood. His need for Kat.

The moon had a lot to answer for, he thought grimly.

And yet, was it the moon's fault that he hungered for her in a way he'd never hungered for a woman before? Or that he'd never felt anything as strong as this in his adult life?

Maybe it was just worry for Janie. Maybe it was the loneliness that had haunted him for the last few years. Maybe it was just a growing distaste for seeking satisfaction from an endless line of faceless women.

Or maybe, as she'd suggested, there *was* something between them.

But if that were the case, it was a seed that was destined to wither and die. Because of the past. Because of Jacinta, who had stolen his heart and his dreams, only to destroy both.

Be honest with her, Gwen had advised. He could at least do that—offer Kat the truth, or as much of it as she needed to know. Because no matter how much he might hunger for her, there was nothing else left for him to give.

For the first time in many years, he viciously cursed the woman he'd once loved, then turned and headed back to the cabin.

KAT HEARD THE CABIN DOOR OPEN. SHE HITCHED THE COMforter closer to her nose and closed her eyes. Soft steps echoed in the living room, then the smell of rain and man entered the bedroom.

She tensed a little, not sure what to expect. Not sure what sort of mood he might be in. But he walked across to the fire, not the bed, and the tension slithered away.

The soft rustle of material told her he was undressing. She resisted the urge to look and tried to keep her breathing soft and even, though she had no doubt he knew she was awake.

When he made no further sound, she opened her eyes. He faced the fire, his hands on the mantel, knuckles white. The glow of the flames caressed his bare body, making his skin appear almost golden. Tension knotted his shoulders, and his breathing was rapid. Because of the moon. Because of what she'd done. Because of what they hadn't finished.

Guilt slithered through her, but as she gripped the comforter to toss it aside, he said, "Don't move."

She hesitated, then obeyed. "Why?"

"Because there's something I need to tell you. Something I need to explain."

Though surprise rippled through her, she said, "You really don't have to."

"I do, because you're right. There's something between us, and I need to explain why it can be nothing more than what it already is."

No explanation could make her believe that. But as the swirl of his emotions began to invade her senses and fill her mind with the echo of his pain, she wasn't so sure.

He hesitated. "I was seventeen when I met Jacinta."

His voice was soft, but full of remembered wonder. And suddenly she didn't want to hear any more, because already it was obvious that despite her determination to believe otherwise, this woman still had what she never would. She briefly closed her eyes and fought the urge to scream at fate for putting this man in her path when it was far too late for them to build anything together.

"She was three years older than me and had come to my hometown for a skiing vacation with several of her friends. She ended up staying long after they'd left."

She briefly closed her eyes. "You don't have to continue."

"I asked her to marry me," he said softly. "She accepted."

It hurt, though God knew it shouldn't have. Especially since he'd warned her going in—not that she'd ever been one to listen to warnings unless they truly suited her.

Her gaze slid to his hands, and she frowned. He wasn't wearing a wedding ring, and she had a suspicion he still would be if they'd actually married. Especially seeing as a werewolf gave his heart for life. "So what happened?"

His hurt swam around her, deep enough to drown in. "She didn't know I was a werewolf. I showed her that night."

"Oh."

"I wish that was all *she'd* said." Bitterness edged the anguish in his voice.

One piece of the puzzle fell into place. "So that's why you loathe your werewolf half?"

"It lost me the woman I loved. It lost me—" He stopped and took a deep, shuddering breath.

And she knew then that there was far more to this

story than what he was admitting now. "So she wasn't a werewolf herself?"

"No."

"She never got over the shock of it?"

"No."

And neither, obviously, had he. She rose from the bed and walked up behind him. He didn't move, didn't react, so she simply put her hands around him and pressed her cheek against his back. He was so tense, his muscles quivered.

"If she loved you, surely she would have eventually seen past that."

"She got a court order to prevent me going near her."

The woman was obviously a fool. A fool who didn't know what she had. "I'm sorry, Ethan." Sorry for him. Sorry for them.

He took another shuddering breath, then turned and wrapped his arms around her. "So am I."

His breath stirred her hair, brushed warmth past her ear. His body pressed against hers, filling her with radiant longing. It felt so good. So right.

So how come it could be so wrong?

She lifted her face and met his gaze. The sorrow evident in the brown depths tore at something deep inside her. There wasn't much she could do about it, except love him in the only way he was willing to accept.

She kissed him. It was a slow and sensual exploration that left them both breathless. He brushed a thumb down her cheek and smiled his sexy smile.

"Shall we retire someplace more comfortable?"

She raised an eyebrow. "You weren't comfortable here last night?"

His smile went up another notch and damn near smoked her insides. "I'm planning something a little slower than last night, and the bed is definitely more pleasant than a rug on the floor."

"I suppose if you insist—"

"I do."

He swept her off her feet and carried her over to the bed. He placed her on it gently, then stepped back, his gaze rolling languidly down the length of her body. It was a heated caress that sent a shiver of expectation through every part of her. Her nipples hardened, and the pooling heat between her legs became an ache that was almost unbearable. His gaze completed its erotic journey, then met hers again, almost drowning her in longing.

"Beautiful," he murmured, lying down beside her.

From that moment on there was little room for talking. As he'd promised, their lovemaking this time was a luscious and thorough exploration. Thought became desire, desire became need, and her whole world became this man who swore he couldn't love her.

His touch pushed her into a place where only sensation existed. The air was hot and thick and almost impossible to breathe. Every inch of her quivered beneath the relentless assault of his fingers and tongue. When he finally raised himself above her, she was slick with sweat and burning with pleasure, unable to think, unable to do anything more than feel.

For several seconds he held still, his arms trembling with the effort as their gazes met. Something twisted deep inside her. Ethan might not be able to love her, but he wasn't exactly immune to her, either. There was caring in his eyes.

Slowly, deliberately, he entered her, sliding so very deep, filling her with his rigid heat. The sheer bliss of it had her moaning. He held still again, his lips claiming hers, his kiss passionate and tender.

She wrapped her legs around him and pushed him deeper still. He began to rock, gently at first, touching places that had never been touched before. She could only groan in pleasure as his body drove into hers and the sweet pressure began to build.

He kissed her neck, her shoulders, her breasts, his movements becoming more urgent. The pressure built, curling through her body, until it became a tidal wave that would not be denied. She grabbed his shoulders, her fingers trembling, her nails digging into his flesh.

"Oh . . . God." Her voice was little more than a fractured whisper. "Please . . ."

He answered her plea, his thrusts powerful and demanding. Her climax came in a rush that stole her breath, stole all thought, and swept her into a world of sheer, unadulterated bliss. A heartbeat later he went rigid against her, the power of his release tearing her name from his throat. He held her for one last thrust, then his lips sought hers, his kiss a lingering taste of heat.

Then he rolled to one side and gathered her into his arms, holding her close as they drifted off to sleep.

It was only later that she realized they hadn't used a condom.

TWELVE

KAT WANDERED INTO THE NEXT CABIN AS ETHAN TOOK A shower. The front door was open, and the smell of rain and pine hung heavily in the air. Gwen was visible through the doorway, a steaming mug of coffee held between her knotted hands. She made herself a cup, then joined her grandmother on the porch.

The sky was still heavy with the remnants of the night's storm, and the chill of winter was in the air. Days like today were best spent huddled in front of a warm fire, chocolate and a good book in hand, not out hunting the dead. Not that they had any choice—not when time was running out for those kids and maybe even themselves.

She ignored the premonition of rising danger and raised her cup to the sky. "If the color of those clouds is anything to go by, it's going to be a bitch of a day."

"At least zombies don't like the cold any more than we do. It slows them down."

Which could be a good thing if there was a houseful of them to contend with. "You think that's where Janie and Karen are?"

"Too easy. But the zombies have to be guarding something, so it's definitely worth a look."

She sipped her coffee for a moment, watching a small brown bird flit from tree to tree. "Has Seline come through with anything?"

Gwen nodded. "She's been able to confirm a lot of what we already know, and has found some additional information. This thing is an extremely ancient spirit and apparently very hard to kill."

"Great," Kat said sourly.

Gwen's gaze became speculative as she continued, "As I suspected, it is similar to a vampire, only it feeds on souls rather than blood. It does have one interesting restriction—it can only feed while at the height of passion. But the same sort of weapons that kill a vampire can kill the mara."

"I attacked it with a stake last night, and it didn't seem to do much."

"Was it in human or spirit form?"

"Spirit."

Gwen nodded. "Apparently it can only be killed in human form. Attacking it at any other time will do little more than wound it."

No wonder it was so hard to kill. "So why is it taking these kids?"

"That's the frightening bit. Apparently, when the mara is coming near the end of its life cycle—"

"I'd be resting a whole lot easier if this thing was actually *at* its end, rather than just near it," Kat cut in, voice grim. "And just how long do these things actually loll about having fun at humanity's expense?"

"Eons. And life never-ending is not all it's cracked up to be."

Kat raised her eyebrows. "Oh yeah? Says who?"

"Says Michael, who's the oldest vampire in the

Circle. According to Seline, he was pretty close to either ending it all or stepping across the line when he met Nikki."

Kat nodded. She'd met Michael only once, but she had been more than a little overwhelmed by not only his good looks and charm, but the dark aura of destruction that had seemed to shadow him.

"Anyway," Gwen continued, "when a mara is near the end of its cycle, it breeds. To do this, it needs to find a supernatural to procreate with. Apparently it's incapable of reproducing with those who are its food source."

"The werewolf said he had sex with her." Her partner could hardly be vampire—vampires weren't fertile.

Gwen nodded. "From here on, it's purely guesswork, but we think it's the children's terror that actually induces fertilization."

"How many kids is this thing capable of having?"

"*That* I don't know, but I suspect it's more than we might wish."

A chill raced across Kat's skin and she shivered. Facing one mara was bad enough. Facing a host of them, whether youngsters or not, was *not* something she wanted to contemplate.

"So it's dark emotions she needs to breed," she said. "Like horror. Terror. Maybe that's why she's keeping them alive for six days. Plenty of time for fear to build."

"Or plenty of time for the current crop of youngsters to siphon off those emotions before the mara uses the kid to create another lot of horrors."

"Possibly." Gwen half shrugged. "Seline hasn't discovered what form the mara's youngsters take."

"My guess is we'll discover that soon enough ourselves."

"You're probably right." Gwen drank her coffee for a few minutes, then said, "So, what's troubling you, Kitty-cat?"

She smiled. She never could keep anything from her grandmother for very long—not even the faintest of worries. "You remember me saying that both of us were more than able to contain our hormones long enough to take care of protection? Well, last night we forgot."

Gwen sighed. "That's always the worry with werewolves. That aura of theirs can be overwhelming sometimes." She paused, then added with a fond smile, "That's how your uncle came into being, you know."

Kat's smile widened. She hadn't known that, though it certainly explained why he was the only wolf shifter in a family of ravens.

"Does Ethan know?" Gwen asked.

She shook her head. "We used one this morning, and I cleaned up afterward. I doubt he even thought about it."

"Are you going to mention it?"

She hesitated. "I don't know. He was so damn vehement about never having kids."

"Yet he's obviously very close to this niece of his." Gwen regarded her thoughtfully. "There's a story in all that, I'd wager."

"If there is, it's not one he's telling me." Not yet, anyway. "Besides, I won't know for a couple of weeks for sure."

"I can tell you tonight. A day passed is all the stones need to see such things."

"I know." But did she want to know? Knowing meant she had to decide whether to tell Ethan or not. He had the right to know, and yet he'd already told her he didn't want a relationship, let alone kids, and she had no right to trap him that way. Especially when she was more than capable of raising a child by herself.

Gwen sighed. "A kiddy will put a serious dent in our Circle activities. At least for a couple of years."

The anticipation evident in her voice suggested it was a dent she'd more than welcome. "Don't start counting your ravens before they hatch."

"Might be a pup," Gwen mused. "Mine certainly was."

"I really don't care what it is."

Gwen grinned at her. "Sounds as if you're certain it happened."

Deep down she was. Gwen might have scrying and visions, but her own second sight was just as strong, if somewhat more erratic. But she wasn't about to admit her certainty. Not yet. So she shrugged. "You're the one who told me they were lethally fertile around moon fever time. With the way my luck has been running of late, it's bound to be a certainty."

Gwen touched her arm, squeezing gently. "You should talk to him. Try to find out why he is so against children of his own."

She sighed. "I'll try. But digging information out of that man is hard."

Footsteps echoed across the wooden floors behind them. Ethan appeared two seconds later, a cup of coffee in hand as he stopped beside her. He was close enough that she could smell the fresh soapiness of his skin, yet not close enough for his arm to brush hers. And she sensed this slight distancing was deliberate. That after last night, he needed to put some space between himself and the emotions they'd raised.

And that annoyed the hell out of her.

"Benton just called," Ethan announced. "The missing kid turned out to be a custody case—just as you'd predicted."

Gwen nodded. "I'm not usually wrong, you know. I gather he's on the way back?"

"Yeah. He's told me to tell you to stay put. He wants to talk to you both about last night."

"We can't stay put." Kat's voice was sharper than she'd intended and earned an amused look from her grandmother. "We have a house to investigate."

Ethan nodded. "I told him as much. He ordered me to wait."

"And are you going to follow his orders?"

"Nope." He took a sip of coffee, his gaze distant. "Janie's time is running out. If we don't find her today or tomorrow, we're not going to find her at all."

"I feel the same way, wolf." Gwen sighed and rose stiffly from the stool. "I've got some packs ready with zombie deterrents and sleep potions in them. I'll just add some stakes, then you're ready to go."

ETHAN WATCHED HER WALK AWAY. HER HOBBLING WAS worse this morning and pain pinched her mouth. "Why is your grandmother doing this?" he asked once Gwen had gone.

Kat's glance was quizzical. "Doing what?"

"This. Chasing bad things. Why do it when she's old enough to retire?"

"She's also strong enough to turn you over her knee and paddle your butt for even suggesting such a thing."

He couldn't help smiling. "I reckon she'd enjoy it, too."

Kat's own smile was fleeting. "You'd better believe it."

Ethan sipped his coffee and studied Kat. There was strain around her eyes and shadows beneath them. He'd thought they'd settled all their problems last night, but looking at her now, he had to wonder.

"So, why isn't your mother here helping?"

Her expression tightened. "My mother is dead."

He hesitated but didn't apologize. He could never understand exactly why people did that, though as a cop, he'd certainly done enough of it himself.

"Did she die on the job?"

She snorted. "No. She overdosed."

"Deliberately?"

She raised an eyebrow. "Does any addict overdose deliberately?"

"Yes." And far too often for anyone's liking.

Her gaze slid from his. "I have no idea whether it was deliberate or not. Gwen probably knows, but I've never asked."

"Why not?"

"Because I barely knew her."

"Were you young when she died?"

Her smile was bitter, and her hurt swam around him. "I was ten. But she never had much to do with me."

"Why?"

"Because I was a hindrance to her social life. Gran raised me from the time I was born."

And if that hurt was anything to go by, she resented the abandonment, if only on a subconscious level. "And she never tried to help your mother?"

She gave him a long look. "Addicts have to want to be helped before you can help them. You should know that."

"I reckon your grandmother could convince a cat to shower if she wanted to."

"I reckon she probably could. But Mom was her daughter and every bit as strong-minded."

"What about your dad?"

She looked away again. "I never knew my dad."

He hesitated. Her stance was still and straight, and the emotions that swam around him thick with pain. Yet he had to ask the question, if only because he sensed this could explain why she was the way she was—strong and independent, yet oddly vulnerable. "Why not?"

She looked at him. Tears touched her green eyes but were quickly blinked away. "Because my mother sold herself to feed her habit. My father could have been any one of the dozen men she'd had on the day of my conception."

It was a familiar enough story—many addicts fed their habit that way. He took a sip of his coffee, then said, "It sounds as if you know who her clients were that day."

She snorted softly. "I do. I stupidly asked her once. She gave me a very detailed account of the possibilities."

A charming woman, from the sound of it. "And you never tried to track any of them down, just to see?"

She looked at him, her expression closed but her eyes filled with sudden anger. "Why should I? Mom was nothing more than a body on which they rutted to relieve themselves. What difference would it make knowing which one of them was my father?"

So they were back to *that* again. "Kat—"

She held out a hand. "I've heard all the bullshit, Ethan. I don't want to hear it again."

"I told you the truth last night." His voice was amazingly calm, given the anger beginning to surge through his veins. "Don't keep pushing for what we both know isn't there."

"You told me part of the truth," she shot back. "As much as you thought I needed to know, nothing more."

"Because there is nothing of importance left to say." Nothing except the reason his world, his heart, had shattered so completely.

Pain rose like a tide, threatening to engulf him. Even now, all these years later, that night still haunted him. The image of Jacinta, deliberately throwing herself down those stairs . . . He shuddered and finished his coffee in one long gulp.

It didn't drown the images of all the blood. On her head, between her legs . . .

"I'll wait in the car." He slammed the cup down on the railing and stalked toward the vehicle.

Kat joined him about ten minutes later. She threw a pack onto the backseat, then fastened her seat belt. He started the car and headed for the mountains.

"I'm sorry," she said after a few minutes.

She didn't sound sorry. "Forget it."

His voice was still brusque, and she sighed. "Ethan, how old were you when you met Jacinta?"

He barely glanced at her. "I told you last night. Seventeen."

"And she was your first?"

He smiled grimly. "Hardly. When puberty hits, so too does the power of the moon."

"But she was the first woman you'd really fallen for, as opposed to just mating with?"

"Yes." He hesitated. "Why?"

She regarded him for a second, her green eyes serious. "If she was the first woman you felt anything for, how do you really know she was *it*, rather than just a rather heated crush?"

"She wasn't a crush." His voice was tight with the anger that rolled through him. "Drop it, Kat."

She sighed again. "You are really the most stubborn and irritating man."

"Takes one to know one."

Amusement swam around him. "I hardly think you can call me a man."

He couldn't help smiling, despite the anger. "Well, no."

"Will you answer just one more question?"

His smile faded as he flexed his fingers against the steering wheel. "Maybe."

"Why do you say you hate kids so much when you're obviously close to your niece?"

He relaxed a little. At least this was a question he could answer with practiced ease. "I don't hate kids. I just don't want any of my own."

"Why?"

Because he didn't want any child of his going through what he'd been through. And the surest way to ensure that was simply not to have any. "That's a second question."

"Given you didn't actually answer the first properly, I think it should be allowed."

She was persistent, he had to give her that. But he also had to wonder why. Was she thinking about trying to trap him by becoming pregnant? He stared at her for a moment, trying to gauge whether she was capable of such deception. While he didn't really think she'd stoop so low, the truth was, beyond the physical, they really didn't know each other all that well.

God, he'd better keep his wits about him and make damn sure they kept using condoms!

"Because," he lied, his voice a little sharper than necessary, "a werewolf's sense of family is all tied up with his heart. I can't physically love any offspring I might sire on any woman other than the one who captured my heart."

"Yet you love Janie."

"But she's not my get, and I don't love her in the same way."

"So what would happen if one of your monthly mates were to get pregnant?"

Tension knotted his gut, and he shot her a glance. "Don't even think about it, Kat. I like you—a lot—but that's as far as it goes. I don't love you, and I certainly couldn't love any offspring you and I might produce."

"I'm not *thinking* about it, believe me." Her voice

was hard, almost bitter. "And that didn't answer the question."

He took a deep breath, then blew it out in exasperation. "If I answer this, will you promise to drop the subject for good?"

Her gaze searched his briefly. He wondered what the hell she was searching for.

"Yes," she said after a moment.

"Good." He hesitated, steering the car around a sharp bend. They were approaching the cabin where he'd found the zombies, and he slowed, needing to look for a place to park. "If one of my mates got pregnant, I would support them financially, but that's it. I wouldn't see them again. Wouldn't see the kid."

"But why? That's what I can't understand."

He stopped the car in a stand of trees and turned to face her. "Because it's never good for a child to see his father treating his mother with utter contempt. And that's all I'd feel for someone who tried to trap me that way."

She raised an eyebrow. "If the vehemence behind that statement is anything to go by, you've seen something like that happen."

"Yeah," he said tightly. "My parents."

Because his mom *had* trapped his dad, even though she'd known what he was. What he was capable of. It was a small town and she'd been scared of ending up alone. Better a freak than nothing, she'd once told him.

But their often bitter relationship was another reason he'd been more than happy to leave that place as soon as he could.

For several seconds there was nothing to be seen in

Kat's expression. Nothing beyond curiosity in the emotive swirl that swam between them. That in itself eased some of his tension, and when she smiled, it dissipated even more.

"I was only asking, Ethan, so relax. In a job like mine, I can hardly afford to be carting a kid around."

Even so, he was going to keep carrying condoms in his jeans pocket. "Good. Because I'd hate to think you'd sink so low."

"Never fear," she said, thrusting open the door almost viciously. "I know you're in it for nothing more than a good time, and I don't intend to forget it. Or the condoms."

"Good," he muttered and climbed out of the car.

And wondered why the thought of her belly fat and round with his child filled him with such fierce and sudden longing.

KAT SQUATTED BESIDE ETHAN AND STUDIED THE OLD SHACK below them. It was a small wooden structure that looked to have been at the mercy of the elements for a good five years. Not the warmest hideaway in the world, though it was doubtful the dead really cared.

She shifted the weight of the pack on her back, then said, "You wait here. Once I'm sure the sleep bombs have worked, I'll call you over."

He placed a hand on her arm, stopping her from rising. "I don't think you should go down there alone."

She bit down on her impatience and ignored the concern in his eyes. "We've been through this already. Gran only included one mask." Truth was, she didn't include *any*. They didn't need them, because these sleep bombs were designed to affect only the dead. But she needed to get away from him for a few minutes. Needed time alone to gather her thoughts. To contemplate the reality of bringing a kid into the world who, like her, might never know his father.

Pain rose. She pushed it away and stood. "I've been doing this a long time. I know what I'm doing when it comes to the dead." It was the living she couldn't understand.

She walked down the slope to the small cabin. The smell of death was so overwhelming she gagged. She took several deep breaths through her mouth to ease the churning in her stomach, then edged around the corner and headed for the nearest window. The glass was grimy, but even so, she could see the dead on the floor. Ten of them. God help her and Ethan if they woke before the sleeping potions had a chance to work.

She kinetically unlocked the window and eased it up. The zombie closest to her stirred. She froze, hoping the gentle breeze playing in her hair didn't take her smell to it.

It turned, then began to snore. She swung the pack off and carefully dug out the four golf ball–sized bombs. They were warm against her palms, their feel almost jellylike. She tossed one into each corner of the cabin, listened for the gentle plop that indicated the outer skin had broken, and watched as pale fingers of red smoke began to ease across the floor. She closed the window and glanced at her watch. They'd have to wait five minutes for the mist to do its stuff, making it safe enough to enter.

She squatted on her heels and leaned back against

the cabin wall. Thunder rumbled overhead, a warning of the storm clearly gathering. The smell of rain sharpened the air but didn't quite erase the smell of the dead. She hoped the storm didn't break until after they'd explored whatever it was the zombies protected. If those clouds were anything to go by, the storm was going to be a doozy. Maybe enough to wake the sleep-spelled dead.

She let her gaze roam across the tree line until she found the shadows in which Ethan hid.

What in hell was she going to do with him?

He kept insisting he wasn't capable of loving her, and yet his touch and his eyes and the emotions that sometimes surged between them suggested otherwise.

Could a wolf lose his heart more than once?

She'd ask him, except for the fact that she'd promised to drop the subject and didn't want to risk alienating him completely. Maybe it was a question Gwen could answer.

She hoped so. Because she very much suspected she was falling in love with the man.

She hugged her arms around her belly. She'd find out tonight whether she was pregnant or not. And if she was, there was one thing she was suddenly certain of.

Her child would know its father.

She'd grown up without that knowledge and knew the pain it caused. If he didn't want any part of his child's life, then fair enough, but her child would know who he was, what he looked like, what he did, and where he lived. That child would have the sense of history, of belonging, that in many respects she never had, no matter how much Gran had loved her. Four simple pieces of information could have made her childhood seem a whole lot less of a mistake.

And perhaps most important, *her* child would never be in doubt that her mother not only wanted her, but loved her. Or him, as the case may be.

She glanced at her watch again, then rose and looked inside. The red mist had almost dissipated. It should be safe enough now to enter without waking the zombies.

She signaled to Ethan, then carefully opened the window. A heartbeat later she felt the warmth of his presence wash over her senses.

"What, no masks?" Ethan asked, voice low and annoyed as she clambered inside.

She hid her smile and met his gaze. "Don't need them with the mist almost gone."

He snorted softly. "Wouldn't be a ploy to keep me at a safe distance while you explored, would it?"

"Of course not," she said absently as she looked around, trying to sense the presence of anything other than the sleeping zombies.

"That's what I figured." He stepped carefully over a zombie. "What are we looking for?"

"I don't know. You check that door." She waved a hand at the door to their left. "And I'll look around here."

He made his way toward the door. She stayed where she was, hands on her hips, as she studied the floor. The air gently caressing her face was damp and smelled slightly musty. It wasn't the staleness of a cellar, but rather that of an old cave. Suggesting, perhaps, there was another access point here besides the window and the front door. One that went down rather than out.

She stepped over a dead man and followed the caress of air into the shadows. And found a trapdoor. One that had a zombie sleeping over the top of it.

"Nothing in this room," Ethan said quietly. "You find anything?"

"Yeah, a zombie in the damn way."

He stopped beside her. "So why not kill it?"

She gave him an annoyed look. "Contrary to popular opinion, I do not run around killing zombies willy-nilly. Besides, if I kill any of these things right now, the person who raised them will know."

"Then let's move it, so we can check out the door." His voice held an edge of impatience. Or maybe it was annoyance.

"I'll move it. You touch it, and it might just wake."

She directed a thick lance of kinetic energy at the zombie, carefully moving it closer to the window. It stirred, tearing at her kinetic hold. Hot lances of fire burned into her brain, and she bit her lip, blinking back tears as she eased the creature back to the floor.

Ethan had the trapdoor open and was squatting near the edge, peering down into the darkness. "It smells damp. Musty."

She nodded. At least the air coming up from the darkness was free from the scent of death—for the moment, anyway. "I'll go down first, check that it's okay."

He glanced at her. "What if we're attacked?"

She slipped off the pack and opened it, grabbing the stakes and zombie deterrents. "Use these," she said, offering him a set.

He just looked at them. "Thanks, but I'll stick to my gun."

"A gun's not much use in a situation like this."

"I'm sure they'll stop if you shoot their damn brains out."

"They would, but it would also make far too much noise." But she put one set of weapons away. He was obviously determined to stick to his gun, and noise be damned.

She handed him the pack, then peered into the hole. It was as dark as hell down there, but the breeze was coming from the right. She looked up at Ethan. "Just how good is your night sight?"

"Wolf keen." He frowned. "I was under the impression *your* sight was pretty damn good as well."

"It normally is, but I can't see squat down there."

"Then I'd better lead once we're down."

She nodded and climbed in, dropping lightly to the stony ground. For several seconds she did nothing more than listen. Everything was still—silent. Almost oppressively so.

She met Ethan's gaze. "It's okay."

He jumped down, then caught her hand, his fingers warm against hers. "Nothing?"

She shook her head. "Nothing dead, at any rate."

"Good."

He tugged her forward. The chill in the air increased, and the ground seemed to be sloping downward, though the darkness was so deep it was hard to be sure. The tunnel was narrow, tight, and her breath caught as she imagined the weight of the walls and the roof bearing down on her. She had only to straighten her fingers and she could brush the cold stone. Sweat trickled down her forehead, and she bit her lip. Damn it, why couldn't she see? It was odd, to say the least. Especially when Ethan obviously could. She would have thought a raven's sight to be nearly as good as a wolf's, but obviously, it wasn't. Or maybe it was just the fact that they were under the ground rather than above it.

Ahead, moisture dripped, lending the darkness a steady heartbeat. The dank smell increased, until it almost felt like they were breathing in liquid.

"I'd say there's a river overhead." Though his voice was soft, it seemed to boom through the tunnel, echoing loudly.

"I can't hear water running."

"You probably wouldn't, with the amount of rock above us."

Right now, she didn't need to be reminded about the weight above them. She swiped at a trickle of sweat and peered past his shoulder. Something glowed up ahead. "Is that light?"

"Torchlight, by the way it's flickering." He squeezed her hand. "It opens up a little up ahead."

"Good." She didn't bother masking her relief. "Can you smell anything?"

"Humans. Two of them."

Though his voice was flat, she could feel his excitement. "It might not be her, you know."

"I know."

But his pace increased regardless. The flickering glow grew until it shone warmly across the damp rocks and finally lifted the darkness. Ahead, the tunnel opened up into what looked like a wide cavern. Relief crawled through her.

There was no one to be seen ahead. Nothing to be heard. But she could certainly smell someone. Or some*thing*.

She pulled Ethan to a stop. "Zombies, dead ahead."

"How many?" His question was little more than a caress of air past her ear.

"Two." She hesitated, then frowned. "But there's something else."

"What?"

"I'm not sure." She let go of his hand and stepped forward cautiously. Energy tingled across her skin, brief but powerful. She raised a hand. The farther she reached, the sharper the buzz, until it felt like it burned across her skin. Eventually it became a wall that resisted her efforts to push any farther. Tiny slivers of energy shot from her fingers, lightning sharp as they crawled up that unseen wall and faded away.

"What the hell is that?"

"Some form of magical barrier. I haven't got the equipment with me to get past it right now."

She kept her hand against the barrier and moved from one side of the tunnel to the other. The barrier appeared to be oval in shape, bowing out into the tunnel from either edge.

"Touch it with your fingertips," she said. "Keep that contact so you know where it is, but don't go any closer."

He nodded. The lightning that crawled away from his touch was sharper, more fiery. He hissed slightly. "Feels like I'm being eaten by ants."

"I think it would be a whole lot worse if you came into full contact with the thing." She edged around to the right.

"Can you see anything from your side?" he said.

"A wall and another tunnel." One that looked carved by nature rather than man. Or magic.

"I can see living dead men." He hesitated, and a wave of emotion hit her, so strong it knocked her backward. "And Janie." Anger, hope, and frustration combined in his voice and speared right through her heart. He really did love that little girl.

"You sure?"

His glance was sharp. "Yes. I can see her face. You've got to break this thing so we can get her out."

"I can't—"

"Damn it, she's here. She's alive, and I'm sure as hell not leaving without her!"

"We have no choice, not right—"

"I will *not* leave her!"

"And if I try to break this barrier without the right tools, I'll risk killing us all. Can't you feel the power in this thing?"

"It's only magic, for God's sake. How dangerous can it be?"

She stared at him. "Have you learned nothing in the last few days?"

"That's my niece in there." A stiffened finger stabbed the air, and the unseen barrier buzzed almost angrily as lightning flared away from his touch. "And if you won't get her back, I will."

"Ethan, no!"

He thrust at the wall, fists clenched as he tried to force his way through. Electricity swarmed around his wrists, locking him tight, then began crawling up his arms. He swore vehemently, tugging to get free as the slithers of lightning reached farther up his arms and began wrapping him in a web of energy.

"See what happens when you don't listen to me?" She swung off her pack and pulled out the slender chain of pure silver—the only metal immune to the effects of magic. It could also be deadly to shifters, but she'd been handling the stuff for so long now she'd developed a fairly strong immunity to it. Ethan, however, would not have the same advantage, so she'd have to be careful not to burn him.

"Now is not the time for an I-told-you-so." His teeth were clenched and sweat beaded his forehead. "Get me free of this damn thing. It feels like it's sucking me dry."

What she *should* do was leave him there a few minutes, so he'd learn to pay magic a little more respect. "Since it was made by a creature who steals souls to survive, I wouldn't be surprised if that's exactly what it's doing."

She looped the chain around his arms—making sure it touched his sweater rather than his skin—and the lightning instantly shriveled away from it. Cut off from the main source, the web of energy wrapping around his body fizzled and died, leaving only his clenched fists in contact.

"Now pull free."

With a grunt of effort, he did. "Thanks," he muttered.

She nodded and unwrapped the chain from his arms. If she'd had enough silver chain with her, she could have created a doorway to crawl through, but neither she nor Gwen had expected the soul-sucker capable of something like this. Though why, she had no idea. An ancient spirit would have had more than enough time to learn a magic trick or two.

"It won't take much more than an hour to go back to the cabin, get supplies, and come back."

His look suggested an hour was fifty-nine minutes too long. "Then go. I'll wait here."

"For what? You can't get past the barrier."

"But I can watch. I can see if she's moved or anything."

And what if the soul-sucker came to taste rather than move? What could he do, other than go insane watching? "The zombies or the mara could come down this tunnel at any time."

His gaze went back to the cavern. "The tunnel will force the zombies to come down one at a time. That I can handle."

"And the soul-sucker?"

"Leave the pack."

She sighed in frustration. "I will, but I insist you wear the chain under your collar." She didn't wait for argument; she simply lifted his shirt collar and looped the chain around his neck. Once she'd folded the collar back down, the chain couldn't be seen.

He frowned. "Why?"

"You saw how the energy reacted, didn't you?" When he nodded, she continued. "That's because pure silver is immune to magic, and as such, repels it. So wear it and make yourself a little less of a target. Just don't touch it yourself, because it will burn you."

"It didn't burn *you*."

"That's because I have some immunity to it."

His frown deepened. "Does that mean I can't shift shape?"

"Magic is magic, whether it's a wall or the ability to shift into another form."

"I think I'd rather *not* wear the chain." When she opened her mouth to protest, he threw up his hands and added, "Go. And be careful going through those zombies."

"I will." She hesitated, wanting to kiss him but not daring to take the step that separated them. Not sure how he'd react to the everyday act of lovers the world over.

He made no move, his attention on the cavern more than on her. She sighed, dropped the pack at his feet, and walked away.

The darkness closed in around her again. She dragged her fingers along the walls to keep her bearings and tried not to think about the tons of rock and dirt hanging overhead. She was trembling by the time the end of the tunnel came into sight, and she shifted shape with relief, flying through the trapdoor and out the window. Out into the wide-open skies. Lord, the freedom of it felt so good!

It took far less than an hour to fly to the cabin, grab the necessary supplies, and get back to the tunnel.

But the zombies were gone when she arrived.

And so was Ethan.

THIRTEEN

ETHAN CROSSED HIS ARMS AND LEANED AGAINST THE DAMP, cold wall. Janie was a bare ten feet away, and it took every ounce of self-control he possessed to *not* attack the wall that separated them. God, all he wanted to do was sweep her into his arms and let her know everything was going to be all right. That he was here and he would protect her against the demons.

But the truth was, he couldn't protect her against those demons. Not yet. And maybe not ever. Kat and her grandmother probably had more chance of doing so than he ever would.

He wished the cabin were only a few minutes away. Hoped Kat was coming back right now with whatever she needed to free the girls. He had a bad feeling that time was running out.

His gaze drifted to the left. In the other cell lay a second little girl—undoubtedly Karen, the kid they'd failed to save last night.

Like Janie, she was asleep, curled up into a ball. Like Janie, she was shivering and crying softly in her sleep. He had no doubt they'd both been drugged. The cave was icy, and neither child had blankets. And it certainly wasn't an environment that induced a restful sleep.

Damn it, they had to get them *both* out! They couldn't leave either of them here in that monster's grip any longer than necessary. He glanced at his watch. Ten minutes had passed. It felt like an eternity.

He shifted his weight from one foot to the other and studied the two zombies. They stood on either side of the small cells, one of them close enough to turn his stomach with its smell. They'd obviously been around for a while, if the withered, gaunt look to their skin was any indication. Did zombies actually grow old? Did they decay? They were dead, so surely they must, eventually.

He snorted softly at the thought. Two days ago he would have considered himself insane for even thinking something like that. God, what a nightmare this was all turning out to be!

Except for Kat.

He certainly didn't regret meeting her. Or making love to her. She was warm and vibrant and so damn sexy he ached just thinking about her. Her scent lingered around him, a taste of sunshine in the cold darkness. He briefly closed his eyes, remembering the way she'd looked at him just before she left—green eyes filled with a combination of passion and hesitation. Doubt. Her mouth had been so damn lush he'd just wanted to reach out, drag her close, and kiss her senseless.

But that was dangerous. Especially if she wanted to take this whole thing one step further, though it was crazy to think anyone could get so serious in such a short time.

It was a thought that made him smile grimly. *He* had. It had taken only two incredible days—and nights—with Jacinta, and he'd been ready to commit the rest of his life to her. It was Luke who'd convinced him to wait the six months.

Luke, who had picked up the pieces when it all went to hell.

God, he had to save Janie for him. *Had* to.

Sound scuffed against the silence. He froze, listening intently. It came again—the brush of a heel against stone. Then the smell of death began to invade the air. The zombies must have awoken and discovered the open trapdoor.

He swore softly, grabbed the pack, and called to the wolf as Kat had taught him. Nothing happened. No golden glow, no rush of power, no moment of numbing emptiness as his body reshaped and the wolf formed. *The chain.* He ripped it free from his neck and shoved it into the pack, burning his fingers despite the small amount of time he was in contact with the metal. He reached again for his wild side, and this time it came in a rush of power that was almost overwhelming.

In wolf form again, he gathered the pack in his mouth and bounded up the tunnel. He'd seen a small fissure in the rock about halfway down—not big enough to hide a human, but just right for a wolf. All he could hope was that the zombies had a lousy sense of smell. As much as he liked to think he could handle ten dead men, he wasn't going to take a chance when Janie's life was at stake. Not unless there was no other choice.

The dragging footsteps moved closer. From the

sound of it, there were only three coming down the tunnel. He wedged himself into the fissure, keeping low to present a less obvious presence to any dead gaze that might happen his way.

The smell drew closer. But with it came something else, something he'd felt before—in the warehouse, just before Kat and the man he now knew was a vampire had entered.

Heat began to burn against his neck. He glanced down. One of the stones in the necklace Kat had made was beginning to glow the color of blood. Hadn't she said the red stone was meant to prevent the mara from sensing his presence?

Did the fact that it glowed now mean the soul-sucker was coming down the tunnel with the dead men?

If she was, he had to hope the stone worked like it was supposed to work. Zombies he could handle, but what hope were teeth and claws against a creature who could disappear into a cloud of smoke?

A zombie shuffled past. It was big and lumbering and looked no more dangerous than a slab of meat. But the dead men he'd fought at the farmhouse had proven just how deceiving that image was. They might look slow, but they weren't. And they were damn strong.

A second zombie lumbered past. The stone at Ethan's neck burned more fiercely, searing his skin with its heat. A third appeared—and above its head, tendrils of white smoke slowly gyrated. He didn't move, hardly dared to breathe in case the soul-sucker sensed him. But his heart was pounding faster than a damn locomotive, and it was a wonder the creature couldn't hear it.

They disappeared into the tunnel's darkness. He waited until the shuffling steps of the zombies had become little more than a scuff of sound and the burning in the stone had faded. Then he slowly eased out of his hiding spot.

Four figures were silhouetted against the flickering light of the torches at the far end. The mara had regained human form and was gesturing with one hand. Air shimmered briefly, then the four of them walked into the cavern.

He padded forward quietly, keeping low to the ground and close to the walls. When the shadows began to give way to the light, he stopped. Two of the three dead men who'd accompanied the soul-sucker down the tunnel had moved into the cells and picked up the girls. The mara was talking to the zombie guards. He flicked his ears forward but couldn't hear anything beyond a singsong murmur.

The two zombies with the girls moved out into the main cavern area. The mara motioned them toward the second tunnel, then her form dissolved and floated after the dead men. One of the guards disappeared inside a cell, reappearing moments later with a box clutched in skeletal hands. Both dead men began to walk toward the tunnel he was in. He cursed softly. While he doubted the mara had sensed his presence in the tunnel, any delay in following the creature could be costly. It had taken days—and blind luck—to find this hideaway. If he lost them now, it might be the end of any hope he had of rescuing Janie alive.

He turned tail and padded back to the fissure.

Water dripped onto his nose as he crouched down. He shook it free and glanced up, noting that the cracks rising from ceiling to roof were oozing moisture. From the look of it, the tunnel slid right under the river in this section. He suddenly hoped whoever was responsible for creating the passageway had allowed enough depth to give the river base support—otherwise the river could end up cutting itself an entirely new path.

The zombies shuffled past. They didn't go far, stopping just beyond his line of sight. They stood there for a good five minutes, their breathing as sharp as their smell, their fingers scraping across the stone. Finally, they moved on.

He edged out. The zombies were shuffling toward the trapdoor, and one still carried the box. He looked up, but couldn't see anything out of place and wondered what the hell they'd been doing. Something, he was sure of that. Something that boded him and Kat no good.

For a second, he was tempted to follow them. Kat was due back down this tunnel in the next half hour, and if the dead men were creating some form of trap, she'd be caught.

But dare he risk losing Janie by watching the dead men?

The answer was a resounding no. Kat was a resourceful woman, and psychic besides. Surely she'd sense any trap the zombies were laying.

Right now, his priority *had* to lie with his niece and the other little girl, not with a woman he'd probably never see again once this mess was over.

He turned and padded after the mara, wondering

why the thought of never seeing Kat again churned his gut and made his chest feel tight.

KAT PEERED DOWN INTO THE DARK TUNNEL FROM THE RELative safety of the empty cabin. She could hear no sound beyond a steady dripping, and Ethan's scent was little more than a caress of warmth across the chill air coming out of the tunnel. He wasn't in there; she was certain of that. Did the absence of both him and the zombies mean he'd been caught?

If he *had* been, he wouldn't have gone down without a fight. But she couldn't smell freshly dead zombie in the air of the tunnel, and surely she would have if there were one or two down there.

She bit her lip. She had an uneasy feeling that it was no longer safe in the tunnel, but unless she went in, she'd never know what had happened. Surely Ethan would have left her some hint, some clue, as to where he'd gone if he hadn't been captured by the zombies or the mara.

Perhaps shifting shape was the answer . . . only her back and legs were aching with the strain of carrying the small backpack so far in her claws. She doubted that her raven form would be able to hold on to it much longer without dropping it—and dropping it would shatter the extra sleep bombs she'd collected. Leaving it here while she explored the tunnel was out of the question. If the mara came back, she'd be left without weapons.

She'd have to risk going in. She really had no other option. Sighing, she grabbed the pack, swinging it over one shoulder before lowering herself into the tunnel.

Her feet hit the stone with a soft thump. She remained where she was, studying the darkness in front of her, listening to the silence. Beyond the steady dripping there was very little sound. The air seemed thick and cold, icing her lungs with every intake of breath. She shivered and was suddenly glad she'd put on an extra sweater.

She rose and cautiously moved forward. The ground under one foot shifted. Something clicked—a sound so soft she might have missed it had she not been so aware that something was horribly wrong. She froze, her heart beating somewhere in her throat and goose bumps chasing down her spine. Nothing happened, yet that sensation of wrongness increased tenfold.

Swallowing to ease the dryness in her throat, she lifted her hand, running her fingers against the damp wall for guidance as she edged forward.

Again, her foot hit something. Again, there was a whisper-soft click.

Apprehension slithered through her. She scanned the inky tunnel, fingers clenched against the urge to release kinetic energy. At what, she had no idea. There was no threat she could see or smell or hear. Yet every instinct suggested she was stepping deeper and deeper into danger.

Sweat trickled down her cheek. She swiped at it, then stopped, suddenly aware that it was beginning to get truly hot inside the tunnel. *Just like the house . . .*

Apprehension turned to fear. She swung around, knowing she had to get out while she still could, before whatever trap the soul-sucker had set could snare her.

Deep darkness slammed down on her. Someone had shut the trapdoor. Cursing loudly, she bolted for the end of the tunnel.

The air around her began to vibrate with energy. The heat increased, until it felt as if her skin glowed with it.

Then everything exploded. She was knocked off her feet by a blast of red-hot air and hammered into the tunnel wall.

JANIE'S BABY-SOFT SCENT LINGERED, GIVING ETHAN A TRAIL to follow. The light of the torches was quickly left behind, but the veil of darkness didn't fully return, lifted by the beams of light filtering in up ahead. Slime hung in tendrils from the ceiling, waving gently in the breeze wafting down the tunnel. Water trickled past his paws, freezing his pads. He half thought about shifting shape, but he knew it was safer to remain as he was, cold paws notwithstanding. The mara was less likely to be on the lookout for a wolf.

The path came to a junction. He stopped, looking both ways. To his left were warmth and light and the promise of an entrance to the outside world. But Janie and her captors had headed right, up the slope and deeper into the mountain.

Why? The cells in the cavern behind them had appeared secure enough, so what did moving the two girls gain? Did they suspect he and Kat had found their hiding place? Or did the move have nothing to do with that and everything to do with the fact that both girls were food for the soul-sucker and its offspring?

Fear began to pound through his veins, and the sensation of time running out increased.

He followed the tunnel, his nails making little noise against the damp stone under his paws. The air grew colder, and the sensation of being very deep under the earth increased. Odd, when the path he followed seemed to be going up rather than down.

The smell of death sharpened the air. He slowed, knowing he had to be close.

Light shimmered up ahead. He stopped, not sure what he was seeing. Then he realized he was viewing the torch through a curtain of water, and the tension in his gut increased. The clothes of the kid they'd found torn apart in the warehouse had been damp. Now he knew why.

He edged closer to the water. The zombies were standing next to a stone table that reeked of blood. Not fresh blood, but old. As if the stone had spent years and years steeped in it.

He couldn't see the two girls, but the soul-sucker stood in front of what looked like a second cave, placing small stones across the entrance. When she'd positioned the last one, she made a motion with her hand, and the air shimmered briefly. Another magic wall, obviously. Only this time, he was on the right side of it. With any luck, all he had to do was shift the placement of those stones and the energy wall would dissipate.

The mara walked past the old stone table to the other side of the cavern. She stood in front of it for several seconds, then made another motion with her hand. The curtain of darkness that shadowed the wall seemed to flow aside, revealing another tunnel. One that had a slightly phosphorescent glow. He had no doubt a sample would match the material under the second kid's fingers.

The soul-sucker glanced at the zombies, and all but one followed her into the greenish passageway. He shifted his feet, itching to attack, knowing this was possibly his best chance. But Kat had said the mara would know the minute one of the zombies died. Right now, he couldn't afford to do anything that would attract the soul-sucker's attention. Not when he was alone and the mara was so close.

Besides, he doubted if he could outrun the zombies, and he certainly couldn't fight when he was carrying both girls.

It left him with very little choice. He'd have to wait and see whether the mara and the zombies intended to leave the girls here. Then he'd have to go back and wait . . .

The thought died as a distant sensation of foul energy vibrated through the air. The hackles along his back stood on end, and he turned, sensing the main source of that power came from behind him.

The buzz increased until the air was thick and electric. The rock under his feet quivered, and hot air blasted down the tunnel. Then energy died and silence fell once more.

He remembered the fissures he'd seen in the tunnel. Remembered the zombies stopping. Knew that Kat was due back any minute. Felt fear engulf him—a fear that was both his and hers.

His four legs had never moved so fast as he raced back to the tunnel.

KAT PUSHED HERSELF UPRIGHT AND SWIPED AT THE WETness running down her face. The sound of the explosion still rang in her ears, but it didn't prevent her hearing the rush of water—water that was up to her knees and rapidly rising.

And the tunnel was no longer dark. Dust danced in the golden slithers of light that thrust into the gloom, and even from where she was standing she could see the gray of threatening clouds.

But those same sunbeams allowed her to see the water. It looked as if half the damn river was being diverted into her prison.

She rose and staggered forward. The water poured in through two fissures. They were large enough to thrust a couple of fingers through, large enough for the water to pour in with sufficient force to tug at her feet and threaten to topple her. But not large enough to allow a raven to escape, let alone a human.

Being caught in a tunnel was bad enough. Being caught in a tunnel rapidly filling with water was the stuff of nightmares . . .

She took a deep breath, trying to calm the rapid pounding of her heart and the fear threatening to lock her limbs.

The water was only at her knees. She had plenty of time to find a way out. She looked up, studying the roof, noting at least half a dozen fissures that dripped water. But move one rock, and she might just bring not only the wall down but the rest of the river as well. Getting to the trapdoor that lay beyond the wall was definitely out of the question.

She turned and went back through the water. The darkness weighed in on her as she moved away from the fissures and the sunlight. She tried to keep her breathing even, tried not to think about the weight of the river above her or the water that was creeping up to her thighs. Tried to think warm, calm thoughts as a chill crept across her skin and made her teeth chatter so hard her jaw ached.

She raised her hands, running one along the wet walls, holding the other out in front as she waded slowly through the swirling water. It wasn't long before she hit something solid—but it was a solid she didn't want to feel. Another wall of rock.

She bit back a curse, ignored the rising sense of panic, and edged sideways. It couldn't be totally solid. There had to be stones she could move. Even if she only made a hole big enough for the water to escape through, it would be enough. Ethan was beyond this wall somewhere. She was sure of that, if nothing else. He'd find her. He'd get help and get her out—if the soul-sucker and her zombies didn't find him and the rescue party first.

Rock tipped under her touch. Kinetic energy surged to her fingertips. She carefully withdrew the stone from the pile and tossed it behind her. Water splashed, creating a wave that lapped past her hips. She bit her lip and grabbed another rock, working methodically to create a gap as dust and pebbles rained down on her and the water continued to rise.

Sweat trickled down her face and a pounding ache settled into her head. She was beginning to push her kinetic limits, but she had no other choice. The water was rising faster now, and creating a hole was her only hope of escape. Her only hope of immediate survival.

She pulled out another rock. There was an odd sound, like an old man groaning as he struggled to rise, then rocks and debris began to rain down on her.

She yelped and jumped back. Her feet slipped and she went under the water, the coldness snatching her breath. Stones rained around her, churning the dark waters, confusing her senses so she couldn't tell up from down. She tried to relax, tried to let herself float, but a rock hit her shoulder, and she cried out in pain, sucking in water, filling her lungs with ice. Then something hit her head and darkness closed in.

ETHAN DROPPED THE BACKPACK AND SHIFTED SHAPE AS HE ran into the cavern. Where the entrance of the tunnel had been was now a wall of stone and rubble. He could hear the rushing of water and knew the fissures must have opened in the explosion, providing the river with a brand-new course.

A course that might kill Kat if he didn't find some way to free her quickly.

He slid to a stop. Near the very top of the wall there was a small gap. No water escaped through it, which surely meant it hadn't reached that high yet.

He scrambled up, dislodging rocks and slipping in his haste. Stones tore at his hands and arms, but he didn't care. Time was ticking away, and so were Kat's chances of surviving. He had to act fast.

He grabbed the rocks and began throwing them down, rapidly widening the hole. The air that rushed out of the tunnel was thick and cold and filled with fear. Or maybe it was his own fear he could smell. His gut churned, and the thought that he might already be too late made his hands shake.

He kept working, shifting a rock, throwing it down, then grabbing another and repeating the process. Over and over, until his arms and back ached and sweat stung his eyes. Water lapped at the widened hole. He climbed a little higher and leaned into the damp darkness.

"Kat?"

His urgent whisper seemed to echo through the darkness. She didn't answer. The steady rush of water was the only sound to be heard.

He swore and grabbed another rock, thrusting it past his feet. A tremor ran through the rocks, then the whole pile shifted and slipped forward, as if the pressure of the water behind it had became too much. He froze for a second, every muscle tensed as he listened to the groaning. The wall shifted again, this time more noticeably. It was going to collapse . . . He jumped down and ran like hell.

There was a rumble of sound, like that of an express train bearing down on him, then a surge of water and rock swept him off his feet. He hit the ground with a grunt and was sent tumbling forward, tossed and turned as easily as the boulders that rained around him.

He slithered into a cavern wall, pain blooming up his side. He cursed, but braced himself against the wall and rose. The wall of rock was all but gone, the water rushing down the other tunnel. He couldn't see Kat anywhere.

Pushing away the rising sense of panic, he ran back to the wall and climbed over the few stones that remained. That was when he saw her. She was facedown in the remaining puddle of water, wedged up against the wall.

He grabbed her, pulled her onto dryer ground, and turned her over. She wasn't breathing, and her lips were blue. Panic surged, and he took a deep breath, trying to calm down. He knew CPR. He'd done it successfully more than once.

Only this was the first time it had really mattered. This was the first time he was trying to save someone he cared about. He pushed her onto her side, then opened her mouth and checked for obstructions. None.

He began resuscitation. Fear was a knife digging deep into his heart. He didn't want to lose her—not now, not like this. Not ever.

And that one thought filled him with as much fear as the thought of not being able to revive her. But he thrust the fear aside and concentrated on breathing for them both, on willing her back.

For what seemed like ages, nothing happened. He continued CPR and hung on to hope. Then she shuddered and coughed. Water spewed from her mouth. Relief surged, so strong it left him trembling. He thrust her onto her side, holding her while she vomited the rest of the water from her stomach.

"God," she murmured. "I feel like I've been sitting in a freezer for a week."

Her teeth were chattering so hard he could barely

make out what she was saying. “Are you hurt anywhere else?”

She shook her head and coughed weakly. “What in hell happened to the magic barrier?”

“The mara came down the tunnel not long after you’d left and took it down. She and the zombies moved the kids to higher ground.”

Her gaze met his. The fear still lingering in the green depths of her eyes stabbed through his heart. He ran his hand down her cheek and brushed a thumb across her cold lips. Lips he ached to kiss. “You up to walking?”

“I think so.”

“Good. We have to get you back to the cabin where it’s warm.”

“We can’t. Not until we get those two kids.”

He rose, then took her hand and pulled her upright. She hissed, and pain flitted through her pretty eyes. He wrapped his arms around her waist and held her close. She was wet and cold, and he wanted her so fiercely his whole body ached.

“You look like something the cat coughed up,” he said softly. “I don’t think rescuing anyone is really an option right now.”

A cheeky smile touched her lips. “So that’s a stake in your pocket and not an indication that you might be exaggerating just a little about how bad I look?”

He grinned. “It’s no stake, and I’m not exaggerating. And I think I’d want you no matter how horrible you looked.”

She raised an eyebrow. “The heat of the moon has a lot to answer for, huh?”

“Maybe.” But it wasn’t the moon surging through

his veins right now. It was her presence. Her closeness. He brushed a kiss across her lips and resisted the temptation to do anything more. Now was definitely not the time.

He stepped away. "You're shivering with cold and barely able to stand. There are at least three zombies guarding the kids, and the mara's with them. I think it's safer to wait until tonight."

"And give her time to set more traps? How sensible is that?" She looked around. "Have you seen my backpack anywhere?"

He ignored the rush of annoyance and said as calmly as he could, "No."

"Then we'd better look for it. We'll need the stakes if the soul-sucker attacks."

"Kat—"

"No." She crossed her arms, her expression a picture of stubbornness. "We're wasting precious time standing here arguing, you know."

"I can pick you up and carry you out."

"And I can slap your ass across the cavern and go on by myself."

And she probably would, if he didn't give in. "God save me from obstinate women," he muttered and swung away to find the backpack.

It was wedged into what remained of the fissure he'd hidden in earlier. He swept it up, then walked back down to her. "At least get out of those wet sweaters."

She raised an eyebrow. "And run around the tunnels topless? As much as you might enjoy that, I don't think so."

"As much as I definitely *would* enjoy that, that wasn't

what I meant." He took off his coat. His shirt was relatively dry, and if he got too cold, he could always shift shape. "Wear this."

She hesitated, then handed him the pack and quickly exchanged her sweaters for his coat. Though it was loose everywhere else, the coat squashed her glorious breasts flat, and she glanced up with a grin. "Well, I guess this proves your chest is not as large as mine."

"I'd be worried if it was."

He handed her the pack and she got out several stakes, handing them back to him. She pulled out one more, shoved a couple of chains and what looked like stones into her pocket, then tossed the bag aside. "Everything else is smashed."

Little wonder, given the small space the backpack had ended up in. "You ready to go?"

She nodded. He caught her hand and led her toward the exit, only to stop when the smell hit.

"That's not good," she said softly.

It certainly wasn't.

The cavern beyond was filled with dead men.

FOURTEEN

KAT SWEPT HER GAZE ACROSS THE CAVERN. THERE HAD TO be ten of them, if not more. At least she now knew where all the dead men from the cabin had disappeared to—they'd been waiting in the shadows to see if she escaped the trap.

"No, they weren't." Ethan's expression was grim as his gaze met hers. "And I certainly would have smelled them if they'd been anywhere else close by."

She studied him for a moment, wondering if he realized just how well he was reading her surface thoughts. "There'd be more than one exit from this place."

"Probably." His gaze went back to the zombies. "What do you want to do?"

"There's only one thing we *can* do."

He looked at her, concern deeper in his nut-brown eyes. "You sure you're up to it?"

Given the fact that it felt like there were a dozen madmen pounding away in her head, she was sure she *wasn't*. But it was either face the dead men or stay here shivering.

She forced a smile. "At least fighting will warm me up."

"I guess there's that." He glanced at the zombies again. "I'll head left, you head right. Hopefully, we'll meet in the middle."

"Just remember: those stakes won't kill zombies."

"That I'll remember." He shoved them through the belt loops of his jeans, gave her a quick, hard kiss that left her lips tingling, then jumped over the wall and ran at the zombies.

They reacted instantly, rushing at him with a deafening roar. She shoved the stake through her belt and followed him out. Two dead men charged at her, bony hands outstretched like claws. She swung and smashed a booted foot into the face of one. The other she hit kinetically, thrusting him back into the pack attacking Ethan, knocking down three of them.

The zombie whose nose she had mashed roared and swung a fist. She swayed out the way, then dropped, sweeping with one leg, knocking the creature off his feet. Then she hit him kinetically, twisting his neck until there was an audible snap. The madmen in her head did a weird little dance, making her eyes water. She blinked away tears and rolled out from under the rush of two more zombies. She jumped to her feet and lashed out at one, her hand smacking into its face. The zombie grunted and bit her palm, teeth tearing at her skin like a dog gnawing a bone. She yelped and punched him hard in the gut with her free hand, but didn't get any response.

The back of her neck tingled a warning. She twisted, kicking out at the dead man reaching to grab her hair. Her blow cracked against his knee but seemed to do very little damage. She swore and hit him kinetically, wrapping the energy around his neck, pulling until bone snapped and the zombie dropped.

Which still left the one gnawing on her hand. She reached again for kinetic energy, but it felt as if the madmen were shoving red-hot needles into her brain and all she wanted to do was throw up. And that certainly wouldn't get rid of the zombie clinging to her flesh. She hit it again, then with as much force as she could muster, lifted her knee and buried it deep in the zombie's groin. It might be dead but it had once been a man, and its reaction was still instinctive.

The zombie yelled, clutched itself, and dropped like a stone to its knees. She wrapped an arm around its neck and twisted hard. Bone snapped. She released it and swung around.

Ethan stood in a pile of the dead. There were scratches on his face and his shirt was torn, but otherwise, he looked unhurt. She sighed in relief.

His expression was grim when his gaze met hers. "Didn't you say the soul-sucker will sense their deaths?"

"Yep." She dragged the stake free of her belt. "And I think you were right before. I think we're better off getting out of here."

It was one thing being sore and cold when they had the element of surprise, quite another now that the advantage had slipped the soul-sucker's way.

He stepped over the dead bodies and held out his hand. "If she's around, we'll have to make her believe we don't think the kids are here."

She nodded. "We couldn't fight her in this condition anyway."

"Especially given the fact you can't use your kinetic abilities right now."

She slipped her fingers into his. They felt so warm and solid and right against her own that she felt like hanging on and never letting go. But let go she would when the time came and he still refused to admit the emotions she could see in his eyes.

"How do you know I can't use kinetic energy?" she asked as he led her into another tunnel that sloped gently downward.

"From the fact that you killed the last zombie with your bare hands." He hesitated. "And because I can feel just how bad the pain in your head is."

So the emotion sensing was a two-way deal. She wondered if he realized just how rare it was for two non-telepaths to connect so intimately. Wondered if he'd been able to feel Jacinta's emotions or read her thoughts. But she couldn't ask because she'd promised not to, so she simply said, "I'll be all right once I rest with my herbal pack for a few hours."

He nodded. The tunnel came to a junction. He hesitated, looking right. She followed his gaze, staring into the darkness and feeling the wisp of evil stirring the air. The soul-sucker was in the shadows, watching them. If they stepped her way, she'd attack. And she wasn't alone. There was another dead man with her, not a zombie but a vampire, and something else as well.

She squeezed Ethan's hand, and he looked at her. The grim set of his mouth told her he was aware of those waiting in the darkness.

"The fresh air is coming from this tunnel," he said, and she knew it was more for the benefit of the watchers than for her.

"Great," she muttered. "I've just about had enough of wet tunnels."

"There was nothing here to find anyway."

"No."

He glanced at her and raised an eyebrow, and she shrugged lightly. If the soul-sucker bought their retreat, then good. If it didn't, well, hopefully they'd return fast enough that it wouldn't really matter. And when they came back here, they'd be coming back armed to the teeth. The only problem was the time they were giving the mara to set more traps.

They retreated. Light began filtering into the tunnels, but it got no warmer. Thunder could be heard rumbling and an icy wind whisked around their legs.

They came out of the tunnel onto a ledge. Trees surrounded them, giving little hint as to their location. She shivered and glanced at the sky. The clouds were low, almost seeming to caress the treetops.

"Either we're about to be hit by the mother of all storms or we've come out near the top of the mountain," she said. "I didn't think we walked that far."

"The darkness can be deceiving. I just hope we get down to the car before the storm breaks."

She grunted in agreement and glanced behind her, staring at the tunnel's entrance as Ethan led her away. Fear rose, threatening to engulf her. Evil was gathering its forces in the darkness. If they got down this mountain without being attacked, they'd be lucky.

If they survived until night, it would be a damn miracle.

So why had they been allowed to walk free? The soul-sucker surely would have realized the zombies' attack had weakened them. It didn't make any sense to simply sit back and leave the attack until later when they had the upper hand right now.

"It makes a little more sense once you know we're being followed," Ethan murmured.

She resisted the urge to look behind them again. "By what?"

"It smelled like a wolf when I first sensed it, but it took off into the sky not long afterward."

"A dual-shifter," she murmured. "That's rare."

"Rare or not, it's probably going to follow us right back to the cabins."

"The soul-sucker must realize we're not working alone."

"I believe it was you who said it wasn't stupid."

"We can't go back." They'd lead them straight to Gwen, and while her grandmother could look after herself, she was their trump card and the one person they could not risk exposing. Not yet, anyway.

"There's a motel up near the main highway. We'll head there and call your grandmother."

She nodded. Once the attack had hit, it should be fairly safe to go back. If they both survived the attack, that was.

She tried not to think about how tired she felt. How cold she was. How bad her head hurt. Tried not to think about facing the oncoming attack with little more than stakes, silver chains, and the protection stones.

Because right now she was more frightened than she'd ever been in her life.

But why?

She frowned as she continued following Ethan down the steep slope. She'd certainly been in far worse situations than this before. If Gran and she could survive a mass attack of demons, as they had in Seattle a few years back, then surely Ethan and she could survive the attack of a couple of vampires and shapeshifters. If that was all the soul-sucker sent at them, of course.

Then it hit her.

For the first time in her life, she had something more to lose than just *her* life. There was a very real possibility that Ethan and she had created a life last night, and it was not giving that child a chance that she feared more than anything.

She lightly touched her stomach. She had to survive, not only tonight, but this whole damn case. The child she carried might be the only good thing to come out of her brief time with Ethan, and she sure as hell was going to make sure they both survived. Because even though she now had something to lose, she also had an extraordinary reason to survive.

They came out of the trees, and she glanced skyward. A solitary bird flew high up, a dark form almost lost against the deeper darkness of the clouds. It was circling, and she had no doubt it was the shifter Ethan had sensed in the tunnel. Given the strength of the approaching storm, most birds worth their salt would be seeking sanctuary right now, not riding the blustery wind.

The storm hit before they reached the car. Not that it really mattered, since she was already soaked and chilled to the bone. Ethan turned the car's heater up to full, but it didn't seem to help melt the ice that had settled deep into her bones.

"We'll be at the motel soon," he said, concern in

his eyes as he glanced at her. "You can have a hot shower there."

She nodded and wondered why he wasn't shaking with cold himself. He was as soaked as she was.

"Werewolves have a strong constitution. The cold has never really worried me."

She studied him for a moment, wondering why he was catching some thoughts and not others. He surely wouldn't be sitting there worrying about her being cold if he knew she could be carrying his child. Or was it simply a matter of neither of them being ready—or willing—to push any deeper than surface thoughts?

"So there are some good points about being a werewolf, after all?"

His gaze returned to the road. "Perhaps."

She studied his profile and saw the tension around the corners of his eyes. In the firm set of his full lips. "Why would one woman's reaction set you so against what you are?"

"I loved that woman." His voice was tight. Angry. At her, at the past.

"But unless you were born and raised in a wolf community, you must have witnessed or experienced such a reaction before. You must have been aware it was a possibility."

God, she'd certainly experienced it. And while a lover's reaction of horror and fear was both disappointing and upsetting, it was also to be expected. It was human nature to fear what you could not understand, and those who were more than human had to accept that and deal with it.

Only Ethan's way of dealing with it had been to

deny that part of himself. And that couldn't be healthy in the long run.

"It wasn't just her reaction. It was what she did—" He bit the words off and gave her a hostile look. "I thought we agreed not to talk about this anymore."

She sighed. "We did. But I'm a nosy bitch, just like my grandmother."

"Then I'll tell you what I told your grandmother. Stop trying to understand me, because once this case is solved, I'm out of here."

If I don't understand what makes you tick, what the hell am I going to tell our child when it asks about you? She swallowed the thought and the rising tide of anger, and looked away. "I know you're out of here," she replied, keeping her voice even. "You keep telling me that at every opportunity. But that doesn't stop me from being curious."

His anger, frustration, and hurt swam around her, an emotive swirl that brought tears to her eyes. What on earth had this woman said or done . . . the thought faded. She remembered him stating that no child of his was ever going to face what he'd had to face. Combine that with what he'd said only moments before—that it was what she did more than what she'd said—and the final piece of the jigsaw finally fell into place. Horror snatched her breath, and for several seconds she could only stare at him.

He glanced at her. "What?"

"She was pregnant, wasn't she?"

His knuckles went white against the steering wheel. He took a deep breath, then ground out in a raw voice, "Yes." There were some wounds that time never healed, and the loss of a child was one of them.

She placed a hand on his arm, feeling the tension under her fingertips.

He shook off her touch almost angrily. "Maybe now you'll understand why I didn't want to talk about it."

All she could understand was that by refusing to accept what had happened, he was keeping the pain of that night alive and festering deep in his soul. She didn't expect him to forget, because something like that you could never forget, but acceptance was vital if he was ever to move on with his life.

"Did she abort the child?"

"No." He took another deep breath and let it out slowly. "She said she didn't want the child of a monster in her body any longer than necessary and threw herself down the stairs."

"And it worked?"

A muscle in his cheek pulsed as he battled to not show the torment she could feel through every pore.

"I rushed her to the hospital. She told the doctors I pushed her."

"Were you charged?"

"No. While accusing me, she accidentally let the truth of what had happened slip out."

"And she lost the child?"

"Yes."

She touched his arm again. This time he didn't shake it off, but he was no more relaxed than before. "Just because Jacinta reacted that way doesn't mean every woman would."

His laugh was a short, harsh sound that hurt her ears. "If the woman I loved couldn't accept what I was, what hope is there of any other woman accepting it?"

I accept it. But he didn't want to hear that. Might never be ready to hear it if he couldn't see beyond the pain of that night. "The question is, did she love you?"

His gaze stabbed hers. "She carried my child. We were going to get married."

"That doesn't mean she loved you."

"Maybe in your free-and-easy world it doesn't, but in mine, that suggests love."

His words knifed right through her. In two simple words he'd summed up what he thought of her. But she'd never been particularly free or *easy,* despite the fact that she'd had more than a couple of lovers. Nor had she ever been inclined to give in to lust and go to bed with a man just for sex. Until Ethan.

But then, deep down she'd always known there was something more than just sex happening between Ethan and her. At least on her side.

He sighed. "Kat, I'm sorry. I didn't mean—"

"Yes, you did." She stared ahead, determined not to let the hurt show. But anger crept past her guard to roughen her voice as she added, "And I guess it's easy for you to think that because that's exactly what I've been with you."

He touched her knee. "You've been nothing short of wonderful and—"

"Yeah, I guess sex on tap is a wonderful thing for a werewolf in the midst of moon fever."

She ignored his touch, ignored the way it made her feel inside. What did it matter? He would obviously never settle for someone like her, even if she could get him to admit he was capable of feeling something more than friendship.

He didn't say anything. Nor did she expect him to, given his continuing insistence that there was nothing more than sex between them. They drove in silence until the motel came into view. He stopped near the manager's office, and she climbed out, went inside, and got them a room and some extra towels.

"I'll call Gran if you want to grab the first shower." She unlocked the door to their room and tossed him the towels as she walked across to the phone.

There was a certain amount of wariness in his expression—as if he wasn't quite sure what he should do or say. "You need to warm up more than me."

"I also need to call my grandmother."

She turned her back on him and began dialing Gwen's number. He moved away, and a few seconds later she heard water running.

"About time you called," Gwen said into her ear. "I was beginning to get worried."

"We had a few problems." Which was the mother of all understatements, but Gwen didn't need to know the details until they'd gotten out of this mess safe and sound.

"Did you find the kids?"

"Yep. But they were too well guarded, and by that time, we had nothing much left in the way of weapons."

"So why are you calling rather than coming back?"

"Because we're being followed by a hawk shifter."

"*Damn.*" Gwen paused, then added, "Where are you holed up?"

"At a motel near the main highway. We'll wait for the attack, then come back."

"I have a bad feeling about this, Kitty-cat."

So did she. Especially given that the soul-sucker had already shown she wasn't averse to using some form of explosive. It might be a case of third time lucky. "We really have no other choice."

"I doubt whether that shifter will be hanging around once he thinks you're stopping. Maybe you should just drive back here."

"He knows what car we're driving. It would be easy enough in a town this size to find it again."

Gwen sighed. "True. And right now, when we're so close to snatching the kiddies back, I don't want to run the risk of letting the mara know she's not only facing a wily young witch, but an old one, too."

Kat's smile felt tight. Right now, she didn't feel particularly wily. Just cold, wet, and annoyed. "I've got warding stones, so I can use those. Just make sure you're doing the same, in case this is all a ruse of some kind."

"I'm sitting in a circle now, and it's primed against magic and evil. I'll be okay. Just make sure you call me when the attack is over."

"Will do."

She hung up the phone and listened to the patter of water as Ethan showered. She had a sudden image of water rolling down the taut muscles of his stomach and legs and closed her eyes, fighting the desire that surged through her. She might be annoyed by the man, might be hurt by his words and his continuing determination to walk away, but she still wanted him so intensely it hurt.

In love for sure, she thought grimly. But she could never let him know. Just as she could never let him know she might be pregnant. While she wasn't so convinced he was telling the truth when he said he didn't want kids, she was sure he meant it when he said he would hate anyone who tried to trap him that way.

But even if that hadn't been the case, she wouldn't have told him simply because she wanted him to stay because he loved her, not out of a sense of honor or duty. And if she couldn't have his love, she didn't want anything else.

She walked across to the window and watched the rain come down, feeling in it an echo of the tears she refused to shed.

ETHAN PULLED A COVER OFF THE BED AS KAT PADDED naked out of the bathroom.

"Wear this." His voice was a little rough as he tossed the blanket her way. "Your clothes are still too wet to put back on."

Her gaze scooted down his towel-wrapped body, arousing him even more than he already was. Then she quickly wound the blanket around her. Obviously, she both sensed and saw just how tenuous his control was right now. Dusk was closing in fast, and the moon fever was beginning to rage in his blood. With the full moon a night away, his need for her was incredibly high. Yet right now he couldn't afford to sate that need. Not when an attack could come at any moment.

He clenched and unclenched his hands, but it did

little to ease the tension riding him so hard. He watched her emptying the contents of her jeans pockets onto the table but found his gaze drifting to her blanket-wrapped breasts. Suddenly his feet were carrying him closer. *Not good.* He swung around and strode across to the window instead. The chill of the storm eddied past the windowpane and caressed his fever-touched skin. He took a deep breath, but all he could smell was the soapy cleanness of freshly washed skin and the heat of feminine wanting. She ached as badly as he, but for an entirely different reason.

He closed his eyes, trying to ignore the little voice slyly suggesting he was kidding himself, that there was very little difference in the cause behind her desire and his.

Which was stupid. He was caught by the moon, nothing more.

He let his gaze roam across the parking lot. He had no doubt that the mara knew he was werewolf. No doubt that she would wait until night had well and truly ignited the moon fever in his veins before she attacked. Which gave them maybe a half hour to prepare themselves.

Footsteps echoed in the silence as Kat walked back into the bathroom. Frowning, he glanced over his shoulder. When she didn't reappear, he gave in to curiosity and followed her.

"What are you doing?" He stopped in the doorway and tried to ignore the way the blanket curved enticingly around her rear as she bent over.

She didn't look up. "What does it look like I'm doing?"

"Placing stones around the bathtub."

"Precisely." Her voice was vague, and there was a fierce look of concentration on her face.

"What for?"

"Circle of protection."

What she was creating was more a rectangle than a circle and encompassed not only the bathtub, but a good portion of the floor. But he guessed the intention was the same. "In here?" He couldn't help the skepticism in his voice, and she glanced up.

"Well, the bedroom is certainly out, isn't it?"

He didn't bother telling her it wasn't the location that posed the danger to his control, but her closeness. "So why not set it up in the living room?"

"Because the bathroom has one door and no windows. Easier to defend. Plus, we're traveling light this trip, so we only have small stones with us."

"And that makes a difference?"

She nodded. "The smaller the stones, the smaller the protection circle."

That made sense. Or as much sense as anything involving magic could ever make. She laid the last of the stones on the floor, then reached for the silver chains sitting on the vanity. These she carefully placed around the perimeter of the stones, hard up against the walls and across the doorway.

"Silver stops magic," he said, clenching his fingers against the urge to reach out and pull her close as she raised up, her face only inches from his.

"And, hopefully, will be our first line of defense."

Her breath was warm and quick across his face, her pupils dilated with desire. He forced himself to step back, freeing her from the aura of the wolf. She licked her lips, drawing his gaze to her lush mouth again. It took all his strength to remain still.

"Why don't you go get some bottled water in case we're here for a while? I need to finish this."

He nodded and swung away. He put on his still-damp jeans, then collected two bottles of water and a couple of chocolate bars and headed back. She was sitting cross-legged in the bathtub and motioned him to sit opposite her.

"Thought you might need some chocolate," he said, placing his collection close to her knees.

Her smile broke loose. Something clenched deep in his gut, and he suddenly found himself wanting to wake up to that smile not only tomorrow, but the day after that and the day after that . . .

"Trying to get into my pants again, huh?"

"I'm a werewolf, and it's one night away from the full moon." His voice was a little harsher than necessary, and her amusement faded. For that alone he was sorry. "What do we do now?"

She took a deep breath. "Now we must complete the circle. Hold my hands."

He placed his hands in hers. Energy seemed to surge between them, an electric touch that pulsed in time with the ache in his groin.

"Close your eyes."

He did. And saw her naked, panting with need for him. Her fingers clenched against his. "Concentrate."

"I'm trying," he ground out.

"Then try harder."

He bit back the urge to swear and forced the image from his mind.

"Breathe deeply. Draw breath until it seems to fill every pore in your body."

Her voice was a monotone. Soothing. He did as she asked and felt the tension begin to slip.

"Now, I want you to raise your body energy by tightening your muscles. Start at your toes and work your way up. Imagine the energy as a mist . . . squeeze it up through your body until it reaches our hands."

He had no idea what she meant, but as he methodically tightened his muscles, the air around him began to crackle with energy. When their fingers clenched against each other, it felt like the air was burning.

"Now, imagine that energy leaving your fingertips and fanning out in a clockwise circle around us. Imagine the two of us encased in an orb of mist. Feel the power of it pulsing through you and out into the night."

As he imagined that orb, she began murmuring. The air seared his lungs with every intake of breath, and energy vibrated through his limbs.

Then the noise died, the energy died, and an incredible silence wrapped around them. He opened his eyes. The air seemed to shimmer above her head.

"Evil and magic cannot enter this place." Her gaze met his almost challengingly. "Not for as long as we touch."

"Touching how?" He edged a little closer so that their knees rubbed and was suddenly glad he still had condoms in his jeans pocket.

"Hands on hands. Hands on body." A smile touched her lips. "Not sex, if that's what you're thinking."

"Well, damn."

She raised an eyebrow, her expression amused.

"Sex magic raises an altogether different type of power. I don't think you're quite ready for that yet."

He stared at her. "You're kidding."

She shook her head. The energy that zipped around them caught her hair, standing strands of it on end. "No. Sex magic raises a very strong energy that can be used in spells, but it's not particularly reliable when it comes to protection spells."

"Have you ever tried sex magic?" Even as the question left his mouth, jealousy surged through his veins. The thought of her with another man made him want to hit something, which was totally irrational, especially given her history and the fact that he could lay no claim on her. Not now, and certainly not in the future.

"My history?" Her green eyes narrowed dangerously, and anger touched her voice. "Shall we compare notes when it come to lovers, Ethan?"

He smiled grimly. "No. I'm a werewolf. I have had as many lovers as there have been full moons."

"Then let's not talk about *my* history. I've only had as many lovers as I have fingers."

If she was counting him as one of those lovers, that was still nine too many in his estimation. He frowned at the thought and wondered if in helping her create the protection circle, he'd somehow short-wired his brain.

"So," he repeated, "have you actually tried this sex magic?"

She hesitated. "Yes. And it was damned amazing."

He released one hand and touched her mouth, running a finger across the warm lips he ached to kiss, then down the long line of her neck. "As amazing as what we've shared?"

Her full lips opened slightly, as if she couldn't drag in enough air. "Yes."

He ran his finger around the outline of one pebbled nipple. Saw the tremor run through her. "You sure about that?"

"Yes. It's just sex with us. You said that yourself."

That he had. But he'd been lying, and they both knew it. What they had went beyond just sex. How far beyond, he didn't know and would probably never find out. But one thing he did know. He'd never experienced this level of desire and need before. Not in all the long years and many lovers he'd had since Jacinta.

Maybe not even with Jacinta.

He tugged the blanket loose until it fell to her waist and allowed her wonderful breasts to spill free. He cupped one, brushing his thumb across her nipple.

She shuddered, but her gaze darted to the door. "They come."

"Can they see what we're doing?"

"Not with this type of circle, no. They'll just feel its presence when they try to get in here."

"And as long as we're touching we're safe?"

She nodded. "I think we'd better keep one hand joined, though, just so it doesn't venture too far into sex magic territory."

He smiled. He had no intention of going that far, but he did have every intention of exploring what he could one-handed. He leaned forward and captured her lips. It became a long and tender exploration that did strange things to the rhythm of his heart and made him want her more fiercely than he'd ever dreamed possible.

He kept kissing her, kept touching her, all the while aware of the noise beyond their haven and the constant rise and fall of the energy that pulsed around them. Through them.

The fever in his blood burned as fiercely as the air itself, but an awareness of the danger that waited beyond their orb of safety was just as fierce. He wasn't about to risk her safety to sate his own needs.

After a while, silence fell and the trembling force of energy grew calm. They'd gone. The silence ticked away.

Alarm ran through him.

Silence didn't tick.

He opened his eyes and glanced toward the door. A small parcel sat in the doorway. "The bastards have left a bomb."

She grabbed him, stopping him from rising. "Don't break the circle. It could be a trap."

"It's not."

"You don't know that."

"I know I can't feel them anymore. Can you?"

She shook her head. "But that doesn't mean you can simply walk out of the circle. We have to close it first."

"We might not have the time—"

"Then we find it. Believe me, breaking this circle right now could be more dangerous that that damn bomb."

He took a deep breath and tried to calm the urge to ignore her advice and run her out of the danger he sensed was slipping ever closer. "What do we do?"

She grabbed his other hand again. "Imagine that misty field of energy again. Draw it back into your fingers and down into your body. Relax with it, loosening the muscles as you work back down to your toes."

He took a deep breath and did as she directed. The energy that pulsed around them swirled across his fingertips and slithered up his arms, easing the tension riding his shoulders before trickling down. But long before the sense of relaxation reached his toes, he heard the ticking stop.

Time had run out.

He flung himself over the top of her as the bathroom exploded into flame.

FIFTEEN

KAT WOKE TO THE WARMTH OF ETHAN'S TOUCH, THE WEIGHT of his body atop of hers, the dampness of earth and grass pressed against her spine. She kissed his fingertips as they brushed her mouth, then opened her eyes. His face was inches from hers, his eyes a heated combination of worry and lust.

"Are you all right?"

She nodded. His voice was as ragged as his breathing, and she knew it wasn't so much pain as desire. He was fighting the moon fever, but if the desperation that surged around her was anything to go by, it was a battle he was rapidly losing.

She swore under her breath and looked around. Metal loomed above them. The bathtub, upside down on top of them. While it had undoubtedly saved their lives, right now it was also trapping them.

She wondered how much time had passed. Wondered how long the mara would leave watchers to see if they'd survived.

Through the noise of the storm she could hear voices, but they were as distant as the sirens. Which was odd, to say the least. Or maybe it just meant they were buried deep under the rubble of the motel room.

"I'm going to lift the edge of the tub and see where we are and what's going on."

He nodded. Sweat dripped down his forehead and splashed onto her lips. She resisted the urge to lick the droplet from her mouth, knowing right now the slightest sexual move could tip his control past the edge.

She reached for kinetic energy and carefully lifted the tub. And gasped. Because they were no longer anywhere near the motel. It lay at the bottom of the slope below them, half demolished and wrapped in flames.

The force of the bomb had obviously blown them free, and she had a feeling the active protection circle had a lot to do with that. That parcel might have been a product of the human world, but the imprint of magic had still been on it. Maybe because the soul-sucker had handled it, or maybe because she'd used magic to put it there. Whatever the reason, that imprint had registered with the remaining magic of the stones. How they ended up this far away she couldn't say, but she wasn't about to question a quirk of fate. Not when it played in their favor.

She lifted the opposite edge of the tub and saw they were close to the edge of a forest. She swept her gaze across the darkness, but she couldn't sense the taint of magic or evil, and the only sound she could hear was the distant gurgle of water. Lady Luck had definitely stepped into their corner for a change.

"Ethan?"

His gaze jumped to hers. His eyes had slipped past humanity to become almost primordial. "I need—"

"I know what you need, but right now, we need to get out of here. Do you understand me?"

He didn't answer. Maybe he *couldn't* answer. His whole body quivered with desire, and his groin ground against hers. While it was a need he was obviously still fighting, it was one he was predestined to lose. And she had a bad feeling that if she did anything untoward—even something as simple as rising—that need would be unleashed. Which meant they had to briefly separate. The last thing she wanted was the mara realizing they'd survived, which meant she had to hide any evidence of it. Thanks to that explosion and a huge piece of luck, they'd bought themselves some time. Time from another attack, time to rescue the kids.

Maybe even time enough to ease the hunger of a moon-snared werewolf.

But that couldn't happen here.

She caught his face in her hand, holding his gaze with her own. It was a wolf in mating heat she stared at, even if that wolf still wore human form—and he was close, so close, to completely losing control. "Can you hear the river?"

"Yes." His voice came out as little more than a harsh growl.

"Your lady awaits you there," she said, wondering who he'd see there—Jacinta, her, or someone else entirely? Wondered if it even mattered when the moon had him in its grip.

"Jac?" It came out little more than a harsh rasp of sound. "No."

"Yes." She closed her eyes against the sting of tears. "She needs you, Ethan. Needs you to hurry."

He didn't reply. Energy caressed her skin, its touch warm and sharp as he shifted shape. She lifted the tub higher, and he sprang away, quickly disappearing into the night.

She loosened the damp and heavy blanket from around her waist, then shifted shape and flew up to the shelter of the nearest tree. She took a deep breath, then kinetically lifted the tub and blanket, and thrust them both deep into the surrounding trees. With any sort of luck, they wouldn't be found until this was all over.

Then she took to the skies again, flying high over the trees until she found the river she'd heard. It was deep in the forest, and she could neither see nor hear anyone close. No one except Ethan, that is. Though she couldn't actually see him, just sense the force of his wanting. It had to be dealt with now, before the fever raged totally out of control and he attacked someone.

Besides, they could hardly rescue the kids when he was in this frame of mind.

She spiraled down through the trees and shifted shape as she neared the ground. The rain stung her skin, and she shivered. This wasn't exactly the best time or place to sate a wolf's desire, but right now she had very little choice. A twig snapped behind her. She turned as Ethan padded out of the trees.

He hesitated, staring at her with eyes that were neither human nor wolf but somewhere in between and far more ethereal. He shifted shape and took off his jeans, tossing them casually into the trees. But there was nothing casual about the way he walked toward her. Nothing casual in the way he watched her. Even in human form, his eyes were otherworldly.

He stopped in front of her. She'd expected the moon-spun lust to be so great that he'd simply grab her and mate with her. That he didn't surprised her.

For several seconds she lost herself in the heated embrace of his eyes. Though the night was cold and the storm continued unabated, she no longer felt it. Barely even heard it. His warmth washed over her, through her, stirring her senses with longing.

He raised a hand, cupping her cheek. It felt like he was branding her skin for eternity.

"My lady does indeed wait."

His voice was little more than a caress of sound, yet it seemed to sing through every fiber of her being. She briefly closed her eyes against the sudden sting of tears. It wasn't Ethan speaking but the wolf. A wolf who was far more romantic than the man would ever allow himself to be.

His thumb caressed her lips. It was a gentle touch that curled her toes with wanting.

"Does my lady know what night it is?"

The heat of his gaze was melting her insides. His desire burned the air around them, even though he held himself still.

"It's the night before the full moon."

"The night of promises."

"The night of destiny." She didn't know where those words came from, and that scared her. She cleared her throat and said, "But there are no promises between us." Could never be any promises between them until he moved beyond the pain of what Jacinta had done.

He stepped so close her breasts were crushed against his bare, wet chest and his erection pressed heat against her stomach.

He slid a hand down her back, his fingers burning warmth against her spine as he pressed her closer still. "I was told I would find you here by the river, with the magic of the night rising all around us."

It felt as if he'd reached into her chest and torn out her heart. She closed her eyes against the pain. It clearly wasn't her he was seeing in the haze of his wolf lust, but rather Jacinta. Otherwise, why would he be quoting her own words back to her?

But in the end, it didn't really matter. She had to sate his hunger so they could rescue those children, and if he thought he was making love to Jacinta rather than to her, then so be it. She could worry about her breaking heart later.

She swallowed against the bitterness in her throat. "I thought you didn't believe in magic."

He brushed a sweet kiss across her mouth. "I believe in destiny."

His breath stroked her lips and made her tremble. "I'm not your destiny, Ethan." She might want to believe otherwise, but the fact that he was seeing Jacinta now rather than her only proved how wrong her hopes had been.

"You are my heart, my soul."

A tear tracked down her cheek. "I'm not Jacinta."

He didn't hear her. Or maybe he chose not to hear her. His hand entwined hers. "Kneel with me."

"We can't do this." He couldn't make whatever promise he intended to make because she wasn't the woman he really wanted. She'd been a fool to believe she ever would be.

"Kneel with me," he repeated and tugged her down in front of him.

The ground was muddy against her knees and legs, and it felt like she was going to slide backward. It was only his grip on her spine that held her close and kept her upright.

She touched a hand to his cheek, holding his gaze with her own. Trying to reach the sanity of the man deep inside.

"I'm not Jacinta. I'm not the woman you love. Whatever it is the moon bids you to do, forget it. Let's just make love."

She pressed her mouth against his, her kiss demanding. His response was immediate, almost harsh. His hands slid down her back and cupped her rear, pressing her hard against the heat of his erection. Then a shudder went through him, and he pulled back.

The wildness was sharper in his eyes. "Not yet."

She ran her hands between them, cupping him, caressing him. "I don't want promises, Ethan." Especially when those promises where meant for another woman. "I just want to feel you inside me."

His groan was more a growl as his mouth sought hers. His kiss was a possession, one that left every inch of her trembling. His body thrust against hers, but he didn't take what she so readily offered. He pulled away yet again.

"There are words to be said to the moon first." His voice was little more than a hoarse whisper.

She closed her eyes, but tears still squeezed past

her lids. "Don't do this. Wait until the moon fever passes."

"The moon calls for this promise. Some things cannot be fought." He touched a hand to her face again. "Look at me."

She opened her eyes. Almost drowned in the love so evident in his. Love that wasn't hers to take. She bit her lip, holding back the anguish that rose up her throat. "I'm not Jacinta. I'm not the woman you love."

"Dance with me," he said softly. Magic began to pulse across the night. His words were the start of some sort of spell, but one she'd never come across before.

"No," she choked, trying to pull away. He held her in place, his grip gentle but firm. "Ethan, stop this, before it's too late."

He didn't seem to be hearing her. "This night and the rest of our nights, for as long as the divine light shines in the evening skies. For as long as we live beneath it."

The pulsing became stronger, tingling across her mouth. Words spilled from her lips, words she couldn't stop, "By her light, I offer you my body."

He kissed the tears from her cheeks, then shifted their bodies, and the heat of him claimed her in the most basic way possible. It felt so right, and yet so wrong. Because it wasn't *her* he was seeing. Wasn't her he was claiming.

He began to rock inside her. She trembled, biting her lip, fighting the urge to move with him. She couldn't do this. Had to stop him. But how, she had no idea.

"Under the divine light of the moon, I offer you my heart." His voice was a stroke of heat across her lips.

She closed her eyes. It felt like her own heart was shattering into a million pieces. "Don't," she whispered, but the magic surged, and she found herself adding, "Under her light, I offer you mine."

His rocking became stronger. It felt so good she wanted to cry. "Don't do this, Ethan. Don't make promises you'll regret when the fever is gone."

He still wasn't hearing her. Or maybe the moon's spell had him convinced he was at last making the promises he'd never had the chance to make.

Would it be so wrong to give in to that dream? To pretend, just for a moment, he was seeing and making his promises to her?

Yes, she thought. It would.

He'd said he would hate anyone who tried to trap him by becoming pregnant. Why would pretending to be someone else to gain his promises be any different?

She wasn't Jacinta. She could never hold his heart, as much as she might have believed otherwise. This night, and this ceremony he seemed determined to continue, were proof of that.

"Under the divine light, I offer you my soul," he continued.

The sting of magic was becoming stronger, his movements more urgent. Sweat bathed her skin as she battled the sweet sensations rolling through her. "Don't do this. Don't say these words." Because she was certain the magic he was raising would be permanent.

She thought about pulling away again but knew it

wouldn't be safe now that the spell was under way. He might not have known what sex magic was, but that was what this spell was. And like all magic, there would be proper protocols to follow in breaking it. Without knowing those, she had no hope of stopping it—not without endangering them both.

Heat and magic shimmered between them, warming the night. Warming her. He was pushing her into a place where only sensation existed, and that was dangerous. She had to keep her head. Had to watch what she said, or she might well bind herself to this man forever.

Though in many respects, there was no need of magic to do that, because she already was bound to him in more ways than he would ever know.

His movements were filled with rising urgency. Deep down the tremors were beginning, spreading through her body like a wave. She gripped his shoulders, digging her nails into his flesh as she fought the sensations. Fought the need to just let go. Fought the words forming on her lips.

But there was no stopping them.

"By her light, I offer you mine." Moisture ran down her cheeks, dripping from her chin. Tears he didn't even see.

His thrusts became more demanding. Jolts shook her, building to a crescendo. "Oh God, Ethan, don't." But the words came out as little more than a strangled groan as her body burned with the need for release.

"Then let our souls become one as our bodies have become one."

Still the words came. "Let the moon bless and rejoice in this union."

"Do you accept the gift of my seed?" he ground out. "Do you accept the promises of the night and the moon?"

His seed. That she could accept because she was already pregnant. "Yes," she gasped. "Yes."

The dance of magic seemed to explode around them, and her climax came in a rush of power that stole her breath, stole all thought, and swept her into a world that was sheer, unadulterated bliss. A heartbeat later he went rigid against her, the power of his release tearing a roar from his throat that sounded so very briefly like a wolf howling her name to the moon.

He held her for one last thrust, then his lips sought hers, his kiss a lingering taste of heat.

"Let our souls become one as our bodies have become one. What the moon has joined, let no man break."

The thrum of magic muted but didn't entirely die at his words. In some ways, it felt incomplete. She hoped that meant the spell of binding—if that was indeed what it was—hadn't worked.

He kissed her nose, her forehead. His lips were warm against her skin and stirred the embers of desire to life. He was still hard inside her, and she wondered if that was the spell or simply the need of a werewolf caught by the moon.

"By the moon's divine light, let us now celebrate this union," he continued.

Magic seemed to flow through every pore of her being. It felt as if the moon itself was blessing her. Blessing them. She fought the sting of more tears. But right now, she could do nothing more than follow this through to the end.

And hope Ethan didn't hate her too much when he came out from under the moon's spell.

KAT BIT HER LIP TO STOP HER TEETH FROM CHATTERING and carefully eased out from under Ethan's arm. He might be immune to the cold, but it felt as if ice had settled into her bones. Making love under the stars was fine in summer, but in the midst of winter it was something close to hell. At least it was when the passion was over and you were left lying on the cold, wet ground.

The moon had long ago waned, but it had been only in the last half hour that their so-called celebrations had eased into sleep. If his snores were anything to go by, he wouldn't wake for at least another couple of hours.

Though any other man would certainly have slept beyond tomorrow.

She rose. While she was muddy and cold and more than half wishing she hadn't so readily discarded the wet blanket, she also felt incredibly invigorated. Maybe the magic he'd raised still pulsed through her blood. Or maybe it was simply all the great sex they'd shared.

Only it was more than just sex. It was a commitment. But not one meant for her.

She thrust away the pain of that thought and glanced skyward. Though the rain had stopped, the night was still bitter, and she didn't particularly want to leave him lying there naked. Frowning, she raised a hand and kinetically retrieved his discarded jeans.

Then she turned the energy on him, lifting him gently and carefully pulling his jeans up his legs.

She took the condoms from his pocket, then eased him back down. He stirred, murmuring something she couldn't quite catch. She waited until he was still again, then gathered a heap of undergrowth and leaves from beneath the nearby trees and covered him. The end result wasn't really adequate—not if she wanted to keep him from freezing to death. She bit her lip for a moment, then changed form and went in search of the blanket she'd discarded. With that retrieved, she cocooned him in its thick warmth, then covered him again with undergrowth. It would help keep him warm and provide some cover from inquisitive eyes—whether human or animal.

She lifted her arms and called to the wildness of her alternate shape. On night-dark wings, she headed back to her grandmother.

Gwen had the door open as Kat approached, allowing her to arrow inside before she shifted shape. "You just missed Ethan's boss and partner. They've been keeping me company while we waited for you two." Gwen hesitated, eyes twinkling and a smile twitching her lips. "Where have you left him?"

Kat kissed Gwen's leathery cheek. "Sleeping the sleep of the well sated. I hope. Do you mind if I shower while we chat? I need to get warm again."

She threw the condoms on the table and headed into the bathroom. Gwen followed her in and sat down on the edge of the bathtub. "Something happened out there, didn't it?"

Kat felt the temperature of the water, then stepped inside the shower. "Yeah," she said, avoiding the intentness of her grandmother's gaze by raising her face to the stream of heat. "The mara tried to blow us up again."

"I know that. Benton got a call from the sheriff stating you and Ethan were still missing after being caught in a motel explosion."

She spat the water out of her mouth and quickly explained what had happened. "If the soul-sucker thinks we're dead, it gives us a huge advantage. One we'd better take immediately."

"Then you're intending to go after her?"

"We don't dare do anything until we get those kids to safety. Once we have, you and I are free to confront the bitch."

Gwen nodded. "I don't hear Ethan's name mentioned in any of that."

"He'll be with me this morning."

"And later?"

"It's you and me. Ethan's task will be to get his niece to safety."

"And you think he'll settle for that?"

She smiled grimly. "It's what he came for. It's all he wants." Other than Jacinta. She grabbed the soap and quickly began washing.

The heat of her grandmother's gaze burned into Kat's back. After a while Kat said, "What?"

"You didn't answer my question, you know."

"That's because nothing of importance happened. You want to work up a kit of goodies I can take into the cave? I have to get back to Ethan in case he wakes."

She knew her grandmother wasn't fooled by her casual tone and words. Tears stung her eyes, but she blinked them away. Right now, she really didn't want to talk about it. Not when there were more important things to worry about.

Besides, she definitely *didn't* want to know for certain that she'd committed her heart, her body, and her soul to a man who would never love her.

Gwen sighed, then levered herself off the bathtub and walked out. Kat closed her eyes and leaned her forehead against the cool tiles. He'd told and told her he couldn't love her, but she'd refused to believe him. Until tonight. Until he'd made his promises and celebrated a union to a woman that she wasn't. It hurt. God, how it hurt!

My fault, she thought. If she hadn't been so pigheadedly certain she was right and he was wrong . . . She took a deep breath and pushed away from the tiles. Right and wrong weren't important. Getting those kids back was. Everything else would save for later.

She finished washing and quickly dried herself before heading into her bedroom to get dressed. She grabbed a sweater and boots for Ethan, then walked back into the living room.

Gwen offered her the backpack. "You've got stakes, sleep bombs that'll affect *both* zombies and shapeshifters—oh, and some masks for you and Ethan for protection—and some holy water. Be careful."

Kat swung the pack over her shoulders and gave her grandmother a hug. "Keep safe."

"I intend to kick this thing's butt, so don't worry about me."

Kat grinned and grabbed her cell phone off the table. "It'll take us an hour to get back up the mountain on foot, and God knows how long to snatch the kids. If you get a car, I'll give you a call and let you know where to meet us."

"I might let Ethan's boss in on the pickup. Might be handy if we can swap the kids into a different car somewhere along the line."

"Good idea." She kissed her grandmother, then headed for the door.

"Kat?"

She hesitated and looked over her shoulder. The understanding in her grandmother's green eyes threatened to shatter the wall she was building around her emotions.

"The promises a werewolf makes under the divine light are very rarely false ones."

"They are if the woman he sees when he's making his promises is not the one he's with," she said, and walked out.

THE SOFT SOUND OF A FOOTSTEP WOKE ETHAN. HE DIDN'T open his eyes, remaining still as he listened. Material scraped against wood, then silence fell again. The wind whispered through the trees and thunder rumbled in the distance. The air was crisp, cold, and filled with the scent of the storm, the ripeness of the wet ground, and Kat.

Her scent was on his skin, her taste in his mouth. Every intake of air seemed bathed in her essence. Longing stirred his body to life, but right now, it was a need he had to ignore. At least until he found out what had happened and how he'd gotten here.

There was only one thing he was certain of—hours

had passed. The storm had eased, and dawn had come and gone. But the full moon was closer than ever, and the hunger in his veins would continue to escalate right through the day until the animal in his soul finally took control. Only then would he be free of the burning need.

He looked around. Kat was fully dressed and sitting cross-legged on a log six feet away.

"Gwen dropped by," she said before he could ask. "She also brought some weapons."

She was lying, though why he was so certain he couldn't say. He pushed away the forest and blanket covering him and rose. Her gaze skated down his body and jumped away, but he could smell her arousal as easily as he could feel his own.

"What happened after the explosion?" he asked.

Her posture suggested wariness, and something churned in his gut. What on earth had he done?

"You don't remember?"

He caught the sweater she tossed him. "Not a lot after the explosion." He hesitated. He remembered the power of the moon singing through his veins, through the very air around them. Remembered howling her name to the moon. He brushed his fingers across his jeans pockets as he pulled on the sweater. Most of the condoms were gone, but that didn't really mean he'd used them. "I remember making love."

Relief flared briefly in her eyes, but he had a feeling it wasn't because of what he remembered but rather what he didn't. And that only made fear tighten his gut further.

"The explosion blew us and the bathtub well clear

of the motel, but the moon had you in its grip. We escaped into this forest."

"And made love?"

She tossed him his boots and looked away again, but not before he'd seen the sheen of tears in her eyes. What in hell had he done?

"Now that the moon fever has abated—"

"It hasn't," he said sharply. "And it won't now. Not until the change comes."

Her eyes widened a little, glimmering brightly in the light. "Can you control it? We need to get back to the cavern. The soul-sucker thinks we're dead, and this may be our best chance to grab those kids."

"I'll control it." He covered the distance separating them in two steps and placed a finger under her chin, turning her gaze back to his. "What happened? Did I hurt you?"

God, he hoped not, but with the heat of the moon burning through his veins, anything was possible.

Her smile seemed forced. "No, you didn't hurt me."

He frowned. She was still lying, and he wasn't sure why. "Then what happened? Why are you so upset?"

"It's been a long few days, and I haven't had much sleep. I tend to get emotional at the stupidest things when I'm tired. Don't worry about it." She pulled her chin from his grip and rose. "We have to move."

His frown deepened. "If you're tired, it might be better—"

"No."

Her eyes flashed with annoyance and something else. Something that looked a lot like desperation. It was an emotion that made no sense, though maybe it would if he could just remember what had happened between them.

"We have the advantage right now," she continued. "And we have to use it to get those kids back. How good is your sense of direction?"

"Very." And she was right about getting the kids back. The nagging sense that he'd stepped beyond some self-imposed boundary could wait until Janie was safe and in his brother's arms once again. He grabbed the pack out of Kat's hands and slung it over his shoulders. "Let's go."

He pushed through the undergrowth, forcing a path where there was none, taking the most direct route back to the cavern. She walked behind him, a silent shadow he was all too aware of.

The totality of that awareness worried him. That he'd be sexually aware of her was natural, given he was a wolf and the moon bloomed almost full. But this went far deeper. He could feel her scent in his pores, feel every breath she took. Her emotions not only swam around him but through him, so that her unhappiness became his. It made him want to turn around, pull her into his arms, and simply hold her until all the hurt faded away. Which was something she neither needed nor wanted.

But it was more than just that. He had a feeling he only had to reach out with his thoughts and he would touch hers. Completely. It was almost as if they had become two parts of a whole.

No, he thought. *It isn't possible.* He cast a troubled glance skyward. Even though dawn had passed by several hours ago and the moon had long faded from the sky, he could feel its presence. Feel its power. The full moon broke tonight, which meant the night just past had been the night of promises. A night when the power of the moon could be raised to bind. A time when soul mates promised eternity.

Kat wasn't his soul mate. He couldn't have performed that ceremony.

But what if he had?

What if, through some vicious quirk of fate, the damn spell had worked?

If it had, he'd bound them together. Heart. Soul. Body. For as long as they both lived. And while the thought sent an odd thrum of excitement through his veins, she deserved far more than just his lustful visits during the bloom of the moon. Deserved more than just his caring.

The spell *couldn't* have worked. It took love to initiate that spell. Love to complete it.

He didn't love her. Couldn't love her. Because of Jacinta.

He scrubbed a hand across his jaw and wished his memory would return. But that didn't always happen when the moon fever burned high. He could ask her, but he had a feeling honesty wasn't high on her list of priorities right now.

The slope steepened and his muscles began to burn with effort. Sweat trickled down his back, and he thrust up his sleeves, needing to get some cool air circulating across his skin. The tang of Kat's sweat flamed the sparks of desire, but her breathing was short and sharp, and that concerned him. She needed a break, needed time to recoup her strength. The thought brought a grim smile to his lips. He'd probably been responsible for sapping a fair amount of her energy during the night. And if he was honest, given half the chance he'd probably waste a whole lot more. But while he wanted her, it wasn't the urgency of the moon thrumming through his veins right now. It was something far more powerful. Something he didn't dare put a name to.

He scanned the trees ahead, listening intently. Above the noise they were making came the sound of trickling water. He angled that way, and they quickly came out in a clearing.

"We'll take a breather here," he said, squatting near the stream.

She dropped down beside him, her shoulder brushing his and sending a flash of desire to his groin. He had a sudden feeling he would always want her, moon or no moon.

But that surely wasn't love.

And it certainly wasn't what he'd felt for Jacinta.

The thought made him frown. Why, after all these years of certainty, was he questioning what he'd felt for her? He scooped up some water, rinsing his mouth before drinking. He swept his gaze around the clearing again, then glanced skyward. "We're only about ten minutes away."

"Yes."

She cupped some water in her hands, sucking at it almost greedily. There were shadows under her eyes, tiredness even in the way she held her mouth, and guilt swirled through him. He looked away, wishing, and not for the first time in his life, that he'd been born human rather than wolf. Maybe then she wouldn't have shadows under her eyes, and he could be free to love her.

"Have you got a cell phone on you?"

His voice was curt, and she frowned as she reached into her pocket.

"Why?" she asked, offering him the phone.

"To call my brother. He'll want to be there when we hand over the kids."

She nodded. He dialed Luke's number and quickly told his brother what was going on. While he couldn't yet give Luke a location to meet them, he did give him Mark's number, knowing his partner would pass the information on regardless of what Benton might say.

He hung up, then offered the phone back to Kat, but she didn't react. Water dribbled down her chin as she stared ahead. Her eyes were distant and unfocused.

"The soul-sucker hungers." Her voice was as remote as her gaze. "She's chosen her next victim—a widower who lives near the beach."

He swore softly, and she blinked. Wariness filled her green eyes again as she looked at him. "We have a choice."

"We have no choice," he ground out. "It's the lives of two little girls weighed against that of an old man."

"We could split up."

"You can't fight that thing alone, and you certainly can't send your grandmother to fight it alone. And I might not be able to handle what waits in the cavern."

"I agree." She studied him for a minute, then rose. "Let's go."

He rose with her, but grabbed her arm and pulled her into his embrace.

"What are you doing?" Her question came out as little more than a breathy whisper that stirred through his soul.

"This." He captured her lips with his own. Kissed her long and passionately. When he finally pulled away, they were both breathing as hard as they had walking up that damn mountain.

She studied him, her lips kiss-swollen, nipples straining against the softness of her sweater. But all she said was, "Why?"

He entwined his fingers through hers. "In case I don't get a chance to do it again later," he said, and led her toward the cavern and the things that waited.

SIXTEEN

KAT PULLED ETHAN TO A HALT BEFORE HE COULD ENTER THE tunnel and tugged the backpack free of his shoulders.

"Take these," she whispered, handing him some stakes. "Remember that they work against shape-shifters as well as vampires, so be careful with them."

"I don't suppose you packed my gun in there, did you?"

His warm breath skated across her skin, and a tremor of desire ran through her. "No," she replied. "Sorry, I didn't even think about it."

He grunted. "I wish you had. I'd much rather have it in my hands than a few damn stakes." But his gaze settled on her breasts, and she had a feeling that given the choice, he'd much rather have *her* in his hands.

She flicked a finger across his nose. When he looked up, she said, "Concentrate."

He didn't smile. Didn't do anything but watch her with those hungry eyes of his.

She licked her lips and regretted it the minute his gaze dropped to her mouth. "I've also got some sleep bombs in here, and hopefully we'll be able to use those." She handed him a mask. "Don't take it off until we get back out of the cavern, because these sleep bombs affect zombies *and* shifters."

He put it on, pushing it down until it was around his neck. His hand closed around hers, so warm and strong and safe somehow. Her gaze met his, and what she saw went far beyond just caring. But it was a lie, she thought, and she looked away.

His fingers touched her chin, gently drawing her gaze to his again, then he leaned forward and brushed the sweetest of kisses across her lips.

"Be careful in there," he whispered. "I'll lead until we get to the cave where the girls are."

She nodded and swallowed the anguish that rose in her throat. How could he have committed his heart and his soul to Jacinta and be so caring, so gentle, so damn *loving,* toward her? It didn't make any sense.

She followed him into the cavern, and the darkness quickly swallowed them. A hush descended. The deeper they walked, the cooler the air got. Up ahead, water fell, a rush of sound that had her suddenly wanting to go to the bathroom. Or maybe the growing knot of fear in her stomach was the reason behind that.

The sound of footsteps came from beyond the rush of water. Someone was moving around. Ethan slowed. Warm light danced ahead, but it was oddly distorted, as if viewed through a moving curtain. She blinked and realized she was seeing the light of a torch through a waterfall.

He glanced at her and held up two fingers, then pointed to the left and the right. She untangled her fingers from his and edged forward until the spray of the water danced a chill across her skin.

She knelt and swung the pack off her back. Two zombies stood guard rather than two shifters, and she couldn't help feeling relieved. In the long run, zombies were a far easier foe.

She took out two sleep bombs and tossed them left and right. There was a hiss of sound, and rust-colored smoke began to curl through the cavern. She put on her mask and motioned Ethan to do the same.

Rising, she stepped back from the water. Ethan's arms slithered around her waist, and he pulled her back against the hard length of him. She frowned and glanced up. The mask hid his mouth, but his smile was there to be seen in his eyes. He was still in control. She relaxed a little and pressed back against him, letting the heat of his body chase the chill from her spine. It felt so good, just standing here with him. So right. She closed her eyes and thrust the thought from her mind. And wondered if she'd even see him again once his niece was safe and sound.

The minutes crawled by. The smoke dissipated, and she pushed her mask down past her chin. "Are there any other entrances to this cavern?"

"There's a tunnel on the opposite side to this, and there's a door hidden by magic to the right." His breath brushed past her ear and sent a flurry of warmth across her senses.

"I'll deal with that first. You keep a watch on the tunnels."

She tried to move away, but his arms held her tight. She looked up, and her breath caught in her throat. Not just at the hunger in his eyes, but at the emotion so evident in his face. And while she might have called it love, she was just as certain he wouldn't.

He ran a warm finger down her cheek. "Would you like to see me again after this is all over?"

His touch was making her ache, but it was an ache she had to ignore. "Ethan, this is neither the time nor the place."

"A simple yes or no."

It wasn't that simple. Not anymore. "What do you feel for me?" she ground out, pulling her arm from his grip. "Because I'm not interested in being just someone you play with whenever the moon makes you horny."

He didn't say anything to that, and maybe it was just as well. She ducked through the water, the iciness snatching the heat of his touch from her body, then followed the curve of the cavern wall around to the right.

Energy began to tingle across her skin and she stopped. She dug the stones out of the backpack, then raised a hand, using the flow of energy across her fingertips to define the boundaries of the soul-sucker's hidden entrance. Once she'd determined that, she set out her stones, softly murmuring the spell that would activate her own wall and stop whatever evil might lie beyond the mara's wall from entering. The soul-sucker would undoubtedly know how to break the spell, but as long as she didn't return before they'd gotten the kids out of there, it wouldn't matter.

She placed the last stone on the ground. Power surged across her senses—a clean, warm touch that told her the spell had worked. She turned and headed across the cavern.

The two girls were lying inside a small cave. Both were naked. Both looked distressed and cold. Anger surged through her. The mara definitely had to be stopped. It was bad enough destroying the lives of grown men, but taking the future of someone so young, someone who'd barely even had time to stretch and grow . . .

"Dead men are heading this way." Ethan's voice was little more than a whisper she heard deep inside.

She raised a hand, feeling the flow of energy, trying to discern what spell the mara had used.

"Hurry," he continued. "Because there are more than one of them."

Hurry was the one thing she couldn't do. She could hurt the girls if she dismantled this spell the wrong way. Light played across her fingers, a fire-fall of energy that whispered secrets to her mind. It was a simple containment spell, one very similar to what Kat had used across the cavern. She glanced at the stones, seeking the one she had to remove first, then began murmuring the words that would dismantle the energy wall.

"They're almost here," he warned her.

She swept away the first stone and continued murmuring the spell. The wall shimmered as she swept away the second. From behind her came the noise of flesh smacking against flesh. She swept away the third stone, effectively creating a doorway in the wall. She finished the spell and swung around to see Ethan in midair, diving feetfirst at the pack of zombies fighting to get into the cavern. He hit the first two hard, forcing them back into those behind. The dead toppled like bowling pins, creating a barrier of flesh that briefly stopped those behind from entering.

"Mask," she said, putting on her own as she tossed a sleep bomb into the writhing pack of zombies.

The dead men at the back scrambled over those still fighting to find their feet. Ethan rose and swung a booted foot, knocking two more back. He didn't look like he was trying to kill them, and of that she was glad. Right now they didn't need to alert the mara to their presence.

She grabbed another bomb and tossed it deeper into the tunnel. As rust-colored smoke swirled, she dropped the pack on the ground and ran at the two zombies trying to get behind Ethan. She reached for kinetic energy and flung one back into the smoke. She slid to a stop and smacked the other across the back of the head. The zombie roared and swung around, clenched fists flying. She ducked, swept a leg around his, and knocked him onto his ass. Then she picked him up kinetically and tossed him back into the smoke as well, toppling more zombies in the process.

Dead men were beginning to drop like flies near the cavern entrance, making it harder for those behind to scrabble past. She grabbed another sleep bomb from the pack and lobbed it deeper, just in case there were more zombies waiting in the tunnel.

"You go get the two girls," she said, putting the pack back on. "Make sure you enter and leave through the gap in the stones."

He nodded and headed for the small cave holding the girls. She reached for kinetic energy again and began to stack the sleeping zombies, creating a wall of flesh that was as tall as she was and at least two arms' widths deep. If there were any more of the dead down in that tunnel, the wall would at least hamper their progress for a while. Though she had to hope there weren't too many more. There were at least fifteen piled in front of her. How many more could the mara have raised in this area without someone noticing something odd was going on?

She half turned to go help Ethan, then stopped. Noise whispered down the tunnel. Nails, clicking against stone.

A werewolf was headed their way.

But how? This smoke was just as effective on shifters as on the dead. Unless the wolf had realized what was going on quickly enough and grabbed something to use as a mask.

"Something else is coming," she warned Ethan, hurrying across to the small cave.

He'd taken off his sweater and put it over one of the girls. Then he carefully scooped both of the girls up. Neither of them moved or showed any sort of reaction, meaning that, like the other children, they'd been drugged. "Let's get out of here."

"You go. I'll deal with the shifter coming down the tunnel." She knew if she told him it was a werewolf, he'd refuse to leave her. Especially after her near escape with the last one.

His expression was grim. "I don't think that's a good—"

She touched a hand to his lips, stopping his words. "The most important thing right now is getting the girls to safety. I won't be far behind, I promise you."

He kissed her fingertips, then nodded. "You'd better not be, or I'm coming back after you."

His words did weird things to the rhythm of her heart. God, it would be so easy to believe he *truly* loved her. Except for that moonlit ceremony. Except for the fact that he'd promised himself to a woman she wasn't, even if it was only in his mind.

She followed him as far as the waterfall and dropped the backpack on the ground. There were a couple of sleep bombs left, and the holy water, but neither was much use against a werewolf.

She ripped free one of the stakes she'd taped to the leg of her jeans, tossing it lightly in her hand as she walked back to the cavern's center.

The radiating heat of the werewolf's aura hit her long before she ever saw him. Ethan might have had the moon heat under some control, but in this wolf, the fever raged free. His hunger was a force that seemed to suck the air from the room, leaving her breathless, hot, and very afraid.

Because it wasn't just lust she sensed. This one hungered for violence as well as sex. *Another of the bitten,* she thought, *and as mad as a rattlesnake*. Maybe that was why the mara chose them as guards—they were fast, powerful, and more important, didn't care who or what they killed.

For an instant she thought about retreating, but she had to give Ethan as much time as possible to get those kids free.

And it was only one werewolf. She could cope with that, surely. She'd certainly dealt with far worse in her time with the Circle.

Yet as much as she kept repeating that statement in her mind, it didn't seem to help the fear churning her stomach.

A blur of brown hair leaped over the sleeping bodies of the zombies. She clenched her fingers around the stake as the wolf came to a halt and shifted shape. As a man, he was big. Bigger even than Ethan. And like the wolf that had attacked her in the restaurant, he was all rippling muscles and golden skin.

He was also naked. And hard with wanting.

His gaze slid down her body, and she felt like a prize turkey at Christmastime—all fattened up and ready for the plucking. The wolf's gaze finally rose to hers again, and all she could see was madness. The heat of his aura blasted her skin with his desire, but beyond her breathlessness, she had very little physical reaction. It was as if she'd somehow become immune to this wolf's fever.

"I smell wolf on you." He ripped off the mask he was wearing, revealing a mouth that was thin and cruel. "I shall enjoy erasing that scent."

Bile rose in her throat. Ethan had all the time he was going to get, because she wasn't about to stand here and play with this madman. She lifted her hand and hit the wolf kinetically, smashing him back against the wall. As he slithered down the rock, she flung the stake at him. At the last moment he saw it and dodged. The white ash stabbed through his side rather than his heart. Deadly, but not immediately so.

His rage washed over her, a force so great it knocked her back several steps. With the stake lodged in his body he couldn't shapeshift, but he didn't even appear to try as he picked himself up and rushed at her.

She dodged and hit him kinetically again. Pain slithered through her brain, and she knew she'd have to watch it. She'd need her kinetic skills to cope with the mara, and she couldn't afford to overexert herself right now.

The wolf hit the wall with a grunt, bounced to the ground, and relaunched himself at her. She ducked away but wasn't fast enough. His fingers hooked around the bottom of her sweater and jerked her to a stop. He laughed—a harsh, cruel sound that made her stomach churn.

She swore, twisted around, and raised her arms, pulling herself out of the sweater. She ripped the second stake free, holding it in front of her like a knife. It was doubtful he even noticed it as his gaze slid down her naked torso. The heat of his need boiled around her, sucking away the air and burning her lungs.

He sprang again, but before he reached her there was a blur of fur and fury that hit him broadside and thrust him away from her.

Anger and relief surged in equal portions.

Ethan.

He hit the ground in human form and rose, standing between her and the other wolf. He had one hand behind his back and was flexing his fingers, as if grasping for something. She kinetically slipped the stake into his hand.

"No one touches what is mine," he growled, and launched himself at the stranger.

The other wolf might have been bigger and more powerful, but he didn't have a chance against Ethan, even if he hadn't already been stabbed with white ash. Ethan was fast and furious, and he gave no mercy. Within minutes, the other wolf was dead at his feet.

He swung around and stalked toward her. His brown eyes were more wolf than human and glowed almost golden in the torchlight. His hunger washed across her senses, and her body sprang to aching life. Reacting to him, and only him.

The spell, she thought. He might have thought he was committing himself to Jacinta, but he'd bound himself to her. Or, at the very least, bound *her* to *him*.

He pulled her into his embrace and plundered her mouth. His kiss was intense and passionate and, in many ways, an affirmation of territory. *No one touches what is mine,* he'd said. Her heart did a joyful little dance, but she had to wonder if he was even aware he'd said those words.

"Next time tell me it's a werewolf coming down the tunnel," he growled when he finally broke away.

His breathing was as harsh as hers, and his desire thrummed through every fiber of her being, stirring her in ways she'd never dreamed possible. But right now, it was a need they both had to ignore.

"Next time, trust me to take care of myself," she bit back. "Where in hell have you left the kids?"

"They're safe." He swept up her sweater and tossed it to her. "Put that on so we can get out of here."

Once she'd pulled on the sweater, he grabbed her hand and led her out of the cave. When they were under the canopy of the forest, she dug the cell phone out of her pocket and dialed her grandmother. "Where are we?" she said to Ethan as she waited for the call to be put through.

"Tell her to meet us on Mountain Road, near the Agness signpost."

"You have the kids?" Gwen questioned in her ear.

"Yes." Kat quickly passed on Ethan's instructions.

"I think it would be wise to get to a safer area before we hand the kids over."

"I'll arrange it."

"Good. And bring a couple of full kits. The soul-sucker still isn't in the cavern, so it might be a good time to check out whether she *is* breeding or not."

"Will do. See you in ten."

She hung up and stopped as Ethan stopped. He whipped away a couple of leafy branches that had been piled on top of each other, revealing the two girls tucked safely in a small depression. He picked them up and glanced at her.

"We haven't got far to go," he said.

No, they didn't. Soon it would be over, and he hadn't yet answered the question she'd raised in the tunnel.

She had a bad feeling he never would.

By the time they reached the road, Gwen was already waiting. Ethan eased the two girls into the backseat of the car, carefully buckling the seat belt around their limp, sleeping bodies. Gwen checked them over and declared them both healthy and unhurt, even though both looked a little gaunt, Janie in particular. He was relieved, but that relief wasn't complete.

Because this case was no longer solely about rescuing his niece. Someone else had entered the picture. Entered his life.

He could feel Kat's gaze on him. She was waiting for an answer, but there was nothing more he could say to her.

He didn't *know* what he felt for her. Yes, he wanted her. Yes, he cared for her more than he'd cared for any other woman since Jacinta. And he'd already told her both those things. If that wasn't enough, then too bad, because he wasn't going to lie.

But at the same time, he had to wonder if he was lying to himself.

He slammed the car door shut, then glanced skyward. Though he could no longer see the moon, the power of it thrummed through his veins. But there was a very different feel about that force now. It was intense, yes, but it was also controllable. In past months, past years, he'd spent this day in bed, unable to do anything more than sate his moon-spun lust with a willing woman. He'd never been fussy about who his partners were, and while in recent years he'd started seeing the same few faces, it hadn't always been that way.

Yet right now, he didn't hunger for just *any* woman, only the one, and the mere act of thinking about her had blood surging to his groin. But it wasn't the must-have-you-now heat of a werewolf in the midst of rutting fever. It was deeper than that. Richer than that.

Love.

But a werewolf couldn't love twice. That was part of what they were. Part of the law of the moon. Once his heart had been given, there was no going back. There were no second chances. He couldn't love Kat because he had loved Jacinta.

Hadn't he?

For the first time in his life, he wasn't so sure. But he wasn't about to say anything to Kat. He didn't want to raise her hopes only to dash them again. And if he couldn't love her, he couldn't stay in her life. He might hunger for her, but she deserved far more than that.

Yet even the thought of leaving her formed a cold, hard lump in his gut.

He took a deep breath, then turned and walked around the car. She was still watching him, her big green eyes both warm and wary.

"All set," he said, stopping beside Gwen.

"I'll just go check the kiddies a final time." Gwen reached up and kissed his cheek. "You be careful, wolf. And if all else fails, talk to your brother."

He gave her a sharp glance, but she merely smiled and turned away. He returned his gaze to Kat's. "What did she mean?"

Her shrug was tired. "I don't know."

He touched her cheek, running his fingers down to the warm mouth he couldn't seem to taste enough. A tremor ran through her and her lips parted, as if she couldn't breathe enough air. This close to her, he felt exactly the same way.

It had never been like this with Jacinta. Intense, exciting, and lustful, yes. But the air had never burned with heat the minute she walked into a room, and her smile had never done strange things to his heart.

"Tell me what happened by the stream," he said softly.

Her gaze searched his, then she sighed. It was a mournful sound. "You thought I was Jacinta."

That explained the hurt he sensed in her. "And?"

Her gaze slide away. "And you said some crazy things to the moon."

So he *had* performed the ceremony. Yet the moon

binding couldn't have worked if it had been Jacinta he'd been seeing in his mind. And it certainly hadn't been Jacinta's name he'd howled to the moon. That much he *did* remember.

"Did you take the condoms from my pocket to hide the fact we hadn't used them?" It was a guess, but it was a fairly safe one.

"Believe me, we didn't create life last night." Her voice was almost bitter, but there was an undercurrent that troubled him.

"How can you be so certain?" Because if he'd performed that ceremony, she *would* be pregnant. New life was part of the moon's gift and always the final outcome. But even if he hadn't finished the spell, werewolves tended to be extremely fertile while in moon fever.

The image of her pregnant, her belly round and full with his child, sent a surge of fierce satisfaction through his veins. He wanted that image. Desperately.

Her gaze flashed to his. "I'm a witch. We know these things."

He cupped her cheek again, then leaned forward and brushed a kiss across her sweet lips. "When I drop off Janie and Karen, I'm coming back." *For you*, he thought, but didn't say the words aloud.

Her gaze searched his. "Why?"

"Because we need to talk."

"Do we have anything to talk about? I think you've already made your intentions more than clear."

Intentions could change. *Had* changed. He might be uncertain about the true depths of his feelings, but he *was* certain of one thing. He couldn't let her go.

"Time to move, people," Gwen said behind them.

"You be careful in there," he said and kissed her again, fiercer and harder than before.

Then he let her go and stepped back. She stepped past him, then hesitated, looking back over her shoulder. "I meant what I said in the cavern. Until you can give me an answer, don't bother coming back."

She grabbed a pack from Gwen and threw it around her shoulders, then the two of them disappeared into the trees. He fought the temptation to follow them and climbed into the car. Janie and the other little girl were his priority, his responsibility, and before he could do anything else, he had to ensure they got to the meeting point Gwen had arranged with Benton.

But it was the longest half hour of his life.

An armada of cars awaited him. Benton obviously wasn't taking any chances. Medical personnel rushed over as he climbed out, sweeping the two girls toward waiting ambulances. His brother appeared out of the flow of people, a mirror image of himself except for the eyes. Luke's were blue rather than brown.

He clapped a hand on Ethan's shoulder, and "Thank you" was all he said. All that needed to be said.

"Go be with her while you can," Ethan replied. "I'll talk to you later."

Luke didn't move. "Nina's with her. I can't stay, because it's too close to dusk. What's wrong?"

Ethan hesitated. "When you performed the binding ceremony with Nina, did you ever remember much of it?"

"No." Luke raised an eyebrow. "Why do you ask?"

He shrugged. "Just curious." Now was not the time

to question his brother. Not when the ambulances would soon be leaving.

Luke half turned away, then stopped. "You were seventeen when you met Jacinta. Neither of us was as wise or as worldly as we thought we were, and she knew a good catch when she saw it."

Arguments he'd heard before. Arguments he was only just beginning to understand. "Go be with Janie."

Luke glanced toward the ambulance, then met Ethan's gaze again. "You spent six moons with Jacinta, yet you were never tempted to perform that ceremony with her. You might have loved her, Ethan, but you weren't *in* love with her. Not in the way the moon demands."

"I think I'm beginning to realize that."

"About time."

"I always was a slow learner." He pushed his brother toward the waiting ambulances. "Go see her before the ambulance leaves. We can talk later."

"With your lady in tow, I hope."

"Yes," he said. Hoped.

Mark approached as Luke walked away. "What's happened to our two psychics?"

"They're going after the thing behind all this."

Mark stopped and thrust his hands into his jacket pockets. "You do know Benton wants this woman caught and behind bars."

"You and I know that no jail will ever hold this thing."

"Maybe." Mark studied him for a moment, his expression giving little away. "We found a fingerprint match for that dead guy you had me check out at the morgue."

Ethan raised an eyebrow. "Really?"

"He's ex-military, and apparently he died twenty-five years ago. The coroner's report suggests death found him in much the same state as that old man we discovered at the farmhouse in Rogue River."

So it wasn't just any old dead the soul-sucker was raising, but her ex-lovers. The poor bastards weren't even allowed peace in death. "She's been killing a lot longer than that, my friend."

"That won't matter to Benton."

"I don't care if it matters to Benton. The only thing I care about is stopping the killing."

Mark nodded and glanced over his shoulder. "Benton's headed this way. If you have any intention of going back to help those ladies, I'd leave now."

By the time he got there, over an hour would have passed. Anything could have happened. "Thanks, partner."

As the captain made his way past the ambulances and toward Ethan, he quickly climbed into his car. He caught a glimpse of Benton's familiar red face.

"Goddamn it, Morgan, get your ass back here!"

Ethan closed the door on Benton's shout, thrust the car into gear, and sped away. And prayed to the moon that he got there before the change hit him.

Prayed that he had something—someone—to go back to.

SEVENTEEN

KAT THRUST THE LAST OF HER WEAPONS INTO THE SPEcially designed tool belt around her waist, then tossed the empty backpack on top of her grandmother's. Gwen stood in front of the concealed entrance, murmuring softly as she undid the soul-sucker's magic. Kat cast another look around the cavern. So far, it had been almost too easy. The zombies she'd stacked on top of each other still slept and would continue to do so for another four or five hours, thanks to the extra sleep bombs they'd released. She'd tossed a couple more down the tunnel, just in case, but Gwen had been certain nothing else waited down there.

But something *did* wait behind the stone wall in front of them.

She couldn't tell what it was. It wasn't the soulsucker, but it projected the same sense of evil. Gwen waved her hand and stepped back. The stone shimmered briefly, then faded away, revealing the darkness of another tunnel.

Kat flicked on her flashlight. Whoever—*what*ever—was down there in that darkness had to know they were near, so she couldn't see the point in feeling their way through the ink any longer.

"The air stinks," Gwen commented.

Stink wasn't a strong enough word. It smelled as if a hundred dead men were disintegrating down there. "I'll go first."

Kat edged into the tunnel. The floor sloped downward, heading deep into the heart of the mountain, and the darkness was so intense it felt like a living thing. Slime hung from the ceiling in long tendrils that brushed wet fingers across the top of her head as she moved forward, and in the distance it seemed to glow luminously. She swept the flashlight's beam up and down the walls, wondering why the air was becoming more and more hot and humid when the rocks were so cold.

Water dripped somewhere ahead, a steady rhythm that almost sounded like a heartbeat. Though she could still feel the evil, there was no sound of movement, no sense of anything else. Only that steady beat.

They walked on, their footsteps echoing across the stillness. The beam of her flashlight was almost moon bright against the darkness, but it didn't seem to penetrate more than a few feet ahead. The smell of meat long gone rancid got stronger, clogging her throat, invading her pores, until it felt like every breath was poison, and she was certain she'd throw up.

"Put on your mask," Gwen advised. "It helps a little."

She did, and it did. "Any idea what that smell is?"

"No. It's not zombie, that's for sure."

Any zombie that smelled *this* bad would be losing pieces of itself as it walked. "What about that beating noise?"

"I don't know."

Kat brushed aside a long green tendril. The strings of slime were beginning to curtain the path, slapping and clawing at her clothes like live things. A soft thrum began to accompany the heartbeat dripping, and magic swirled through the heat, dancing like fireflies across her skin. Sweat dripped down her face and back, its cause not just the furnace conditions but fear.

"I suspect we're getting close to the soul-sucker's hatching ground," Gwen murmured. "Be careful."

If she was any more careful she'd be standing still. "Did you ever find out how exactly this thing breeds?"

"No. The text Seline found turned out to be a false lead. All it really did was reinforce the belief that what kills a vampire will kill a soul-sucker."

"*If* we can get it in human form."

"If," Gwen agreed.

The slope began to ease off, until they were walking on level ground. Kat slowed further. Light glowed up ahead, but it wasn't the greenish fire of the surrounding slime, more a sickly red luminescence.

Her stomach began to churn. Ahead something stirred as if agitated, followed by a sloshing sound. She stopped, not liking the feel of this. Not wanting to discover the horror she sensed lay ahead.

But standing here shaking was achieving nothing. She grabbed a silver knife from her belt and edged forward. This close to that odd red glow, the mossy tendrils had become dry and harsh, so that it felt like she was forcing her way through a forest of dead fingers.

She pushed through the last veil and stopped. The

cavern before them was small and round. Fire burned in several stone circles, and it was their sickly radiance that warmed the room. The thrumming she'd sensed earlier was stronger here and seemed to ebb and flow in time to the dancing flames. That odd-sounding heartbeat had two echoes, and the noise set her teeth on edge. Magic flowed around her, through her, and the sparks skipping across her skin were almost painful.

The floor was sand rather than stone, and spotted with wide black globs she sensed were old blood. But from what? Heart suddenly in her mouth, she looked up.

And discovered not only the reason for the smell, but the way the soul-sucker bred.

Men hung from the ceiling. They weren't zombies, simply because they were still alive—and being eaten from the outside in by the creatures in the silky white sacs attached to each of their stomachs.

Kat's stomach finally rebelled, and she staggered to the side and vomited. Gwen handed her the water canteen, then moved farther into the cavern. "They look like caterpillars," Gwen said, her voice a mix of horror and fascination. "But they have human faces."

Kat rinsed out her mouth and spat the water out. "I don't want to know."

"These men aren't in any pain. Quite the opposite, in fact."

Taking a deep breath, Kat looked up. Her stomach stirred but stayed down. Her grandmother was right. They looked damn near orgasmic. She took another swig of water, then capped the canteen and slung it over her shoulders. "If this thing is similar in makeup to a vampire, then maybe it has the same sort of sexual aura that a vampire has when it feeds on humans."

"Probably." Gwen shifted. "Wonder what it needed the kids for, though."

"Does it really matter at this point?" She let her gaze roam across the men. There were five men hanging feetfirst from the ceiling, but only two had the sacs attached. The other three looked asleep—and were dreaming of sex, if their expressions were anything to go by.

Two children dead, and two larvae created—though the mara had obviously intended to create five offspring.

"Well, of course it did. It's not like this mara is the only one—" Gwen paused, then swore violently. The trepidation crawling across Kat's skin sharpened. If her grandmother was swearing *that* strongly, something was seriously wrong. "What?"

"Their faces. Look at their damn *faces*."

She did. And saw what her grandmother had seen. These things were the image of the two dead children.

"*That's* what's she's using the souls for," Kat whispered, sickened to the core. "She's somehow transferring them into her offspring."

"Yes, and I suspect that's how a mara gets its human form."

"Meaning if we kill these things, we're killing the two kids all over again?"

"No." Gwen's gaze was hard as it met Kat's. "The mara devoured their souls. They are dead, both in this lifetime *and* future ones. What we see here are grotesque echoes of what they were."

"Then how—" Kat hesitated, glancing quickly behind her. Though she heard no sound and couldn't feel the approach of anything evil, she had a vague suspicion they were no longer alone under the mountain.

She backed toward Gwen, knuckles white with the force of her grip on the knife as she watched the cavern's entrance. "How do we get rid of these larvae?"

Gwen hesitated. "We're going to have to stake them, then burn their carcasses with the holy water."

Kat's stomach was on the move again. Maybe it hadn't been such a good idea to swallow that extra water. "What about the men those things are feeding on?"

"They're mostly shifters. Staking should kill both host and parasite."

Interesting, given that the kids the mara had stolen were also shifters of one kind or another. Maybe she could infuse her young with the echoes of only those who were not human.

Awareness crawled across her skin, sharper than before. She gripped the stake tighter. "Then we'd better hurry, because I've got a bad feeling the soul-sucker is headed our way."

"If she isn't, she soon will be." Gwen's voice was grim. "I'll handle this. You keep track of the mara."

Kat stepped out from under the human chandeliers, stopping close to one of the sickly fires. Heat caressed her legs, but it was more magic than actual warmth. Yet it had a different feel than the magic that throbbed all around them.

There was a grunt of effort from her grandmother, followed quickly by a high-pitched, inhuman scream. The cavern seemed to shudder as if in pain, then fury rent the air. Kat pulled a small jar of holy water free from her belt and waited.

A second scream followed. The air around her burned, and the tremor was more noticeable this time. Evil was an express train bearing down on them.

"Gran, I don't think we're in a real cave," Kat said, raising the jar and getting ready to throw.

"No, we're not," Gwen responded. "The mara has changed the structure of the mountain to make this cave. It exists only through magic."

The ground pitched, rolling like an animal in pain. Kat rode the waves and tried not to think about the force of hate and rage and desperation headed their way. Tried not to think about the fact that they still weren't exactly certain how to kill this thing.

Smoke roiled into the room as Gwen flung holy water at the first of the soul-sucker's offspring. Kat flicked the top off the jar and hurled the water at the angry, turbulent smoke, keeping it back and away from her grandmother. The air screamed, and the vibrations under their feet became more erratic.

Gwen flung a second vial of water. The smell of burning flesh joined the cauldron of smells, and Kat's stomach began to heave as violently as the floor. The smoke twisted and writhed, as if it, too, was being burned by the water finishing its offspring. With another scream, it arrowed its way toward Gwen. Kat hit it kinetically, forcing it back again. She grabbed a stake and dove forward, slashing at the soul-sucker with the white ash.

Only to find the stake gripped in a fist of iron as the mara found form. Black eyes gleamed malevolently at her as the soul-sucker snarled, revealing teeth as pointed as any vampire's. Kat didn't give the bitch a chance to bite. She thrust her back kinetically, ripped free another stake, wrapped it in energy, and flung it hard. The soul-sucker dodged, but not fast enough. The stake buried itself deep into her thigh—not a deadly wound, but one that pinned the mara to human form.

But a human form that had a vampire's speed.

With another scream, the soul-sucker blurred, arrowing straight at Gwen.

"Look out!" Kat ripped another jar of holy water free, but the earth rolled and heaved underneath her, and she staggered sideways. She swore, battling to keep her balance as she tossed the water. Most of it soaked Gwen as she rolled out from under the soul-sucker's grasp.

Wood flashed, and her grandmother screamed. Fear hit Kat like a punch to the gut, and for an instant she couldn't even breathe. All she could see was the blood flowing freely past the stake that pinned her grandmother's arm to her side. Kat screamed a denial, grabbed another stake, and launched herself at the mara.

It swung and raised a hand. Energy bit through the air, but Kat hit it with her own, holding the surge in place as she rolled under the flashing flow of power and stabbed upward with the white ash.

Flesh and bone briefly impeded the white ash's progress. Kat swore and thrust it through kinetically.

A shocked look crossed the mara's face, then the flow of energy died, and so did the soul-sucker.

An explosion rent the air, and the floor's thrashing became even more violent. With a sob, Kat scrambled toward her grandmother, barely able to see through the tears coursing down her cheeks. The wound in Gwen's side was bad, blood flowing freely, but the stake had also shattered bone as it had gone through her grandmother's arm. They wouldn't be flying out of here—that was for sure. Ripping out the stake, she grabbed a bandage from her belt and thrust it hard against the wound in Gwen's side.

"Gran?" she sobbed, touching her grandmother's face, then feeling her neck for a pulse.

Gwen's eyes opened, the green depths hazy with pain. "Those little pigstickers sure do hurt when they bite into your flesh, don't they?" She reached up, gently patting Kat's cheek. "Don't worry, Kitty-cat. I'll live to give those kids of yours hell."

Relief surged along with more tears. "Kid," she said, helping Gwen into a sitting position. Kat grabbed the last of the bandages and quickly dressed the wound on her grandmother's arm.

"Nope." Gwen's voice was little more than a wheeze. "I did a scrying. It's twins. Runs in his family, apparently."

Dust and bits of blackened flesh began to rain on them. Kat glanced up and saw a huge fissure snake across the ceiling. "This place is coming apart."

Gwen nodded. "The mara's magic created it and sustained it. Now that she's dead, there's nothing to hold it together."

"Then we'd better get the hell out of here."

"Best idea I've heard yet."

Gwen pressed her hand against the bandage as Kat slipped her arm under her grandmother's shoulders. They staggered forward, but any sort of speed was impossible against the pitching floor. It felt like they were wading through a sea of earth. The dust raining down became stone, and Kat swore as chunks got bigger and bigger, forcing them to duck and weave.

Her fear stung the air, and every breath was a rasp that tore at her throat. She was shaking as badly as her grandmother by the time they reached the tunnel. The moss slapped and swayed against them, wrapping around their arms and legs like dried snakes, impeding their progress even further.

They were never going to make it out of here. Not at this speed. There was only one thing she could do . . . She took a deep breath, then kinetically lifted her grandmother and ran like hell back up the slope.

Behind them, the vibrations erupted, and a deep, rumbling roar that sounded like a wave of water headed their way. Hot air punched her, pushing her forward at knot speed. She battled to keep upright, battled to keep her grandmother wrapped in kinetic energy and moving far ahead of the immediate danger. But there were madmen in her head, pressing white-hot needles into her brain, and her vision was blurring with pain.

It couldn't be helped. This was the only way she was going to get both of them out of there alive. Dirt and stone began to dance around her feet, racing her up the tunnel. The roar behind her was getting closer, and the floor cracked and heaved so that it felt like she was climbing unstable steps.

With a clap as sharp as thunder, the roof split and fell. She screamed, flinging up her arms to protect her head as dirt and rock rained down. Stones hit her back with bruising force and she crashed to her knees, tearing her jeans and skinning her knees against the jagged flooring. The madmen in her head were going crazy, and it felt as if her brain were about to tear apart. Her kinetic skills slithered away, and from up ahead came a distant grunt as Gwen hit the ground. Kat hugged her body, rocking back and forth, fighting to breathe and unable to move, yet knowing she had to if she and her grandmother were to survive.

The roar behind her was so close she could feel its approach rumbling across her skin. Waves of moist earth were lapping at her feet, getting thicker and deeper with every rapid breath she took.

Move or die, she thought, and thrust upright. Her stomach rolled, and for a second, the world went black. She staggered forward, trying to find her grandmother in the heaving, disintegrating darkness. The floor lurched again and she slipped, going down on both knees. Pain was a wave of red heat radiating down from her head. Her breath tore at her throat and every muscle trembled. She briefly closed her eyes, trying to find the strength to rise. To go on.

Hands grabbed her and pulled her upright. The warm scents of earthy spices and forest spun around, momentarily warming her soul.

Ethan.

He swung her into his arms and ran. She struggled against his grip, fighting to get loose. "We can't leave Gran!"

"She's safe." His reply was little more than a throaty growl that vibrated through her.

Relief surged through her, even though she knew neither of them was safe yet. But if she had to die, at least she'd die in the arms of the man she loved. She wrapped her arms around his neck and held him tight. The river of dirt and stone was almost knee-deep, but it didn't seemed to impede his progress as he raced them out of the tunnel.

Light began to invade the darkness, but it was the dusky glow of evening rather than the brightness of afternoon. Alarm spread through her, and she glanced quickly at Ethan's face. His expression was fierce, determined. His eyes were the eyes of a wolf, and a golden halo of energy seemed to be forming around his dark hair. The arms that held her so close, so safe, were trembling, and his heart raced. Not with the effort of running her out of the tunnel, but fighting the change dusk was bringing ever closer.

The wave of earth behind them broke, then exploded, and it seemed as if the whole damn mountain was coming down on top of them. Ethan's curse echoed in her ears as he dove for the tunnel's entrance. He twisted as he flew through the air, cushioning her against him as they hit the ground and slid down the path and into a tree.

For a moment, neither of them moved. Rocks and dirt raced past them, but the flow quickly eased and silence fell.

Kat closed her eyes and breathed deeply. They'd survived. Against all the odds, they'd survived. She looked up as Ethan brushed his fingers across her cheek, momentarily losing her soul in the warmth of his wild eyes. But before she could say anything, before he could say anything, the firefly dance of energy flashed down his body, and it was a wolf she was staring at, not a man.

She silently cursed the moon and rolled to one side. He scrambled to his feet and leaped away into the trees. She climbed to her feet, waited until the world stopped spinning, then went to find her grandmother.

EIGHTEEN

ETHAN WALKED INTO THE SMALL HOSPITAL WARD AND WAS relieved to find Gwen sitting up and looking well. He knew without looking that Kat wasn't here, but she had been. The air still carried her warm scent.

Gwen didn't seem all that surprised to see him, and her smile was full of mischief. "I told Kat it wouldn't take you long to find us."

It had taken him two days once the effects of the moon had worn off, and that was precisely forty-eight hours too long. "I'm a cop. Finding people is part of my job." He handed her the roses he'd brought her and leaned forward to kiss her offered cheek. "But I was more than a little pissed that you and Kat didn't leave contact details with someone." In truth, he hadn't been as angry as he'd been afraid that Kat had come to her senses and wanted nothing more to do with him.

"You know where we live, Detective. You would have found us there eventually."

Eventually wasn't good enough. There was too much left unsorted between him and Kat, and so much he had to tell her. "There are lots of good hospitals in Oregon. You didn't have to fly to L.A. to get treatment."

Gwen patted him with her good hand. "I won't be flying anywhere for a few days yet. Not with this arm."

He raised his eyebrows. "So you can also assume the shape of a raven?"

She nodded. "It's not something we want the world to know, and especially not something we want the medical profession at large to be aware of."

He glanced around the room. "So this hospital caters to your—our—kind?"

She nodded. "Funded by the Circle and staffed by its members. There are six centers altogether. This was the closest to Oregon."

"And the private jet that swept you down here?"

"You *have* done your homework." A smile dimpled her cheeks. "Also thanks to the Circle."

This Damask Circle was obviously a whole lot bigger than what his investigations had led him to believe. "When are they letting you out?"

"In an hour or so, after the doc sees me." Her eyes twinkled. "I know you didn't come all the way down here to chitchat with me, Detective. If you want to see her, she's in the gardens, getting some fresh air and having a cup of coffee. Seeing it's so hot, I suggest you try the gazebo first."

"Thanks."

He kissed her cheek again and headed out of the room, making his way down the corridor and out the rear entrance. Sweat began to trickle down his back almost as soon as he entered the sun, and he beat a hasty retreat to shade, his heart racing a mile a minute as he followed the path through the trees. It felt like forever since he'd last seen Kat. Forever since he'd last held her.

He came into a small clearing and saw the gazebo—and her. The sheer force of love and passion that tumbled through him made him stop. All he could do was stand there and drink in her image. She leaned against the arch of the doorway, staring at the small waterfall dribbling into a lily-filled pond. She wore a short T-shirt and a soft, swirly skirt that caressed her thighs. She had never looked prettier or more desirable. He wanted to grab her and make love to her right there in the gazebo, but first he had to apologize for his stupidity. And for hurting her.

He took a deep breath, then continued on to the gazebo.

THE WARM SCENT OF SPICE AND FOREST HIT KAT. FOR A second she froze, certain it was only wishful thinking. Then she heard the soft footsteps behind her, and her heart leaped. Joy surged, but just as quickly fled. Because while she could hear him, she couldn't *feel* him. It was as if he was keeping his emotions in check, and that scared her. What if he couldn't answer the question she'd asked in the cavern? What if he decided it was simply easier to walk away? But if that was his intention, would he bother coming all this way to say good-bye? She didn't know. She might love this man, but they really didn't *know* each other. And right now, she wasn't certain they ever would.

She put down her coffee and turned around. The nut-colored eyes that had haunted her dreams the last few nights met hers, his gaze all but consuming her. Her breath caught somewhere in her throat, and for a second all she could do was stand and stare. Then his hands slid under her shirt and around her waist, his touch sending a flash fire of desire across her skin as he pulled her close to him. But that flash fire was nothing compared to the heat in his eyes. Her heart snagged right along with her breath, and the whole world seemed to spin around her. He leaned forward, his mouth capturing hers, his kiss passionate and tender and oh so wonderful.

"I missed you," he whispered, his breath warm against her lips when he finally pulled away.

"It's was only two days." Even though it *had* felt like an eternity.

"Two days and one night," he corrected, gently brushing the back of his finger down her cheek. "You have no idea how angry and how scared I was to arrive back at our cabin the following morning to discover you and Gwen gone."

His words sent hope and joy tumbling through her. She wrapped her arms around his neck and lightly kissed his chin. "You were scared? I can't even imagine that."

"Then walk away from me now, and you'll see true terror."

His words seemed to echo through every fiber of her being. Never had she heard eleven sweeter words. She smiled and let her gaze search his. "Do you want me to walk away?"

"Not ever." He hesitated. "Can you ever forgive me?"

She raised an eyebrow. "For what?"

"For hanging on to a dream that didn't exist."

"Jacinta?"

He nodded. "I loved her, but I don't think I was ever *in* love with her. As my brother pointed out, I was never tempted to perform the moon ceremony with her."

Her throat went dry, and the giddy sense of happiness died a little. "But you did perform it—the night before the full moon. It was Jacinta you were seeing, not me."

The smile teasing his wonderful mouth made her heart do another heady dance. "Did I ever say her name?"

"Yes. When I told you your lady was waiting, you said Jac—"

He raised an eyebrow. "I also said *no*, if you remember."

"Because somewhere deep inside, you knew she *couldn't* be waiting for you?"

"Or I was simply denying that *she* was my lady."

And with that, he kissed her. Long and hard. When he pulled back a second time, his feelings were in his eyes. The air sang with the sheer depth of them, so that it felt like she was breathing in his love with every breath.

"I was seeing *you*," he said. "It was your name I howled to the moon. It appears my animal half was certain that I loved you even when my human half continued to dither."

"Then I'm glad the full moon was close and the wolf took charge, because I think I fell in love with you the first time I met you."

"Then marry me. Let's finish what the moon began."

The tears in her eyes made his face shimmer before her. "Yes. Though there is something I should tell you."

"That you're not the only shifter in your particular family unit? I know. Gwen told me."

"I bet she didn't tell you I'm pregnant."

"No." Amusement tugged his lips, and his eyes shone. "I figured that out myself. There could only be one reason why you were so certain you didn't get pregnant the night we made our promises—because you already were." He brushed his hand down her hair. "I don't think I can ever describe how happy I am. Or how fiercely I want to see you round and fat with our child."

"Children," she corrected with a smile. "Gran tells me I'm carrying twins."

He didn't seem surprised. "I hope they're girls. I hope they have their mother's beautiful green eyes and midnight-colored hair."

She cupped a hand against his cheek and ran a thumb over the lips she could kiss forever. "I thought most men wanted sons."

"I'm not most men."

She let her fingers trail down his chest and stomach until she touched the hard length of him. "Definitely not."

He grinned and pressed her back against the gazebo's wall. "I can feel the wolf taking charge again."

His hands slid up to her breasts and slowly, teasingly, he brushed his thumbs across her aching nipples. As the ripples of sweet sensation flooded across her body, she found herself hoping there were no other people in the garden. If there were, they'd be seeing a little more than trees and shrubs all too soon.

"This wolf of yours seems to have an exhibitionist nature," she gasped.

His touch slid down her waist, and the sound of the skirt's zipper being pulled down filled the silence. "It's the company I keep. She drives me insane."

A feeling that was totally mutual. "Promise me two things."

"Anything," he murmured, pushing her skirt past her hips.

"Promise to give me lots of children."

He looked up, and his eyes were filled with such fierce love, her heart quaked. "I intend to."

"And promise never to curb the wolf's desires."

His wicked grin was the only answer she would ever need.

If you loved *Circle of Desire,* be sure not to miss the first book in the thrilling Spook Squad series:

Memory Zero

by

Keri Arthur

And stay tuned for the next two books in the Spook Squad series—*Generation 18* and *Penumbra*—which will follow at one-month intervals.

Here's a special preview:

IT WAS THE TYPE OF NIGHT ONLY THE DEAD COULD ENJOY—as dark as hell, and as warm as the Antarctic. Add to that the bonus of rain that bucketed down, and it was no wonder the streets were deserted.

Well, almost deserted, Sam amended, glancing at the alleyway across the street. An old man in a threadbare coat rummaged through the garbage bins that were lined up behind the Chinese restaurant, filling a plastic bag with God-knows-what. And not five minutes ago, two prostitutes had come knocking on her car's window, their faces almost blue with cold as they'd tried to convince her to take them for a ride. Their expressions, when she'd flashed her badge, were almost relieved. But then, a warm cell-block was certainly more enticing than trying to ply their trade on a night like this. Had she not been waiting for her partner to turn up, she might have taken them downtown and charged them with soliciting, just to get them off the street and warm again. Prostitution might be legal these days, but it was restricted to certain areas, and this particular street wasn't one of them.

But she'd had no choice except to let them go with a warning. To say they weren't happy with this stroke of fortune was an understatement. Obviously, they'd been looking forward to being locked up in a warm cell. And right now she knew exactly how they felt. Even a cup of the shocking coffee they served at the station house would be heaven right now.

She glanced down at the onboard computer and noted that it was already after three. If her goddamn partner didn't turn up soon, she was heading home. Why the hell he'd insisted on meeting in this ratty section of the city in the first place was beyond her. It wasn't even close to their patrol zone.

Sighing, she crossed her arms and glanced out the car's side window again. A plastic bag tumbled down the road, ghostlike in the darkness. Unease pricked across her skin, though she wasn't sure why. Maybe it was just nerves. After all, it wasn't every night she got an urgent call from a man who'd been missing for weeks. And it certainly wasn't every night that she went against department policy and agreed to a secret meeting.

She glanced back to the alley. The old man had disappeared. While she knew he'd probably just moved beyond her line of sight, that vague sense of unease increased. She stared through the rain-washed darkness, watching for some form of movement that would indicate the old man was still there.

Nothing.

And instinct was insisting something was very wrong in that alley.

She rubbed a hand across her eyes and silently cursed her partner's tardiness. She didn't need this, not after a fifteen-hour shift—and especially not in a patrol zone that wasn't hers. Just thinking about the extra paperwork made her head ache.

Still . . .

She leaned forward and pressed the locator switch. The onboard computer hummed to life, producing a map of the immediate vicinity. The only way out of the alley, besides the entrance she could see, was via a fire escape on the building that housed the Chinese restaurant. She stabbed a finger at the screen and the computer immediately listed other occupants. The top two floors were empty, but the second floor was rented to an R. C. Clarke.

She frowned again. The name rang a bell, though she didn't know why. She pressed the screen a second time, but the computer had no additional information. For several seconds, she blindly watched the rain race down the glass. It was very wet out there. But the sooner she got out and investigated, the sooner she could get back to the relative warmth of this icebox they had the cheek to call a squad car.

With a slight grimace, she opened the glove compartment and retrieved her wristcom. In reality, it wasn't just a communications unit, but more a two-inch-wide minicomputer capable of doing just about everything but make coffee. She wasn't supposed to be using it after hours, but there was no way she was going into that alley without it. Not when unease sat like a lead weight in her belly. If things went wrong, she wanted an electronic record of everything that happened.

After fastening the unit onto her wrist, she flicked the Record button, checked that it was working, then collected her gun and climbed out of the car. As the door automatically locked behind her, she zipped up her jacket and eyed the dark alley. It was quite possible that this was some sort of setup. In the last few weeks, five detectives had disappeared, one of them Jack, her partner. And while he'd finally contacted her earlier this evening, it was extremely odd that he'd called neither headquarters nor Suzy, his wife. She knew, because she'd checked.

It worried her.

And it was what held her still, even as the drenching rain sluiced off her coat and soaked through her boots. Jack loved Suzy more than life itself, and there was no way he'd contact Sam before he contacted his wife.

Though the fact that he had would only add fuel to Suzy's almost obsessive jealousy. Suzy had always resented Jack's closeness to his partner, and while Sam respected Jack's relationship with his wife, she'd never warmed to the woman.

The wind lifted her hair and wrapped icy fingers around her neck. She shivered, but it had nothing to do with the cold. Suddenly, the night felt very wrong.

Which was crazy. It was probably just the cold, the rain, and her severe need for sleep. If Jack hadn't made an appearance by the time she checked the alley, she was going home. She didn't need to be involved in another of his stupid games, in the dead of the night, after a very long shift. If he wanted to talk to her, he could do so during the day. He knew where she lived—and knew he was welcome there anytime. She clipped the gun to her belt. Its familiar weight offered a sense of comfort from the unease that still stirred through her as she walked across the road.

The rain eased a little as she entered the alley, but the wind danced through the darkness with a forlorn moan that made the hairs on the back of her neck stand on end. She hesitated, her gaze skating across the shadows. The old man's possessions were strewn across the ground near the garbage bins. They amounted to little more than a few old books, a couple of credit cards, and the scraps of food he'd ferreted out of the bin.

She bent and picked up the cards. The names on them were all different—Joseph Ryan, Tom King, Jake George. Obviously, the old guy had not been above a little credit fraud. She dropped the cards, then stepped across the books and cautiously walked deeper into the alley. The darkness was blanket-heavy, but her eyes slowly adjusted. Shapes loomed through the ink of night. On the right-hand side of the alley, a dozen or so large boxes were stacked haphazardly against a graffiti-covered wall, and to her left was the fire escape that zigzagged up the restaurant wall.

She walked past the rusted metal ladder, then stopped. With the full force of the wind blocked by the buildings on either side, the smells that permeated the alley came into their own. Rotting rubbish, puddles of stale water, and the faintest hint of human excrement all combined into a stomach-churning stench. She shuddered and tried breathing through her mouth rather than her nose, but it didn't help much.

Twenty feet away the alley came to a dead end, blocked by a wall at least fifteen feet high. Unless the old guy had springs for legs, or wings hidden under his threadbare coat—both of which were certainly possible in this day and age—there was no way he could have gotten over it. She glanced across to the boxes. It didn't make any sense for him to be hiding there, either—especially when he'd abandoned his belongings to do so. Most street people clung to their few possessions with a ferocity only death could shatter. Besides, the rain had turned the boxes into a sodden mass that would have collapsed with the slightest touch.

Which left only the fire escape.

She glanced up. Moisture dripped from above, splattering across her face. She wiped it away with her palm, then frowned and glanced down. Why did the rain suddenly feel warm?

In her heart, she knew the answer to that question even as it crossed her mind. Grimly, she pressed a small switch on her wristcom. Light flared from the unit—a pale yellow that glowed uneasily against the darkness. She raised her arm and shined the light on the metal walkway above her.

As she thought, it wasn't rain dripping down from the fire escape, but blood. But there wasn't a body—or, at least, not one that she could see from where she stood.

For a moment, she considered contacting headquarters about a possible homicide. But Jack had asked her to come here alone, had specifically asked her not to contact them. She didn't understand why and, in the end, she didn't really care. He'd been her partner for close to five years, and she trusted him more than she trusted the boneheads and politicians back at headquarters.

Wiping her palm down her thigh, she reached back for her gun. Then slowly, cautiously, she began to climb.

Three flights up she found the old man. He'd been thrown against the far edge of the landing, his body a broken and bloody mass that barely resembled anything human. She closed her eyes and took a deep breath. Death was never easy. In her ten years on the force, she'd come across many of its faces, yet it still had the power to shock her.

Especially when it was as gruesome as this.

The old man's eyes were wide with fear, his mouth locked in a scream that would never be heard. His flesh had been stripped from his face, leaving a bloody mass of raw veins and muscle. No vampire had done this. In fact, none of the nonhuman species currently on record were capable of an act like this.

She took another deep breath, then knelt by the old man's side and felt his neck. No pulse, as expected, but his skin was still very warm. The murderer had to be close.

Really close.

Metal creaked above her. Her pulse rate zooming, she grabbed her gun and twisted around, sights aimed at the landing above her. Nothing moved. No one came down the stairs. The wind moaned loudly, but nothing else could be heard beyond the harsh echo of her breathing.

Cautiously, she rose and walked back to the ladder. One more flight and she'd reach the roof. Whoever—or whatever—had done that to the old man might still be up there.

She had to call for backup. There was no other choice, not in a situation like this. Pressing the communication switch, she waited for a response and quickly asked for help. The closest unit was seven minutes away.

Her gaze went back to the landing above her and she bit her lip. Was there anyone up there? Was Jack up there? Or was this all some sort of weird setup? No, she thought. He wouldn't do that to her. And it had been him on the com-link. Her security system had identified his voice. So the fact that the old man had been murdered at the same time she was supposed to have met her partner had to be coincidence.

But where was Jack?

She glanced down at her wristcom. It was twenty-nine minutes past three. It wasn't unusual for him to be late. In the five years she'd known him, he'd managed to be on time only for his wedding.

Maybe he was here. Maybe he was a victim of the creature who'd destroyed the old man.

Panic surged at the thought. God, she couldn't risk the wait for backup, not when Jack's life might be at stake. She had to go on. She had to try to find him. If the department decided to discipline her for leaving a crime scene, then so be it. As long as she found her partner safe and sound, she didn't really give a damn.

As she reached the top landing, the full force of the wind hit her, thrusting her back a step before she regained her balance. Shivering, she dragged her coat zipper all the way up her neck, but it didn't stop the rain from getting past the collar and trickling down her back.

"This is great, just great," she muttered, wiping the water from her eyes—a totally useless gesture, given the conditions.

Visibility was practically zero. If there was someone up here with her, all they had to do was remain still and she'd never even see them. With a final, regretful glance back to the fire escape, she moved forward. After a dozen steps, a dark, boxlike shape loomed out of the grayness. Stairs to the rooms below, presumably.

She found a door and tested it cautiously. The handle turned. With her back to the wall and her gun raised, she pushed the door open and listened for any sign of movement. Still nothing.

Yet instinct told her the murderer had to be inside. There was nowhere else he could be, nowhere else he really could have come from. Unless, of course, he could fly. But if he could fly, why would he have used the fire escape? Why wouldn't he have just dragged the old man's body down to the end of the alley rather than up the stairs, then flown away?

No, he was here, down those stairs, somewhere.

She switched the com unit's light back on, then crossed her wrists, holding the gun and light to one side of her body as she edged forward.

The light gleamed off the metal stairs and puddled against the deeper darkness of the room. Three steps down, she halted again, listening. The silence was so intense it felt as if she could reach out and touch it. With unease growing like a weight in her stomach, she frowned and edged down the remaining steps.

In the small circle of light she could see several stacks of chairs lined up against the wall. Beyond that were the vague shapes of upturned tables. Obviously, someone was using the empty floor as a storage facility. She moved across to the first stack of chairs and stopped again.

Something hit her—an invisible force that came out of the darkness to slam her back against the wall. Her breath left in a whoosh of air, and for several heartbeats, she saw stars. Then her senses seemed to explode outward. Just for an instant, the darkness became something that was real, something that had flavor and taste and body. And then she realized that it did have bodies, and that she was sensing its inhabitants through every pore and fiber of her being. As if, in that one moment, she inhabited the skins of the beings out there in the shadows, learning their secrets, feeling their thoughts.

One of those who hid in the shadows was a vampire.

The other wasn't human, wasn't vampire, and wasn't anything she actually recognized. But it was filled with an evil so complete it seemed to seep into her very bones and made her soul shake.

The sensation then disappeared with a snap that left her weak and shaking. She collapsed onto her knees and took a deep, shuddering breath. What the hell had happened? Never in her life had she experienced anything so weird . . . or so frightening. For a brief moment, she'd become one with those others. Had felt the uneven pounding of their hearts, the rush of blood through their veins. Had felt their desire to kill seep through her being and become her own.

She wiped a trembling hand across her brow. The sooner backup got here, the better. A vampire intent on grievous bodily harm she could handle. That other thing, whatever it was, tipped the odds way too far in favor of the bad guys.

She forced herself upright, pressing her back against the wall as she listened to the silence. Still no sound or movement. Warily, she took a step toward the stairs and then stopped. A light prickling sensation ran across her skin.

Someone approached.

Not understanding what was happening, she nevertheless clicked the safety off her gun and held it at the ready. "Police! Come out with your hands up."

Laughter ran across the stillness, soft and warm. Laughter she'd heard before. Laughter she knew.

"I never could sneak up on you, Ryan."

Jack stepped into the small circle of light and stopped. She lowered her weapon, but she didn't relax or reapply the safety. Not until she knew what the hell her partner was up to. Not until she knew whether he was with those other two she'd sensed. Trust was one thing, complete stupidity another. "What the hell is going on? And why haven't you phoned Suzy or the department?"

He smiled, and there was something decidedly odd about it. "I didn't come here to talk about Suzy. Or the department."

There was a chill in his green eyes she'd never noticed before, an edge to his voice that spoke of violence. This was the Jack she knew—and yet, in many ways, it wasn't. "Why not? What are you up to?"

He smiled and lowered his gaze, silently studying the floor. She had an odd notion that time was running out, that this man, her partner, had come here to kill her. It was a ridiculous thought, it really was, but it was one she just couldn't shake. Licking dry lips, she raised her gun a little.

Just in case.

"There's a war about to begin, Ryan."

The abrupt sound of his voice made her jump slightly. She met his gaze squarely and saw in the green depths only death and determination. She felt no safer about his intentions.

"What sort of war?"

He shrugged. "A war in which man will play no part, and yet will ultimately be the loser. The wise will choose sides."

She frowned. Since when had Jack begun speaking in weird riddles? "And that's what you've done? Chosen a side?" She shifted her feet a little, strengthening her stance. If Jack came one step closer, she'd fire, partner or not.

So much for trusting this man beyond all others.

He smiled his strange smile. "Yes. And now it's your turn."

She stared at him, wondering what was really going on. Surely he hadn't called her down here just to pick a side in some upcoming mythical war. "We're cops, Jack. We're supposed to be impartial and all that."

He snorted heavily. "Yeah, right. Tell that to someone who doesn't know the truth."

The cynical edge to his voice made her feel no easier. If there was one thing Jack had always been proud of, it was his badge. "So why do I have to choose?"

"Because, for you, there can be no standing in the middle. It's one side or the other."

She wondered if pinching herself would wake her from this weird dream, or make sense of what Jack was saying. "That doesn't actually answer the question. I mean, why me? Why not the thousands of others who work for the department?"

"Most of them don't have your intuitive nature, or your determination to act on a hunch." He shrugged. "And we need more people who can move around in the daylight."

Right now, her so-called intuitive nature was telling her he was lying through his teeth—at least when it came to the reasons for wanting her to join them. "Who are you actually working for, if not the department?"

She might not have spoken, for all the notice he took. "We could continue as partners," he added.

God, how deep did he think their partnership had become? "Sorry. But it still doesn't appeal to me."

"That's unfortunate. Already, too many good men and women have gone missing."

A chill ran down her spine. "So you know about the disappearances?"

"Of course. They are, unfortunately, dead. It does not pay to be too inquisitive in this world."

"Meaning what? That they knew about you? About whatever it is you are up to?"

"Something like that."

His smile sent more chills down her smile. There was nothing pleasant about that smile. Nothing rational. She licked her lips and tried to remain calm. "I really think you should come back to headquarters with me—"

She hesitated. The odd, prickling sensation ran across her skin again, whispering dark secrets to her mind. She stared at Jack, her gaze widening. Her partner, and friend of five years, was the vampire she'd sensed earlier.

And that thing out there in the darkness, the creature she could not name, was with him.

He studied her for a moment, then sighed, almost sadly. "So you know."

Her finger curled around the trigger, and it took every ounce of strength she had to resist the urge to shoot him. Not all vampires were evil—how often had he told her that? Certainly she had no evidence that Jack himself had crossed the line between good and evil when he'd taken the step from life to death.

Only instinct, and the oddly ferocious look in his eyes, said that he had.

"Yes. But I still don't know why," she said.

"Why does one normally undertake the ceremony?" Amusement touched his green eyes. "I have no wish to die, Ryan. With the eve of the war at hand, I had no option but to cross over. Humans have no place in what is coming."

Well, that, at least, explained his recent absence. While it took only a couple of days for a human to become a vampire, it could take anywhere between a week and a year for the newly turned to master the sensations and control the bloodlust that came with being a vamp. Some people *never* mastered it, and it was generally these few who were responsible for the rampages that sometimes swept the city. Given the relatively short time Jack had been missing, he'd obviously fallen into the lower end of the control spectrum.

Though looking at him now, she wasn't entirely sure he *had* actually mastered being a vampire.

The sensation of danger was becoming so strong her muscles were twitching under the force of it. She took a deep breath, trying to calm down. Yet if Jack were a vampire, he would know her fear, her uncertainty. Would hear it in the thunderous pounding of her heart. "So why call me here?"

"Because, as I said earlier, it's your time to choose."

"I made my choice long ago." And her badge was all she really had. She wasn't about to walk away from it, even for her best friend. "I intend to stick to that choice."

Sadness briefly touched his eyes. "I'm asking you, as a friend, to join me."

Her finger tightened reflexively on the trigger, and it was all she could do not to fire the weapon. "No."

"One last chance." He took a slight step forward. The

touch of sadness in his eyes was quickly giving way to the certainty of death.

"One more step, and I'll shoot."

He smiled. "I don't think so."

Sweat trickled down the side of her face. "I mean it. Stay where you are."

He took another step forward. "We're friends, Ryan. Partners. You can't shoot me."

There was no humanity in his eyes now, only that certainty of death. She'd seen that look in vampires before and knew it precluded an attack. "Please, Jack. Don't make me shoot you."

He raised an eyebrow. "You won't. You can't," he said, and took another step.

She aimed low and pulled the trigger.

Through the booming report of the gun, she heard his curse, heard him stagger away. She lowered her weapon, hit the panic button on her wristcom, and ran for the stairs.

Heat flowed over her, whispering secrets. The thing with Jack was after her, running swiftly and silently through the darkness. If it caught her, she would die, as the old man had died. Quickly, but horribly.

She grabbed the railing with her free hand and took the stairs two at a time. At the top she hesitated and glanced down. A shadow flowed across the bottom step, then stopped and looked up. For just a second she found herself staring into eyes that were milky white and as bright as the stars. In them was a hunger unlike any she'd ever seen before.

Get out, she thought. *Just get the hell out of here.*

She scrambled through the door and slammed it shut behind her. An inhuman roar followed her into the wildness of the night. She ran for the fire escape stairs, but the wind hit her with the force of a gale, thrusting her sideways. Somehow, she managed to stay on her feet and keep running. Behind her, the door slammed open, the sound like a gunshot ricocheting across the force of the storm. Swearing, she leaped onto the fire escape and scrambled down the slick metal stairs.

One flight down. The old man stared up at her, a grim reminder of her fate if she wasn't fast enough. Onto the second flight. Was that a footfall? She didn't dare look up; she just kept on running.

She hit the lower landing, then grabbed the rail and leaped over it. She landed awkwardly, and pain curled like fire up her leg. But she ignored it and ran for her car.

A sighing sound carried across the howl of the wind. She caught a hint of movement out of the corner of her eye, but before she could react, something hit her hard and flung her sideways.

She struck the ground with a grunt of pain, her weapon flying from her hand. She twisted, throwing punches at the heavy weight that had landed on top of her. His curses stung the night, and then he caught her hands, his grip like iron as he held her still. She found herself staring into eyes that were an odd, green-flecked hazel, and not entirely human.

Not Jack or the creature. Someone else entirely. Someone she hadn't sensed.

"If you want to live, remain still and be quiet," he ordered, his gaze burning into hers for a second before flicking away.

"Get the hell off me and I may consider it," she muttered, twisting left and right in an effort to dislodge his weight.

"That creature hunts by sound and movement alone. Remain still, and we might escape with our lives."

A soft snarl ran across the wind. She stopped fighting and turned her gaze to the fire escape. A kitelike shape leaped off the second flight of stairs and landed awkwardly near the boxes. It made several odd snuffling noises before turning blind eyes in their direction. Her fingers twitched, pressing the trigger of a weapon she no longer held. The stranger glanced down at her, his odd-colored eyes holding a warning.

It went against her every instinct to remain still, to not fight, and her muscles quivered as she fought the desire to do both. The creature took a lumbering step in their direction. Her breath caught somewhere in her throat. At the other end of the alley, the howling wind tugged at the garbage bins. One fell and rattled toward the road, spewing paper and food scraps across the pavement before rolling away. The creature roared, then swung around and ran out of the alley.

The stranger released her and scrambled to his feet. She lurched forward and grabbed his wrist.

"Oh, no, you don't. You're not leaving until you tell me what the hell that thing is."

A slight smile creased the corners of his lush mouth. "And what gives you the right to detain me?"

"I'm a cop, mister. You're under arrest."

"For what? Saving your life?" He pried her fingers away from his wrist, his fingers warm and slightly rough against hers. "Sorry, but I have a creature to stop. Arrests will have to wait."

He moved so swiftly that he almost seemed to blur. One blink and he was gone.

The night didn't appear to be getting any saner, she thought sourly. First her partner had become a vampire, and then she was hunted by a kitelike monster, only to be rescued by a man who could blur his form and soar like the wind. Even shapechangers didn't move *that* fast—did they? She didn't really know, despite her years on the force.

Knowing she probably didn't want an answer to that question, she slowly climbed to her feet. Pain fired up her right leg, and her ankle suddenly felt encased in iron. Great, just great. The night from hell and a busted ankle to boot. Maybe the best idea was just to sit here and wait for the cavalry to arrive. The thought made her frown, and she glanced at her wristcom. Four minutes had passed since she'd pressed the emergency beacon, and nine since she'd first requested help. Why wasn't anyone here?

She glanced around for her weapon and saw it sitting in a puddle ten feet away. She hobbled to it, doing her best to ignore the protests from her ankle. As she bent down, that weird sliver of heat prickled a warning across her skin.

Jack was behind her. And this time, he felt wrong in a way she couldn't even begin to explain.

Slowly, warily, she picked up her weapon and turned around. He stood ten feet away. Blood ran from the wound in his thigh, gleaming darkly against his rain-soaked jeans. Fear swept her again. On a night like this she shouldn't even be able to see the blood.

She flicked off the auto safety catch and pointed the gun at him. "I have to take you back. You know I have to."

He didn't smile. Didn't do much of anything, really. "Can't. Kill if you want."

She didn't pull the trigger. Nor did she lower her weapon. "Why did you really call me here tonight?"

"To join."

The sense of wrongness was growing. And why was he speaking like that? Like he'd suddenly lost all capability of speech? Surely it couldn't be blood loss—if the wound in his leg was *that* bad, he wouldn't have been standing on it, vampire or not.

"And that thing you were with. Did it kill the old man?"

He lowered his gaze, but not before she'd seen a brief flash of amusement. A chill ran down her spine. Jack had watched that thing strip the old man of his humanity. Had enjoyed it.

"Dreg. Didn't matter." His gaze flashed up again, cold and hungry. If there was any humanity left in her partner, it quickly fled as the vampire rose fully to the surface.

"Sorry," he continued. "We were good."

Were. Not are. She swallowed. It didn't ease the aching dryness in her throat. "Don't move, Jack. This time I'll shoot to kill."

His laugh was a low, almost inhuman sound. It wasn't the laugh of the Jack she knew. It was the laugh of a stranger. "Wait for help to arrive?"

Sweat trickled down her back, and her palms felt slick against the cool metal of the gun. "That's my plan, yes."

"Not mine." He flashed a familiar smile, all confidence and teeth.

Too many teeth, in fact.

The vampire was getting ready to feed.

"*Don't* make me kill you," she warned softly. *Please don't.*

The sudden ferocity in his eyes made her take a step back. Even as she did so, he leaped.

Jack had once told her the best way to kill a vampire was to blow its fucking head off.

So that's exactly what she did.